DATE DUE			
JA 19 '15			

BY ALAN DEAN FOSTER

PUBLISHED BY THE RANDOM HOUSE PUBLISHING GROUP

THE BLACK HOLE
CACHALOT
DARK STAR
THE METROGNOME AND OTHER STORIES
MIDWORLD
NO CRYSTAL TEARS
SENTENCED TO PRISM
STAR WARS®: SPLINTER OF THE MIND'S EYE
STAR TREK® LOGS ONE–TEN
VOYAGE TO THE CITY OF THE DEAD
. . . WHO NEEDS ENEMIES?
WITH FRIENDS LIKE THESE . . .
MAD AMOS
THE HOWLING STONES
PARALLELITES
STAR WARS®: THE APPROACHING STORM
IMPOSSIBLE PLACES
EXCEPTIONS TO REALITY

THE ICERIGGER TRILOGY
ICERIGGER
MISSION TO MOULOKIN
THE DELUGE DRIVERS

THE ADVENTURES OF
FLINX OF THE COMMONWEALTH
FOR LOVE OF MOTHER-NOT
THE TAR-AIYAM KRANG
ORPHAN STAR
THE END OF MATTER
BLOODHYPE
FLINX IN FLUX
MID-FLINX
REUNION
FLINX'S FOLLY
SLIDING SCALES
RUNNING FROM THE DEITY
TROUBLE MAGNET
PATRIMONY

THE DAMNED
BOOK ONE: A CALL TO ARMS
BOOK TWO: THE FALSE MIRROR
BOOK THREE: THE SPOILS OF WAR

THE FOUNDING OF THE COMMONWEALTH
PHYLOGENESIS
DIRGE
DIUTURNITY'S DAWN

THE TAKEN TRILOGY
LOST AND FOUND
THE LIGHT-YEARS BENEATH MY FEET
THE CANDLE OF DISTANT EARTH

QU●FUM

QU⊙FUM

A NOVEL OF THE COMMONWEALTH

ALAN DEAN FOSTER

BALLANTINE BOOKS · DEL REY · NEW YORK

Copyright © 2008 by Thranx, Inc.

All rights reserved.

Published in the United States by Del Rey Books, an imprint of The Random House Publishing Group, a division of Random House, Inc., New York.

DEL REY is a registered trademark and the Del Rey colophon is a trademark of Random House, Inc.

Library of Congress Cataloging-in-Publication Data

Foster, Alan Dean
Quofum / Alan Dean Foster.
p.   cm.
ISBN 978-0-345-49605-8 (hardcover : alk. paper)
1. Humanx Commonwealth (Imaginary organization)—Fiction.
I. Title.
PS3556.O756Q64   2008
813'.54—dc22   2008027590

Printed in the United States of America on acid-free paper

www.delreybooks.com

9 8 7 6 5 4 3 2 1

First Edition

Book design by Liz Cosgrove

For Todd Lockwood,
who did this beautiful cover

PROLOGUE

It was easy to believe that Quofum did not exist because most of the time it didn't. Lying along the inner edge of the Orion Arm and outside the boundaries of the Commonwealth, the rest of the system as apprised by the exploration robot seemed normal enough. The G-type sun burned slightly hotter than Sol but was otherwise unremarkable. It was orbited by half a dozen proper planets: two outer gas giants, ornamented by the usual regalia of variegated moons, and four inner rocky spheres. While all of the latter clung to atmospheres of varying density and composition, none supported life more complex than elementary bacteria. There were also a couple of asteroid belts and attendant clouds of comets.

And then there was Quofum.

It was not there when the robot first arrived. Its abrupt, unexpected appearance put a strain not only on the probe's scientific instruments but on the logic circuits of its rudimentary AI. Though it was a rare occurrence, even a machine intelligence could be startled. The sudden materialization of an entirely new and previously unobserved planet in the spatial interstice between worlds two and three was an event of sufficient magnitude and lack of precedence to unsettle even the most efficiently designed artificial intelligence.

Confronted with an apparent impossibility, and a very sizable one at that, the probe's first response was to backscan its accumulated data. It did this several times before concluding that the new observation was not a consequence of some prior instrumental malfunction. All preceding observations were incontestable. Subsequent to its arrival within the present system its instruments had observed and made recordings of six planets, twenty-two moons, two asteroid belts, and assorted free-ranging comets, meteors, and other characteristic planetary system debris. It had manifestly not overlooked an entire world some twelve percent greater in diameter than Earth.

While this rather massive contradiction was distressing, it did not prevent the probe from continuing its work. Resigning itself to leaving the conundrum to be resolved at some future date, it set about following up on its most recent discovery. It promptly set a course for the new world, assigning it a number according to built-in internal protocols, and embarked upon the usual round of standardized observations. Like its brethren, the previously unobserved planet had an atmosphere. Unlike them, this consisted of nitrogen and oxygen in a combination sufficient to support terrestrial-type life. The presence of an unusual variety of largely inert gases was duly noted without comment—the probe's task was to observe and record, not evaluate.

There were pink skies. Beneath the pink skies, puddled oceans composed of liquid water, noble salts—and approximately nine percent alcohol. Landmasses gave clear evidence of supporting life, though the probe did not linger long enough or descend low enough to document specific examples. It did note the important fact that there were no signs of higher intelligence.

Having fulfilled its programming for the present system the probe prepared to activate its integrated KK-drive and move on through space-plus to the next on its list of designated systems to be explored. There were a lot of uncharted, unstudied, unrecorded systems on the fringes of the ever-expanding Commonwealth. The larger the Commonwealth became, the more far-reaching its borders. Survey probes were expensive and the time they could spend studying individual systems was therefore limited. If no sentient life was found, they were programmed to fill a prescribed portion of their data banks and move on—no matter how unusual a particular world or system might initially appear.

As the probe was accelerating toward changeover, rearward-facing instruments duly recorded one last interesting fact about the third planet of the new system. It had disappeared again—vanished as if it had never been. But it had been. The probe's records were proof of that.

The robot did not attempt to put forth an explanation for the phenomenon. It merely recorded the relevant data. Like the rest of the facts and figures it had accumulated, this would be reviewed, discussed, and analyzed by the scientists who built and serviced the flotilla of deep-space probes. Eventually they might decide to do something about it.

It took years for the probe to fill its storage facilities to capacity and finally head homeward. The data it had acquired on the world that one bemused researcher promptly dubbed Quofum was initially presumed to be a consequence of equipment failure. When this was found not to be the case, a good bit of agitated discussion ensued. Some shouting transpired among a number of celebrated and knowledgeable individuals more accustomed to quiet, if often energetic, dialogue. There was spirited debate about throwing good money after what many felt must be evident nonsense.

In the end it was decided that the ramifications posed by the probe's data concerning this particular new world were worthy of a much closer and more detailed look, if only to determine firsthand their validity. A compromise was reached. Funding for a follow-up hands-on expedition was authorized, but at the bottom end of the customary survey scale. If Quofum did indeed exist and was found to be worthy of a full-scale study, that could and would be sanctioned to follow in due course. There was only one problem. The approved expedition could not set course for a world that long-range scrutiny insisted was not present. The system in question was therefore subject to continuous monitoring.

When Quofum unexpectedly did reappear, or at least when observation seemed to coincide with the historical record, things moved quickly.

QUOFUM

1

Like everyone else on the *Dampier,* Tellenberg was a volunteer and a polymath. With a full crew of only half a dozen there was no room on the low-budget expedition for specialists. At least among the scientific complement, everyone had been chosen for their ability to do work in several disciplines. Tellenberg hoped he would have the opportunity to exercise all of his considerable range of knowledge. Like the others, his greatest fear had been that they would emerge from space-plus to find that the world they were charged with surveying and exploring was nothing more than a myth.

If it accomplished nothing else, the mission had already put that particular worry to rest.

Quofum was there, a thickly cloud-swathed world situated between the orbits of the system's second and third planets, exactly where the much earlier robot probe had predicted. As the *Dampier* decelerated toward its destination, he hurried forward to catch a first glimpse of the new world through the sweeping port that dominated the bridge. Screens in his cabin and the lab could have provided much more detailed representations. But experiencing a new world in the form of a projection as opposed to viewing it in vivo was not the same thing. In this manner Tellenberg had previously been privileged to experience first contact with two newly discovered planets. Quofum would be his third and, if the preliminary survey turned out to be valid, the most unusual.

An unusual world fit for an unusual researcher. Twenty years ago Esra Tellenberg had suffered the loss of both arms and both legs in a laboratory accident. Only the telltale darkening of his skin below the shoulders and the knees marked him as a multiple regenerate. From research devoted to studying echinoderms skilled gengineers and doctors had long ago learned how to manipulate genes to induce severely damaged human beings to regrow lost limbs. A far better and more natural option than mechanical prosthetics, these bioengineered replacements were indistinguishable from the appendages they replaced—except for one unanticipated difference. No matter how hard the cosmetic biologists worked at solving the problem, they always had a difficult time matching melanin.

Tellenberg's own body had regrown his arms and legs, but from shoulder and knee down his flesh was noticeably darker. Body makeup would have rendered hues the same. Being a scientist and not a fashion model, he disdained their use. Thus clearly and unashamedly colored as a regenerate, it was to be expected that he would be nicknamed "starfish." He wore the label amiably, and with pride.

He was the last to arrive on the bridge. With a full complement of six, it was not crowded. Though its intensity and size had been greatly diminished by changeover and the drop back into normal space, the luminous violet of the posigravity field projected by the ship's KK-drive still dominated the view ahead. As the *Dampier* continued to decelerate, the field's strength steadily moderated, revealing the rest of the view forward and allowing them a first glimpse of their destination.

"Pretty substantial-looking. Not like something that would go popping in and out of existence."

While he was a master of multiple skills who could lay claim to several specialized credentials, Salvador Araza simply preferred to be called a maintenance tech. As well as a way of showing deference toward those from whom he had learned, it was also an honest expression of modesty. Tall, slender, and as dark as Tellenberg's regenerated forearms, he tended to keep to himself. So much so that the xenologist was surprised to hear the expedition's jack-of-all-trades venture an unsolicited opinion. More expressive even than his face, Araza's hands were by far his most notable feature. Tellenberg had seen them loop alloy he himself could not even bend, and in the next moment exhibit the skill of a surgeon while realigning components under a technician's magnifying scope.

Araza was standing just behind Boylan. In the case of the *Dampier*, the captain was the crew. Appointed though he was, he was still almost a figurehead. Interstellar KK-drive vessels essentially flew themselves, their internal operations and requisite calculations being far too byzantine for mere human minds to manage. Still, on any expedition someone had to be in charge, if only nominally. That responsibility fell to the gruff-voiced Nicholai Boylan. With his flaring black beard, deep-set eyes, stocky build, and an occasionally distressing lack of personal hygiene, he struck Tellenberg as an eventual candidate for brain as well as body regeneration.

Contrastingly, the stunted and Neanderthal-looking captain was quite an accomplished amateur microbiologist.

Moselstrom N'kosi (everybody called him Mosi) stood as close to the port as the sweeping instrument console would allow. He also hovered as near as he dared to his fellow xenologist Tiare Haviti. Tellenberg didn't blame him. When opportunity allowed, he endeavored to do the same. It was always a delicate dance when single men and women were compelled to share the limited, enclosed space on board a small interstellar vessel. Given the uncertain and potentially risky nature of their destination, it was an application requirement that every potential crew member be unattached. All being mature adults, everyone knew their limits. When a fellow researcher was as alluring as Haviti, however, time tended to produce an accelerated compression of those limits. Aware of her unavoidable attractiveness and as adult and worldly as her male colleagues, she knew how to handle the inevitable attention. Proximity was tolerated: indeed, within the limited space on the ship that was allotted to living quarters it was inescapable. But that was all.

Haviti, Tellenberg found himself reflecting, was not unlike plutonium. Though potentially dangerous it was also heavily shielded. With care, one could get quite close. Actual contact, however, might prove physically injurious. Having previously lost and subsequently been obliged to regrow four major appendages, he had no intention of risking any others. There was also the daunting and very real possibility that she was smarter than any of them. Wielded by the right tongue, lips, and larynx, a word could be as damaging as a whack.

Of the five males on board, she let only Valnadireb get physically close to her. This intimacy occasioned no jealousy among Tellenberg and his colleagues. Not because Valnadireb was anything other than a virile adult male in his physical prime, but because their fellow xenologist was thranx. Though intellectually simpatico, Valnadireb and Haviti were as biologically incompatible as a chimp and a mantis, the latter being the Terran species to whom his kind's appearance was most often compared. A bit over a meter tall when standing on all four trulegs and the front set of foothands, rising to a meter and a half when standing on trulegs alone and utilizing both foothands and truhands for purposes of digital manipulation, the insectoid Valnadireb completed the ship's complement. Like the rest of the ship, the air on the bridge was permeated by the delicate perfume that was the natural body odor of his species.

Surrounded by colorful hovering projections both statistical and representative, a busy Boylan grunted a response to Araza's observation.

"It's there, alright. Every reading, she is coming back normal. Iron core, stony outer shell, breathable atmosphere, tolerable gravity. Lots of liquid water she has in her oceans. All normal." For an instant his crusty demeanor gave way to a twinkle in both eye and voice. "Except for that remarkable alcohol content in the seas."

"Nine percent," Mosi reiterated unnecessarily. Unnecessarily because each of them had committed to memory every known fact about their objective since long before their departure from Earth.

"Maybe the place was originally discovered by a wandering race of long-lost master distillers," a deadpan Haviti commented. Though not unanticipated, the joke still generated a few chuckles on the bridge.

Tellenberg shared the captain's phlegmaticism. Gazing at the slowly rotating image of the solid globe floating before them, it was next to impossible to imagine something so large and substantial suddenly not being there. He tried to imagine it winking out of existence in the blink of an eye. To further the metaphor, he blinked. When he opened his eyes again, Quofum was still there.

Instrumentation malfunction, he told himself confidently. There was no question about it, could be no other explanation. All down the line that had been focused on this world, there had occurred a succession of instrumental malfunctions. As Boylan methodically recited aloud one hard, cold, incontrovertible reading after another, Tellenberg felt increasingly confident he would be able to set his regenerated feet down on the target planet's surface without having to worry about them abruptly passing through it.

Having concluded the not-so-insignificant business of confirming the world's existence, he was now eager to explore its surface to study the profusion of life-forms that the initial survey probe had insisted were there. It was an anticipation and excitement he knew was shared by his colleagues. This being such a small expedition there could well be ample discovery (and subsequent professional kudos) to go around.

"I will run a final prep on shuttle one." As Araza turned to go Boylan put up a hand to halt him.

"Not so fast, my friend. You know the procedure." He let his gaze touch on each of those present. "You all know the procedure."

The captain's declaration gave rise to a chorus of groans that was more resigned than resentful. Everyone knew you just didn't settle into orbit around an entirely new, unexplored world and dash down for a ramble. First, a prescribed number of observations and measurements would have to be made from orbit.

These would then have to be analyzed and their results approved by the ship's AI, the latter not being susceptible to complimentary words or physical blandishments by folks in a hurry to set foot on unfamiliar ground. Boylan would then review the final breakdown. If approved, only then would the anxious scientists be permitted to crowd into the shuttle with their equipment and their expectations and allowed to descend to the alien surface.

Though as impatient as any of his colleagues, Tellenberg understood the need to follow procedure. Especially at a new site with as unusual a background as Quofum. With every orbit, the world below became more and more familiar to the team and to the ship, less and less potentially bizarre.

With the exception of its unusual potent oceans and pink-tinged atmosphere, they saw nothing from orbit to mark the globe as anything out of the ordinary. Viewed from high above, it boasted nothing as dramatic as the frozen seas of Tran-ky-ky or the endless metropolitan hive that was the thranx world of Amropolous, both of which Tellenberg had visited. There were mountains and valleys, rivers and deserts, islands and peninsulas, volcanoes and icecaps. A slightly larger pink-tinged Earth. Hopefully the flora and fauna would offer a bit more excitement than anything they were able to discern from orbit.

A week later the always reluctant, ever-circumspect Boylan grudgingly allowed as how it might finally be safe to go down and have a look around.

Anxious as the scientists were to commence their research, everyone knew that the first order of business was to choose an amenable location and establish a base camp. Lively argument ensued over whether to do this on the edge of a desert, mountain, riverine, or oceanic zone. Using his vote, Boylan settled the matter by opting for a temperate zone set-down where a sizable river running through native forest entered a shallow sea, a physical location that hopefully addressed as many requests as possible at the same time. Not a single member of the expedition's scientific team was entirely pleased with this choice, which showed that the captain had made the correct one.

Even though all the essential equipment was prefabricated and compacted, it took several round-trips in the shuttle to convey all of it safely to the surface. Arriving in a much larger vessel than the *Dampier*, a normal-sized expedition would have been equipped with a proper cargo shuttle. Still, the team managed. Only when the last tool, the last wall panel, the last section of roofing and self-routing sealant had been landed according to regulations, did Boylan give the go-ahead for construction to begin.

It was hard. Not because the trio of largely self-erecting buildings proved difficult to put up, but because as soon as they set foot on Quofum, every one of the scientists was overwhelmed by the incredible fecundity of their surroundings. It took an effort of will on the part of every member of the crew in addition to continuous cajoling by an exasperated Boylan to get them to attend to the business of putting together a place to sleep, eat, and work. Everyone wanted to explore the alien forest or the alien beach or the alien river.

There was life everywhere. Mosi N'kosi, who thought he had been on bountiful worlds, avowed as how he had never seen anything like their new planetfall. Haviti was visibly overcome by both the opportunities that surrounded them as they worked to erect the camp and by its beauty. Being thranx, Valnadireb had never lived on worlds that were anything other than tropical in nature, but even he had to confess that for sheer richness of biota

Quofum surpassed any place up to and including the incredibly lush thranx mother world of Hivehom. For its part, what the researchers initially took to be the more advanced native life-forms appeared as interested in the new arrivals as they did in them.

It took less than a week to set up the tripartite portable facility: living quarters in one extended rectangular structure, lab in another, equipment and gear storage in the third—all laid out like the spokes of an incomplete wheel around the domed main entranceway and biolock. Each successive day they spent on Quofum without succumbing to local bacteria or other infectious microbiota, the less necessary the formal double entrance became. Still, no one suggested doing away with the additional security. Just because they had not yet encountered any hostile life-forms did not mean they did not exist. As experienced xenologists, they knew better.

They also knew that since there were only four of them in addition to Boylan and Araza, it was necessary to stay and work closely together until they had a far better conception of their surroundings. While having four researchers go off on four different tangents might prove to be individually gratifying and scientifically productive, it could also prove singularly fatal. So for the present they restrained themselves.

At least there were no arguments over what to do with the skimmer. None of the scientists requested its use. With a lifetime of work easily accessible within walking distance of the camp, none of the researchers felt a need to make use of the long-range vehicle.

While Boylan and Araza stayed behind to finalize and set up the remainder of the camp's internal components, everything from the food processing gear to the research lab, the energized scientists paired off. Haviti and Valnadireb chose to focus on the life in and around the river while N'kosi and Tellenberg elected to study the transition zone where forest met the coast.

Appropriately equipped and armed, the two men restrained themselves from stopping every meter to spend an hour collecting samples of local vegetation. Had they chosen to so indulge themselves, they could have spent weeks without passing beyond view of the camp. This exploratory conservatism would have pleased the ever-cautious Boylan, but not so the sponsors of the expedition. So both men hiked a straight line through the foliage to the beach, resolutely resisting the urge to stop and take samples of blue-orange blossoms and elegantly coiled growths whose trunks glistened like pale green plastic beneath a cloud-scrimmed sun.

It did not take them long to reach the shore of the alien ocean. In the absence of a moon, there was hardly any wave action. To the alarm of his shorter companion N'kosi, the very first thing Tellenberg did was wade into the shallows, dip a sampling tube, and instead of sealing it and replacing it in his backpack, take an experimental sip of the liquid he had bottled. It was bad science. Still, the host of expressions that played across Tellenberg's face showed that at least one portion of the initial survey probe's report had been right on the mark.

"Nine percent seems about right." Tellenberg grinned at his concerned colleague. "I expect you could get good and proper drunk on it. But you'd have to like your drinks with a good dose of salt." Wading back to the beach, the lower third of his field pants drying rapidly, he extended the tube toward his partner.

Raising a hand, N'kosi demurred. "No thanks. If you don't mind, I'll wait until we've had a chance to analyze the contents. See if it contains anything interesting besides alcohol. Swarms of parasitic alien foraminifer, for example."

Tellenberg made a face as he slipped the tube into its wait-ing receptacle slot. "You're no fun."

"Alien parasites are no fun. Horrible, painful death is no fun," N'kosi countered.

"Like I said, you're no fun." A stirring at the foot of the alien growths that grew right up to the edge of the beach drew Tel-lenberg's attention. "Are those worms?" Disagreement immedi-ately forgotten, the two men climbed the slight slope in the direction of the movement.

Inland, Valnadireb slowed as he and Haviti approached the river. Though not large or deep, it continued to flow swiftly out of the foothills to the east. Like most of his kind Valnadireb had an instinctive fear of any water that rose higher than the breath-ing spicules located on his thorax. Furthermore, lacking the large expandable air sac/swim bladders their human friends called lungs, a flailing thranx would sink if immersed over its head. Though some thranx were known to participate in water activities, they were universally considered worse than mad by their contemporaries.

So Valnadireb held back while Haviti walked down to the river and took samples. At her urging and with her encourage-ment he edged closer and closer, until he was standing just be-hind her and to one side. There he was able to assist in storing and cataloguing the water samples she dipped from the shal-lows. The involuntary quivering and barely perceptible buzzing of his vestigial wing cases was the only visible evidence of his unease. The chitinous thranx, of course, did not sweat.

"I know that was difficult for you," she told him as they moved away from the rushing water and back toward the edge of the forest. While she was perfectly fluent in symbospeech, she did not hesitate to speak in terranglo. Her thranx colleague was equally fluent in both, and certainly more at ease with her language than she would have been attempting the clicks, whistles, and glottal stops of Low Thranx.

The valentine-shaped head with its golden-banded compound eyes swiveled around almost a hundred eighty degrees to focus on her as she used both hands to adjust the pack that was slung across his upper abdomen.

"Water is for drinking and ablutions," he declared firmly. "I can never watch humans voluntarily submerging themselves without incurring distress to my digestive system."

Grinning, she stepped away from him and adjusted her shirt. The air was pleasantly warm: a bit cool for a thranx, perfect for her kind. Abruptly, the grin vanished and she froze.

As sensitive to flexible human expression as he was to the intricate multiple limb and hand movements of his own kind, Valnadireb instantly dropped a truhand toward the small pistol that resided in his thorax holster.

"You see something that provokes anxiety. Where?"

Raising one arm, the now wholly serious Haviti pointed. "To the right. Between those two large red-orange growths." She stood motionless and staring.

"I have no idea what it is," she concluded, "but I do know that it's looking straight at us."

2

Even though every part of the camp from the walls to the laboratory equipment to the furniture was designed to essentially erect itself, a certain amount of supervision was still required to ensure that, for example, the compressed bed erectors were placed in individual rooms instead of the kitchen area. Preprogrammed automatics from the shuttle did the heavy lifting and set everything in place after which Boylan and Araza activated the self-contained shipping crates. That done, all that was necessary was for them to stand back and ensure that the self-powered installations unfolded smoothly.

It took several days of steady work with everyone pitching in to set up all three sections of the camp and get them connected to the domed entrance lock. It was while the first of these was being furnished and equipped that the captain noticed Araza staring at him.

"Something wrong, Salvador?" Stepping back from the first

of the expandable beds they were installing, Boylan eyed the technician expectantly.

"No, nothing, sir. I was preoccupied, that's all."

"Time enough for that later. I want every installation done right first time." He grunted softly. "Nobody want their bed collapsing under them in middle of night, or food processor failing to deliver after hard day's work."

"We are ahead of schedule," Araza observed mildly. The sultry heat of afternoon saw both of them perspiring heavily.

"That's way I like it." Something in the tech's voice . . . "You are maybe needing a break?"

"No, I am fine. I was just wondering, that is all. . . ."

Boylan paused while the bed finished installing itself. "Whatever is on you mind, don't keep it to youself."

Turning, Araza indicated the rest of the longitudinal chamber. By tomorrow it would be properly sectioned off and the individual living quarters filled with practical, solid gear as well as items of a personal nature. At present, except for the bed that was rapidly unfolding and positioning itself, it was an empty shell filled with sealed containers waiting to be activated.

"Did you ever stop to wonder why the government authorized such a small expedition?"

Boylan snorted. "Of course. There was no point in spending lots of money to send a big ship and big team to a place that might not exist. Based on what we report, I would anticipate a follow-up investigative team to be much larger."

Araza nodded thoughtfully. "Assuming we all get off here alive."

Boylan's heavy brows drew together. "We have been here less than day and already you are contemplating catastrophe?"

The technician did not look in the captain's direction. "I just think maybe one reason the Commonwealth sent such a small team was so any losses would be minimized. In the event of an unforeseeable disaster."

Boylan was not pleased. This wasn't the kind of talk he wanted to hear from a team member so soon after touchdown. "You are maybe having something specific in mind?"

Shouldering an installer whose label declared that it contained a compacted chest of drawers, the tech looked back at his superior. "While spotty, what records there are of this world show it not being here much of the time."

Boylan let out a short, derisive laugh. "Well, it sure as hell here now!" Raising his right leg, he stomped down with enough force to cause the tough integrated flooring to vibrate slightly underfoot. "It my personal conclusion after past several days working here that I don't think it or we have to worry about disappearing anywhere soon."

"Maybe not soon," a seemingly reluctant Araza muttered.

The other man squinted at the tech. "What was that?"

"Nothing, sir." He set down the installer he was carrying. "You want this storage unit against the wall or freestanding?"

Boylan shrugged indifferently. "I not an internal decorator. Just activate it. Whoever picks this room can place it wherever they like."

Araza complied. Boylan might have found the technician's current expression of more than passing interest, but the bigger man was presently focused on the task at hand and as a consequence his face was not visible.

"What the hell was that?" His attention focused on the tree line, N'kosi took a step backward. Behind him, Tellenberg looked up from where he had been staring in fascination at something long, soft, and multitentacled that was undulating its way through a shallow pool of alcohol-infused seawater.

"I don't see anything." Reluctantly, he abandoned the promising tide pool and walked up the beach to rejoin his colleague.

N'kosi was standing and staring at the riot of twisted, intertwined growths that formed a wall of green, orange, and russet vegetation above the highest berm. Every square meter of sand was a treasure trove of small, dead alien life-forms. In the absence of strong tides the skeletal flotsam underfoot consisted largely of what had been cast ashore by storm surge.

"Well, I did." Checking his gear to ensure that everything was in place, the other xenologist started inland. "It was watching us."

Tellenberg was hesitant to follow. "If you did see something and if it was watching us, I'm not sure pushing into dense unknown forest is the appropriate procedure for preliminary follow-up. We just got here and we know next to nothing about this place."

Standing at the transition zone where sand met soil, N'kosi looked back at him. "Then here's an opportunity to add to our limited store of knowledge in a hurry." Reaching up to make sure the recorder clipped over his right ear was working, he pushed aside a low-hanging branch of what looked like a giant white rosebush and stepped into the verdure. With a reluctant sigh, Tellenberg moved to catch up.

Walking was easier once they had progressed a little ways from the beach. Forced to compete for available sunlight, plant growth diminished, leaving adequate room to step around or between the various boles. Moist ground revealed the tracks of whatever it was that had been spying on them.

"See?" A crouching N'kosi pointed out the path: two sets of dashes like parallel dotted lines. Whatever creature had made them walked on a very narrow foot.

Looking down, Tellenberg nodded. "I suppose tracking unknown creatures through wild forest is a talent you inherited from your ancestors?"

Staring straight ahead, N'kosi straightened. "All my ancestors have been scientists or teachers, except for one who was an inventor of cheap kitchen appliances. At least, that's how it has been in my family for the past several generations. Further back than that, I couldn't tell you."

Who could? Tellenberg reflected. Like that of most people, his own personal ancestry was lost in the mists of time, buried in the ancient history of the homeworld when humankind had, difficult as it was to imagine, been restricted to a single planet. He trailed N'kosi as the other researcher led the way deeper into the forest.

There was no risk of them becoming lost. Disoriented, yes, but a quick check of their individual communits would guide them back to the camp. He checked the time. If everything was going according to plan, Boylan and Araza would have at least the life-support basics up and running by the time the two teams of xenologists returned from their initial exploratory forays into the surrounding environment.

The fecundity they had detected from orbit was no illusion. In addition to the vigorous plant life, the forest was alive with a remarkably dynamic fauna. Serpentine shapes of varying length, color, and pattern slithered along the forest floor or burrowed into its rich soil. Vertebrates with two, four, six, and more legs scurried away from their approach. Such instinctive wariness suggested that they were hunted, or at least harried. Long-armed, tentacled, and sucker-equipped arboreal residents made their way through the branches, traveling from tree to tree. Splashed with the color of perpetual sunset, the pink sky was awing with all manner of flying things. Quofumian taxonomy, he reflected as he stepped over an arching root the color of burnt sienna that was spotted with mauve fungi, could easily be a full-time career.

Not theirs, however. This was a preliminary survey. Their job was to observe, record, and where time and gear permitted, collect. The task of classification would fall to scientists back home blessed with more time and better-equipped labs.

The longer they walked the more troubled he became, though he could not identify the source of his growing unease. The forest was a wonderful place. No xenologist could ask for more varied, exhilarating, stimulating surroundings. Every minute it seemed as if his eyes and his recorder saw something new and exciting. Nothing had threatened them. The local life-forms appeared alternately curious and chary of their presence. It was almost as if, he reflected, the many and varied creatures had encountered humans before. Or something like them. More likely, he decided, local predation was governed by a set of rules yet to be revealed. Perhaps the resident carnivores only hunted at certain times of the day, or according to species-specific biocycles. So much to see, he mused. So much to learn. A whole new world, wide-ranging and vast.

He ought to have been quietly ecstatic. Instead, an imperceptible *something* he could not define continued to nag at him.

He forgot about it when N'kosi halted abruptly and gestured. Tellenberg did not have to squint to see what his partner was pointing at. The subject of their search was staring right back at them.

There were four of the natives. They wore no clothing. Tellenberg was not surprised by their nakedness. How would you clothe something that looked like a stack of sticks encased in translucent rubbery jelly? Attached to a ganglion of nerves, what must have been eyes floated around in the top of the vertical mounds. The shadows of other internal organs were clearly visible. Where the base of each mound had split, the gelatinous material had hardened into a pair of flat-bottomed, hard-edged runners. Their method of locomotion and the source of the peculiar dashed tracks N'kosi had found were revealed when one of the creatures retreated slightly. They slid, rather than stepped.

Upper-body appendages curled to grip sharpened sticks. A couple of these were aimed in the direction of the two explorers. One stick-wielder used his primitive weapon to make what could have been construed as threatening or warning gestures in the humans' direction.

"This is too abrupt," Tellenberg found himself arguing aloud. "We tracked them down. That kind of action leaves too much room for misinterpretation." Keeping his hands in plain view, he started to backtrack. Not too rapidly, lest it suggest fear.

"I agree." An utterly enthralled N'kosi lingered, reluctant to leave. "But just think of it! Contact with intelligent indigenes, in the *first week*." As he joined his friend in retreating, his enthusiasm was matched by that of his more cautious companion. "Physically, they're different from anything in the directory."

"I've certainly never seen anything like them." When possibly hostile stick thrusts were not followed by an attack, Tellenberg began to relax. Their ear-mounted recorders continued to document every aspect of the encounter, from the natives' physical appearance to internal heat and anything else their bodies might be emitting. "I suggest we leave now and try to reconnect tomorrow, after both sides have had time to digest their reactions to first contact."

"Also, we can come back with the others, and with trade goods and other gear," N'kosi concurred. "What a fabulous first day!"

They continued to back up until they were out of what they guessed to be stick-throwing range. At that point the gelatinous natives turned and slid away into the forest. Tellenberg noted that throughout the course of the entire encounter the natives had not made a sound. It left him wondering if the indigenes were not capable either physically or intellectually of verbal communication. With luck, they would find out tomorrow. He could not wait to share the discovery with Haviti, Valnadireb, and the others.

But as he and N'kosi retraced their steps back toward the beach, he still could not escape the nagging, irksome feeling that despite everything they had seen and accomplished in the course of a single day, something was not quite right.

Valnadireb stood frozen halfway between the forest's periphery and the river's edge, staring out of glistening, attentive compound eyes at the same sight that had caught his human colleague's attention. There were four—no, five—of the natives. Each was as tall as Tellenberg, who was the biggest member of the science team. All five were slim of body and covered from head to foot in fine gray fur. Bipedal and bisymmetrical, their attenuated torsos left little room for legs and necks. Proportionately short arms terminated in hands that boasted opposing thumbs but no fingers. Aside from these limbs they had no tails, horns, or other outstanding appendages. The eyes were small but with disproportionately large, round pupils. Pencil-shaped tongues flicked rapidly in and out of small, round mouths. The function of an oval fur-rimmed crater that dominated the center of each forehead was not immediately quantifiable. Ragged attire fashioned from various plant materials hung from high, bony shoulders while their twin-toed feet were shod in thicker, tougher floral shavings.

Observing the two aliens gazing back at them, one raised the stone-tipped club it was holding and shook it in Haviti's direction. This action inspired a chorus of modulated squeals from the others.

"Primitive, but they cooperate." Her voice was calm and composed as she panned her head from left to right to ensure that the recorder clipped to her ear took in the entire display. "Mastery of language is questionable, but they have advanced as far as clothing and tool-making."

Valnadireb's equipment was also recording the confrontation for posterity as well as for future study. "Interesting sensory equipment. I recognize organs of sight and hearing, possibly also of smell. Except for the hole visible in the upper portion of the cranium one might almost classify them as primates."

She glanced over at her colleague. "These are no relatives of mine, Val. Take away the bifurcation and everything else, from the shape of the ears to the limited number and size of digits, is radically different from humankind." She took a step back. "Careful. . . ."

Three of the natives were advancing toward the visitors. One of them hefted a kind of rock-loaded sling while the other two brandished stone-tipped clubs. Opening their mouths to reveal hard palates devoid of teeth, they issued a series of louder, higher-pitched squeals. Valnadireb and Haviti had no way of knowing if these constituted challenges, insults, welcomes, or queries. In the absence of any specific knowledge, they had no choice but to exercise caution. Both human and thranx unenthusiastically drew their weapons.

Instinct shouted at Haviti to flee. Education and experience countered by telling her to hold her ground. The latter won out. Besides, the river was close behind them and while retreating into it might offer some measure of protection to her, Valnadireb did not have that option. She edged a little closer to her companion, both for strategic reasons and to show the natives that despite radical differences in appearance, the two visitors were indeed together.

More squeals were forthcoming, accompanied by further flourishing of primitive weapons. Refusing to be cowed, human and thranx held their ground. Recognizing this, one of the indigenes who had held back now ambled forward on too-short legs, ejected something from its mouth, and gibbered in low tones at the trio who had advanced. Despite their greater size and superiority of numbers, they waddled backward.

Among humans, the deliberate discharging of spittle in another's direction was usually taken for an insult or a challenge. Trained xenologist that she was, Haviti knew that on this world and among these natives it might mean something entirely different. Clutching her pistol, she did not react. To her right, Valnadireb raised both foothands and truhands to execute a thranx gesture of friendship. Speaking formal High Thranx, he directed whistles, words, and clicks in the direction of the indigenes.

It could have been something in the complex four-limbed gesture. Or perhaps the natives were put off by the flow of strange sounds and syllables that issued from the thranx's mouth. Whatever the cause, their pale oval pupils got very wide. Squealing like a posse of panicked piglets, they whirled as one and disappeared back into the forest as fast as their stumpy legs would carry them. In their wake they left behind a pair of exhilarated, if somewhat bemused, xenologists.

"Not bad for a first contact." A relieved Haviti reholstered her unfired hand weapon.

Next to her Valnadireb turned away and back toward the swiftly flowing river. "They did not attack, and we did not have to respond. Words—we may presume for now they were words—were exchanged." Bending his head, he reached up with a tru-hand and began to groom his left antenna. "I do wonder why my greeting caused them to flee so precipitously."

Haviti grinned. "Maybe they were just surprised to see a big bug talking back to them. If you remember your history, something of the same reaction afflicted my kind when we first encountered your species."

"The shock was no less among my kind when it finally had to be acknowledged that stinky soft-bodied creatures with internal skeletons had actually developed intelligence." Pivoting on four trulegs, he looked back at the forest. "Quite an eventful afternoon." Tilting back his head, he considered the alien sky. "We should be getting back."

Removing a collecting net of fine mesh from her backpack, Haviti headed for the water. "Not until I've taken some samples of aquatic life-forms. If the terrestrial fauna is any indication, they should be plentiful and fascinating." Reaching the water's edge and wading out into the cool liquid until it was halfway up to her knees, she paused to look back. "Aren't you going to help?"

"Very funny." Extracting a soil sifter from his own pack, Valnadireb commenced a search for a suitable patch of ground from which to take samples. "I'll restrict my efforts to sensibly dry land, thank you."

As they worked, this or that new discovery would occasion a cry of delight from Haviti or a whistle of pleasure from her colleague. Even as they labored to satisfy their intellectual needs,

however, they would periodically engage safety and security equipment to scan the looming wall of green and orange forest.

They were focused on their science, but they were not stupid. Wielded skillfully and with strength, a rock on a stick could end a life as effectively as the most sophisticated pistol.

Wiping perspiration from his forehead as he considered the rapidly darkening sky, Boylan struggled to contain his irritation. Here he and Araza and the automatics had worked their tails off to get the camp in some kind of shape for the science team and they did not even have the courtesy to return on time. Was it going to be like this every day they went out into the field? he wondered. It could not be allowed. Words would have to be spoken. As commander of the expedition both on board and off the ship, security was ultimately his responsibility.

He knew he shouldn't be surprised. Having worked with scientists before, he was aware that when they were working in the field they believed that every day consisted of twice twenty-four hours—irrespective of the rate of revolution of the particular planet they happened to be on at the time. He understood, even if he did not sympathize, with their desire to accomplish as much as possible in the limited time allotted to an expedition. But having seen on one unfortunate occasion that death had a way of putting a serious crimp in one's research, he knew he would have to be steadfast. Everyone back in camp at the prearranged time and no night work until they had a much better idea of their surroundings and any potential hazards.

Not that the prescribed hourly report-backs had revealed anything other than excitement at each new discovery. At least his current quartet of highly intelligent but frequently preoccupied charges had had the courtesy to call in on schedule. Wholly engaged in supervising the camp's fitting-out, he'd had no time to listen to the details, replete as they were with often incomprehensible scientific jargon. It was enough for him to know that no one had suddenly dropped dead or been consumed by some fascinating new local predator.

Tomorrow would be better, he told himself. With the camp now complete except for the final fill-ins and last adjustments, there would be time for occasional relaxation and the enjoyment of small luxuries. He would lecture them sternly on the importance of returning to the camp on time. With luck he would not have to mention it again.

Movement off to his left drew his attention. "Salvador—that type of processor is for specimen analysis. It goes in the laboratory module, not the kitchen."

The technician responded with an indifferent shrug. "Blend food, blend specimens—what is the difference?" But he obediently turned the lifter on which the equipment in question was presently balanced in the direction of the correct corner of the camp.

Araza was a strange bird, Boylan thought. Excellent worker, never talked back, versatile as hell. Except that when his expertise was not required he had kept largely to himself throughout the entire voyage. Which was alright, since it was all too easy for such a small number of travelers to get on one another's nerves when crammed together on a comparatively small interstellar craft. By removing himself from the social equation at every opportunity, Araza reduced the potential ingredient for intrasocial conflict by one. Boylan might not praise the technician, but neither could he find any real cause for complaint.

In addition to the man's natural reclusiveness, only one other personality trait of the technician stood out in Boylan's mind.

Araza showed absolutely no interest in Tiare Haviti. Even Boylan, who being in a position of dominant authority had to be extra careful in such matters, could not keep his eyes off the xenologist or his mind from pondering highly unscientific possibilities. This was perfectly natural. The hormonally driven stance was similarly evinced by Tellenberg and N'kosi. Whatever Valnadireb might think or feel had no relevance, of course. But one would have expected at least the occasional glance or comment from Araza. Nor had the tech, taking the topic to its logical extreme, shown any inclination toward or interest in any of the other xenologists, either. Where such matters were concerned, he appeared utterly indifferent.

Boylan shrugged inwardly. So long as it did not affect the technician's job performance, it was not really a captain's province to worry about the other.

As sunset approached, his discomfort increased along with the gathering darkness. He did not fully relax until the last pair of researchers were safely back in camp. They hardly listened to the stern admonition he had prepared that chided them for their respective late returns. They were too busy comparing notes on the day's discoveries. One in particular dominated the discussion over the dinner table as they took turns calling up meals from the camp food preparation equipment. Conversation was lightning-fast and overlapping. Feeling lost and left out, Boylan felt that if he could not participate he could at least referee.

"If you will slow down and let each other finish, you might actually be able to communicate something," he bellowed reprovingly.

The immediate result of this loudly voiced suggestion was an awkward moment of total quiet. Staring in dead silence at one another after jabbering nonstop resulted in some self-conscious laughter. It was left to Haviti to restart the conversation. To Boylan's relief, when it resumed it was at a more measured and comprehensible pace. Off to one side and apparently indifferent to the general excitement, a tool-laden Araza was fine-tuning the camp's climate-control instrumentation. He would eat later, when everyone else had finished. Boylan considered ordering the tech to join the evening meal but finally decided against it. If the man wanted to work through dinner, let him work.

"As we said via the general comm channel, we had a confrontation, a first contact," Haviti was declaiming breathlessly. "Definitely sentient, though of a low order. Simple tool-making skills in evidence, substantiation of interpersonal communication, clear signs of internal hierarchy—one would assume they have reached the tribal level."

N'kosi and Tellenberg exchanged looks. "We also encountered the natives, though we saw no evidence of tool-making skills. Hierarchy perhaps, person-to-person communication certainly."

Relaxing prone on his narrow horizontal lounge, Valnadireb provided confirmation as well as explication. As the thranx spoke, his truhands described delicate arcs through the air that even the most knowledgeable of his human colleagues could follow only imperfectly. In any case, the digital punctuation was more reflexive than necessary, as the xenologist's terranglo was virtually devoid of any accent.

"It was very interesting. The five of them watched us for a while. Then three, presumably the boldest of the group, came toward us. When I addressed them, they turned and ran. My appearance startled them, perhaps, or something in my voice. One of them expectorated in our direction and—"

N'kosi interrupted, "One of them spat at you?"

The thranx xenologist nodded. "Hard to tell if it was a gesture of defiance, an insult, an attempt to open some kind of nonverbal communication, or simply a natural reflex. The forming of the mouth—"

This time it was Tellenberg's turn to break in. "Mouth?" Glancing over at N'kosi, he was met by equal bewilderment. "What mouth? From what little we were able to observe, the semifluid, gelatinous nature of the natives' bodies would seem to preclude—"

"Semifluid? Gelatinous?" Her appetite beset by her intellect, a confused Haviti pushed the rest of her meal aside. "Are we talking about the same natives here?" Removing her communit from its belt pouch, she thumbed open the tiny integrated tripod and set it on the dining table. Across from her, Valnadireb did likewise.

"Of course we are talking about the same natives." Valnadireb hesitated. "Aren't we?"

Responding to Haviti's directions, the compact device she had activated played back the recording it had made earlier. The imagery automatically synched with Valnadireb's footage. As yet unedited or modified, the encounter at the river was shown in full detail complete with sound. As three-dimensional images materialized above the center of the table, it was as silent in the dining area as it had been noisy and excited only moments earlier. Everyone's attention was focused on the pooled projection that now dominated the room. Even Araza had paused in his never-ending work to glance in its direction.

Chosen by integrated AIware, the point of view alternated between thranx and human. In bright sunshine was revealed the river, the forest, the taking of specimens. Then the appearance of the native quintet, their brandishing of primitive weapons, followed by advance and bluster and then retreat. When it was over, the dimensional projection winked out. Picking up and re-folding her unit, Haviti looked first at N'kosi, then Tellenberg.

"Well? The only thing that I can see in the entire combined recording deserving of the designation 'semifluid' would be the spittle that the one native spat in our direction."

N'kosi was already setting up his communit. Next to him Tellenberg was doing the same. "Have a look at this." He flicked his device to life. The two playbacks combined.

Everyone seated at the table was treated to a hovering view of the alien seashore, the pink sky, and the specimens the two xe-nologists were collecting. Then the scene shifted to the forest's edge. The trio of stick-jellies emerged. Confrontation was brief but unmistakable, leaving both men stunned by the experience.

No more stunned than Valnadireb and Haviti as Tellenberg and N'kosi resecured their gear.

"I think the explanation is as clear and unavoidable as it is hard to believe." Valnadireb's truhands were now very active in-deed. "Living in close proximity to one another and in a small corner of this world, we have encountered not one but *two* sen-tient species. Most remarkable."

"That's not the half of it." N'kosi was checking his unit to make sure it had copied the information previously displayed by his colleagues. "Not only are we presented with the prospect of two native intelligences, physically they are as different as can be imagined. It's as if worms on Earth achieved sentience alongside humans, and at the same rate."

"Perhaps not the same rate," argued Haviti. "Your natives brandish more primitive weapons and show no sign of clothes-wearing."

"You saw them." Tellenberg eyed her challengingly. "Why would they need clothes?"

"They might as well come from two entirely different worlds." N'kosi was turning philosophical. "They've apparently evolved here. It's not a situation like on Fluva, where you have two sentient species living side by side but one consisting of long-term immigrants."

"Still, we can't be certain that both are native to this world until we have more information." Haviti was insistent. "If such proves to be the case, it will be a fascinating development." Her gaze roved around the table. "The next question is, which species do we first pursue contact with? I would vote for the fuzzies."

"Why?" countered Valnadireb vigorously. "Because they most closely resemble primates? Who is to say that the jelly-creatures are not more advanced? Or more amenable to further contact?"

Boylan put his foot down. "It's a scientific decision to be made, but I don't want to see any of my team strain their brains. You will work out details and I will support you. Enough first contact for tonight. I myself would like hear what else you found today."

Araza turned back to his work. Though reluctant to comply with the captain's directive, the scientific quartet had enough common sense to recognize the wisdom of giving so contentious a matter a rest. Talk turned to methods of photosynthesis, pro-ductiveness of alcohol-blended seawater versus that of fresh, density of microfauna, and other less controversial discoveries. Eventually adrenaline grew drained, eyes became heavy, and one by one the team stumbled off to sleep. Not a one of them be-lieved that the day's discoveries had been anything less than inestimable or a red-letter day for Commonwealth science. Given what they had accomplished in a single twenty-four-hour period, who knew what wonders waited to be quantified and recorded over the forthcoming weeks? Only exhaustion finally mitigated excitement and allowed any of them to even think of sleep.

No fool he, Boylan retired first, followed in close order by N'kosi and Valnadireb. Even the seemingly tireless Araza had disappeared into his personal cubicle by the time Tellenberg and Haviti found themselves walking together down the corridor. They had not so much resolved their disagreements as run out of the physical and intellectual fuel with which to power them.

Tellenberg studied the door that opened into his individual space. "I've stayed in prefab field rooms like these before. They're pretty solid. They may look skeletal, but they're perfectly soundproofed."

Haviti stepped easily around him. "Forget it, Esra. It's too early in the expedition, too soon in our relationship, and I'm too excited by what we all learned at dinner tonight."

He smiled helpfully. "I could assist you in relaxing."

She smiled back. "I don't recall requiring any assistance in relaxing on the journey out."

He persisted. "There are interesting variants on the concept of space-plus that involve the utilization of drives of the non-Kurita-Kinoshita variety."

"Sounds like pretty elementary physics to me." Reaching out, she gave him a friendly and (worst of all) semimaternal pat on the arm. "I already know enough about alternate drive systems, thanks. For one thing, when improperly engaged they have a disconcerting tendency to fail at critical moments. We wouldn't want that to happen, now would we?"

"Uh, no, I suppose not." He blinked at his door. Recognizing the relevant visual and electrical patterns, it clicked open. "I hope you sleep well, Tiare."

"I always sleep well; on Earth, on other planets civilized and elsewise, on unexplored worlds." She blinked at the door to her own room, which was next to Tellenberg's. "It's good that our individual living quarters are so well soundproofed. I wouldn't want my snoring to keep you awake." As the door slid aside, she stepped through. "Myself, I sleep like a stone. After everything that's happened today, I anticipate doing so with no trouble to-night."

But she was wrong, and the cause of her *slumber interruptus* had nothing to do with either her occasionally errant breathing or the self-conscious desires of her captivated neighbor next door.

3

Tellenberg had been only partly correct. The surface life-support modules were very well soundproofed—but their sound-dampening properties were not perfect. Certainly not when large, heavy objects came banging and rattling against them in the middle of an otherwise peaceful, dead-silent night.

Sliding off his inflatable sleeping platform, he stumbled to the hallway door and opened it. Illumination panels emitting their own soft blue internal glow allowed him to see both up and down the corridor without having to touch either wall to inten-sify the light. Nor did he need anything in the way of artificial amplification to allow him to hear an incensed Boylan roaring in the distance. The captain's impassioned bellows soared even above the general clamor that accompanied them, like a brass choir rising above the rest of a fully-engaged orchestra.

Another door opened farther down the corridor and N'kosi stepped out. The xenologist was already dressed. Not only that, he gripped his standard-issue field pistol in one hand. Eyeing his alert colleague, it occurred to a still-awakening Tellenberg that this was an eminently sensible reaction to unexpected violent noise accompanied by the initial inklings of mounting chaos. As relevant neurons responding to his increased wakefulness began to fire with greater frequency, he considered returning to his own room to put on some clothes and pick up some gear. On the other hand, he told himself as he struggled toward full aware-ness, the racket that had awoken him was likely due to nothing more than an unusually unruly equipment malfunction. From the tone of the captain's voice, Boylan was already on the case.

As a cautious N'kosi came up beside him both men peered up the dim but adequately illuminated corridor. "Any idea what's going on?"

Tellenberg shook his head. "Something banging on the out-side wall woke me up. Now it sounds like it's moved inside."

"Same here." The other xenologist gestured. "I think maybe that's Boylan coming this way now."

Since his eyesight was not as sharp as that of his companions, N'kosi could be excused for his mistake. The error rectified itself as the figure barreling toward them resolved itself into a shape. Not only was it not the captain; it was not even remotely human.

Squat and thickset, it was shorter than either of the two gap-ing scientists; shorter even than Valnadireb. Instead of moving in sequence like the limbs of a terrestrial quadruped, the crea-ture's four legs appeared to rotate from front to back in the style of a tracked vehicle. Powerful but stubby arms terminated in circular hands that were tipped with inward-curving talons. Ad-ditional claws were visible on the feet while the wide mouth set in the middle of the half-spherical skull was festooned with fangs that arced in all directions; a Vesuvius of dentition. Set in pairs at the top and bottom of the skull, a quartet of crimson eyes flashed in the reflected light of the hallway. Additional sharp spines jutted from joints, back, and flanks.

One arm cradled a bucketful of rounded stones. Letting out a roar, the creature reached in, selected a rock the size of a fist, and flung it in the xenologists' direction. N'kosi ducked to one side and a startled and nearly naked Tellenberg to the other as the rock sailed between them. The assault demonstrated tool-using of the most primitive kind, but tool-using nevertheless. The actual degree of decision-making brainpower being employed by the alien would have to remain a question for future study since at that moment neither man was in an analytical mood. Speedily shunting aside any hesitation about employing advanced technology against indigenous primitives, N'kosi fired. As a marksman, he was an excellent scientist. His wild shot blew a neat round hole in the corridor's outer wall.

Firing from behind him, Valnadireb put an explosive shell in the center of the onrushing entity's virtually nonexistent neck. Able to grip his weapon with four hands, the thranx had the advantage of a steadier natural firing platform than did his human companions. Emitting a loud noise halfway between a belch and a bleat, the spiny quadrupedal horror collapsed less than a meter from Tellenberg's feet. Deprived of its head by Valnadireb's timely shot, the corpse proceeded to spew greenish-red blood all over the tall xenologist's lower legs and feet.

By now Haviti had come up alongside the thranx. She was half dressed and armed. If anyone had bet Tellenberg that under such circumstances he would not have stared, he would have accepted the wager. He also would have lost money. Having a ferociously hostile and violently decapitated alien primitive gushing bodily fluids all over his lower body instantly reduced any incipient libido to less than zero. Shaken, Tellenberg rose from where he had been crouching. He began brushing weakly at his legs in a futile attempt to wipe himself off.

Crashing, splintering sounds punctuated by echoing gunfire continued to reach them from the vicinity of the camp's entrance dome. A grim-faced Haviti pushed past the three males.

"We'd better get up there."

N'kosi and Valnadireb followed her lead. Tellenberg started to join them, remembered something, rushed back into his room to get his own weapon. He had to run hard to catch back up to them. Focused on recovering his gun, he had not bothered to take the time to get dressed, correctly assuming that his relative nakedness made not the slightest difference either to his colleagues or to the native intruders.

The domed entry chamber was a mess. Equipment and fixtures were scattered everywhere, much still intact, some shattered and broken. As the scientists arrived Boylan and Araza were just stepping out from behind a worktable they had overturned to form a makeshift bulwark. Enough alien body parts to make up four or five of the spike-and-claw-equipped invaders lay scattered around the room or splattered against the walls. A dull, sweetish stink like milk left out too long in the sun permeated the air. Boylan was unhurt while Araza paid no attention to the bloody parallel gashes that creased his right side from beneath his arm all the way down to his hip.

Boylan did not say hello. Gesturing with the pulse rifle he held, he started deliberately toward the gaping entrance. "Quickly! The others have pulled back, but for all we know they re-forming for another try. If so, we have to disrupt them before they can organize themselves!"

This is ridiculous, Tellenberg thought as he and the others followed the captain. *I should be breaking down and recording the*

*microscopic structure of water-dwelling proteins, not running around
in my underwear waving a gun at belligerent natives.* What had
begun as a normal, pleasant evening had degenerated into a se-
riocomic tridee episode.

As it turned out he was not forced to engage in the unwel-
come activity for very long. Contrary to Boylan's fears, a quick
survey indicated that the camp's surviving attackers had fled.
That they had taken their wounded with them only confirmed
their sentience. Rock-throwing animals would have left any seriously injured behind. Compassion for the wounded was a surer
indication of intelligence than any amount of rock-throwing.

The scientists waited while an irate Boylan and the ever-
phlegmatic Araza walked the camp perimeter. Once they were
convinced no natives were lying in ambush, they moved on to
inspect the shuttle. Even though the sealed craft possessed its
own automated defensive devices, the captain was taking no
chances. This gave Tellenberg and his companions time to catch
their breath as well as to reflect on the extraordinary cacophony
of nocturnal noises from which they had initially been insulated
within the buildings.

"Quite amazing." N'kosi was squinting up at a trio of multilimbed arboreals who were cavorting in a nearby tree. Tellenberg
could not tell if his colleague was referring to the outrageous
growth itself, which resembled a cross between a giant spiny suc-
culent and a cluster of amethyst crystals, or the softly hooting
animals capering aerobatically among its branches/thorns. As
unclassifiable as the growth in which they were performing, the
animals smoldered with a weird, internal green light. Seeing
the watching scientists edging closer to their tree, they fled into
the forest depths like a trio of oversized many-armed fireflies.

"Look there." Haviti was pointing excitedly. It was almost as if the attack on the camp had never taken place. This instinctive displacement from reality in the face of new knowledge, so characteristic of scientists in the field, was shared by all of them. No exception to the rule, Tellenberg found himself gazing at the slight bulge in the soil where his colleague was pointing.

The bulge was moving. It approached to within a few meters of them before halting. Dirt and ground cover was pushed aside as a drill emerged from the earth. Made of some dark siliceous material, the drill lay in a slot on the back of a small, flaccid-skinned lump that showed only two front legs. Two more heads popped out of the ground on either side of the drill-bearer. Vestigial eyes regarded the awestruck researchers. Apparently seeing or smelling something they didn't like, the two newcomers picked up the drill-bearer in their front flippers and bodily turned it around. Following it back into the soil, the three subterranean dwellers once again vanished underground.

The astonished researchers had observed a new species in the trees. They had encountered a new species that lived underground. Taxonomically, physiologically, none bore the slightest resemblance to the other. Then there was the matter of the natives who had attacked the camp. Heavyset and ponderous, they possessed a unique method of locomotion. Quadrisymmetrical and belligerent, their bodies were adorned with an armory of fangs, talons, and spikes. Tellenberg's mental discomfort grew. He did not like it when the rules of science were toyed with. This continuously surprising world might well have an ace or two to show them, but so far the local planetary deck seemed to consist entirely of jokers.

He wondered if anyone else shared his growing unease. Without asking, there was no way of knowing. He considered confiding in one of his colleagues. Haviti, perhaps.

No. A general feeling of disquiet was not a scientific tenet. Before he could discuss it with someone else he needed to better codify his distress.

His attention and that of his companions was disrupted by the return of Boylan and the silent Araza. The captain had shouldered his rifle. A good sign, Tellenberg decided.

"Expeditions are rarely greeted with open hospitality," Boylan muttered, "but this is first one I've been on where I was attacked before contact was even offered." Araza had walked over to a storage shed and was unsealing the locks. "Some of you might want gloves," Boylan continued. With one hand he gestured at a gap in the perimeter wiring where the attackers had broken through. "We going to have to put up a full-charged barrier. Salvador and I can do it, but it go a lot faster if all of you pitch in. I not ordering any of you to assist." He mustered a lopsided grin. "But the sooner main barrier is up and activated, the better we all of us sleep."

Boylan was lying, Tellenberg knew. As captain, commander, and the man in charge of military affairs for the undersized expedition, he very well could have ordered them to help with the work. Sagely, he had phrased the necessity as a request instead of a command. Having been roughly roused from their rest and frontally attacked, the researchers wanted to see the charged barrier erected as quickly as did their leader.

With all six of them contributing, one post after another was rapidly and efficiently put in place. Even so, securing the camp's perimeter required them all to work through most of the night. Boylan's prophecy proved correct, though. As soon as the emplaced defensive system was completed and successfully tested, every one of them promptly retired to their cubicles to sleep the sleep of the exhausted. This included Boylan and Araza. Utterly drained, the lot of them were compelled to rely on the automatics they had set up to warn them if another attack by the natives was imminent.

Fortunately, nothing came creeping out of the remainder of the night or the early morning to test the newly erected defensive barrier. A couple of small hopping things inadvertently impacted the crisscrossing beams and were promptly flash-fried. The system's integrated AI was sufficiently sophisticated to analyze these encounters, determine that they did not represent a greater threat to the camp it was charged with protecting, and leave the alarms inert.

The desire for knowledge being a more powerful motivator even than caffeine and its synthetic derivatives, the following morning saw all four of the xenologists assembled in the camp's living area. Less driven and perhaps more tired, Boylan and Araza did not join them. Around cups of reinvigorating liquid and self-heating breakfast packs, the expedition's science team discussed the previous night's onslaught and the afternoon's prospects. The two were now unavoidably entwined.

"I want to get back into that river." Devoid of the makeup she did not need anyway, Haviti was shoveling down food with energy and an appetite more suited to a burly heavy-lift operator. "The sand and mud shallows alone are swarming with the most incredible assortment of arthropoidal wrigglers and bizarre bivalves I've ever seen in one place. And that doesn't even take into account the big stuff that keeps swimming, paddling, or jetting past." She paused her rapid-fire speech and consumption long enough to meet each of their gazes in turn. "But we can't work under conditions like last night."

Sipping his breakfast through the spiraling siphon of a distinctive thranx drinking vessel, Valnadireb readily concurred.

"The next attack, should there be one, could well occur in the middle of the day in less defensible surroundings." He gestured in Haviti's direction. "While one or two of us are working alone at a field site, for example. Under such conditions and given a sufficient disparity in numbers, even modern weaponry might not suffice to hold off an assault by truly determined antagonistic natives."

"I don't understand." On the other side of the table, Tellenberg was shaking his head. "There was no attempt to communicate, nothing at all. I talked to Boylan. He confirms it. It was a straightforward, headlong charge by the spikers. Fortunately, the external sensors alerted him and Araza in time." He sipped at his chosen brew. "You'd think that when confronted by something as utterly beyond their experience as this outpost, curious primitives would try to learn something about it before trying to destroy it."

N'kosi shrugged. "Maybe it wasn't destruction on their minds. Perhaps it was simple loot and pillage."

Tellenberg turned to his colleague. "How do you loot and pillage something the likes of which you've never seen before? How do you know if it contains anything worth looting and pillaging? Or that you could perhaps obtain everything you want from it just by asking? It doesn't make sense. They were clearly intelligent, but they didn't act intelligently."

"Not to you," Haviti pointed out. "Maybe a Quofumian native operates in accordance with a different philosophy."

Tellenberg caught his breath. "You're right, of course. But I'm not just addressing the events of last night from a human perspective. The general rule among newly contacted primitive races is that they don't attack outright. If nothing else, they take the time to try and discern their new opponent's strengths and weaknesses. Not these folk. We land, set up camp, and a few days later they launch an all-out frontal attack without even trying to establish the most rudimentary contact."

"Sounds like it could be a religious reaction." As he spoke, N'kosi was scrutinizing something on his communit's readout. "Maybe we arrived on the day deemed locally most propitious for launching all-out attacks on strangers from the sky. Right now we know as little about the locals as they do about us."

Drink container in hands, Valnadireb slipped daintily off his resting bench. "A situation that clearly must be rectified as rapidly as possible before we can pursue any additional field studies in our preferred specialties. I, for one, have no intention of mucking about in these exceedingly fantastic alien woods until I can be reasonably certain I can do so without having to worry about getting a spear thrust into my abdomen the first time I turn my full attention to my work."

"The next item on the program, then, is second contact." Haviti wiped her lips with the back of a recyclable cloth. "The question is—who with? We're faced with the remarkable and, insofar as my recollection allows, unprecedented situation of having to deal with not one but three distinct indigenous sentient species inhabiting the same geographically limited area."

N'kosi nodded. "I know of worlds where two different races were encountered living in close proximity to one another, but as far as I know this is the first time a survey team has made contact with three existing in such circumstances. And in the first week, no less."

"The place is a veritable metropolis." Valnadireb had walked up to the table to be closer to his colleagues. "We already know what the spikers think of us. It would be useful as well as interesting to know what the stick-jellies and the fuzzies think of them as well as of each other."

Spikers, Tellenberg found himself thinking. Stick-jellies and fuzzies. Taxonomically surreal but descriptively useful. The application of proper scientific nomenclature could wait until, as their thranx colleague had colorfully put it, their backsides were as safe as their ship.

"We should proceed according to a plan," he advised. "Try contacting and studying one species at a time." He repeated the recommendation he had made previously. "I propose that we initiate initial formal contact with the stick-jellies."

Haviti looked at him sharply. "Why? Are you continuing to favor early contact with them because those are the sentients you and N'kosi happened to encounter?"

He bridled slightly at the implication. "You ought to know me well enough by now, Tiare, to know that I wouldn't base a decision as important as this on something as inconsequential as that. We're not jockeying for an award here. It doesn't matter which of us encountered which species first. I am proposing we pursue contact with the stick-jellies because they are the group that has so far shown the least hostility toward us. The spikers' aggressiveness is beyond dispute, and according to your own report, the fuzzies approached you in a manner that was both armed and threatening."

"I'd rather say 'challenging.'"

"Fair enough. The nature of the fuzzies' confrontation remains open to interpretation. That of the stick-jellies was clearly less antagonistic."

"You reported that they waved sharpened sticks in your direction."

"They gestured with sharpened pieces of wood, yes," Tellenberg admitted. "They might have been hostile gestures. They might also have been simple acknowledgment of our presence, or even a type of salute."

Haviti tried another tack. "You also reported that they made no sounds. If they communicate by methods other than speech it will be difficult to exchange complex concepts and ideas."

"It could be managed." By way of emphasis Valnadireb executed an intricate gesture in High Thranx that required the simultaneous use of all four of his hands.

The lively debate ate another hour. At the end of the discussion the decision was put to a vote. Trying to make contact with the spikers was obviously, for the moment anyway, out of the question. It was finally decided that they would make the formal attempt at second contact with the fuzzies. Not only because the representatives of that species had demonstrated the ability to express themselves verbally, but because they were the only one of the three encountered whose possible location could be guessed at. The spikers and the stick-jellies had emerged from the depths of the forest and vanished back into it, leaving no trails behind, whereas the fuzzies had made their appearance on the riverbank and had subsequently been observed by Haviti and Valnadireb retreating upstream. If not a direct path through the woods, the river at least offered a route that could be followed.

Furthermore, traveling on the river in a simple inflatable meant they could move upstream in comparative safety in a craft that, if necessary, could provide a means of rapid escape while simultaneously not revealing the kind of advanced technology that use of the shuttle's skimmer would necessarily entail. When despite his innate fear of water Valnadireb bravely agreed to participate, Tellenberg felt he had no choice but to go along with the majority decision. Attempts at further contact with the fascinating stick-jellies would have to wait.

Three biologically distinct primitive native intelligences, he mused wonderingly to himself. If ever a planetary survey called for the personnel and resources of a full-scale expedition, this one did. In lieu of returning straight home and turning their discoveries over to the administrators of Commonwealth Science Central and the Xenology division of the United Church, however, the four of them would just have to manage on their own.

At least, he reflected, there would be none of the usual backbiting and infighting for credit among the scientific staff of the mission to the outlying system of Quofum. Already there were more than enough in the way of exceptional discoveries to go around. Why, each xenologist could virtually claim to have discovered a new intelligent species all by themselves. That was not how further research would progress, of course. As was only right and proper good science, they would continue to feed off one another's sub-specialties.

He sighed. It was settled. They would begin by studying the fuzzies. He would duly make his contribution. Examination of the silent stick-jellies and the belligerent spikers would follow in due course. Only one other individual had to be convinced that the proper decisions had been made before they could get started.

Perhaps not unexpectedly, Boylan was less than eager to grant his imprimatur to their request. He looked down from the roof where he and Araza were putting the finishing touches on a long-range communications array that would allow anyone at the camp to engage in simultaneous chat with every other member of the team no matter where they were on the planet, so long as they were within range of the main relay on the orbiting starship.

"Let me get this straight: despite what happen last night, you want to leave safety of camp and take an inflatable upriver to study these club-wielding bipeds?" Behind him, Araza was spraying a network of circuitry onto the parabola of the main antenna.

"To do proper fieldwork," N'kosi explained patiently and with a commendable absence of sarcasm, "you have to get out into the field."

Boylan sat down, his legs dangling over the edge of the completed lab module. It had not been damaged in the previous night's attack. "Isn't this enough 'field' for you?" With a sweeping gesture he took in the swath of fantastic forest that surrounded the campsite.

Haviti stepped forward. "Captain Boylan, when confronted by a previously uncontacted alien species that rises to a minimum level of sentience it is our primary duty as xenologists to open inter-humanx dialogue with that species. We are confronted here with not one but three such potential species. Our expeditionary mandate is limited both by charter and supplies. We have no time to waste and, having no time to waste, cannot afford to be as circumspect as we ourselves might wish to be. We have no choice but to forge ahead with these multiple contacts as quickly as possible."

Boylan responded with a hard stare. This was followed by a husky laugh. "If you were running for Commonwealth office, Ms. Tiare, I think I would take risk to vote for you twice. You are human mind-wiping machine that takes away all my common sense. All right, go and take your river cruise." His gaze shifted to the figure standing next to her. "Even the bug is going?"

Valnadireb made a gesture none of his human companions could translate, which was just as well. "In the event of a catastrophic capsizing, I know that I will be able to utilize three bloated human sacs for flotation."

Boylan roared louder than ever. Behind him, even Araza cracked a smile. The tech said little but missed nothing, Tellenberg observed.

It helped that there were numerous preparations to be made. In addition to amassing extra gear in case necessity required that they be away from the camp overnight, it took several of them to help with the inflation of the boat. Suspended on its own lifters, the finished craft could be guided to the river by one person. But first a path had to be cut through the forest. Their carbonizing shafts sweeping back and forth parallel to the ground, beam-cutters made quick work of most of the growth that blocked access to the water's edge. A small copse of narrow, silvery poles simply would not be cut down, however, and this required a small but delaying detour.

By the following evening, the expandable boat rested with its bow on the sandy shore and its stern in the water. The attached compressing engine would power it effortlessly upstream against the current and in comparative silence. As for the hull itself, it was composed of reinforced aerogel froth that would shed water and floating debris with equal efficacy.

They would not load stores until the following morning. Boylan saw no reason to tempt marauding spikers or curious fauna by leaving supplies out on the craft overnight. As for the boat itself, the latter were unlikely to bother the beached vessel and the former had shown no interest in anything where the crew was not present, including the shuttle that lay outside the camp's perimeter.

Later that night Tellenberg lay flat on his back on his bed, unable to sleep. While the inbuilt soundproofing of the camp's buildings provided peace and privacy, they also shut out the splendid melodious tumult sung by the surrounding forest. Straining to hear beyond the silence he could not keep an endless stream of questions from running through his head.

Had the natives mastered higher pursuits such as music, or art, or storytelling? Had any of the three sentient species the visitors had encountered learned the use of materials more advanced than wood and stone and sinew? Hopefully, they would begin to answer such questions tomorrow. With luck they would encounter not only the lanky indigenes that Haviti and Valnadireb had stumbled across, but perhaps indications of embryonic civilization. Crude shelters, perhaps, or maybe even a village. Primitives who had learned to utilize scraps of hide or plant material to make clothing, however crude, could also employ them to fashion roofs and other items indicative of higher thought.

As he lay on his back staring at the smooth, seamless ceiling, he found himself listening for the sounds of rocks thudding against the module's exterior wall. None were forthcoming. The spikers were lying low tonight, he mused. It was an encouraging sign. Maybe tomorrow he and his companions would actually be able to spend an entire day doing nothing but science. It would be a change from their first few days on Quofum.

Even better, the world beneath their feet had not winked out of existence. The planetary reality might be outré, bemusing, even impressive, but it was also thankfully a good deal more solid and stable than that first robotic probe and subsequent singular astronomical conclusions might have led one to believe.

With that comforting thought in mind he drifted off into a deep and restful sleep.

4

It did not take long to load the boat. Self-contained travel modules fit neatly into larger containers that were impervious to the local flora and fauna. Thermosensitive packaging would alternately cool or warm food supplies to maintain them at their optimal temperature and prevent spoilage. Armaments were checked and charged. The presence of these weapons was necessary not only for defense in case of another attack by the belligerent spikers but in the event they encountered dangerous carnivorous fauna. Their brief time on Quofum had already revealed an enormous variety of animal life. If experience and history held true to biological form, it was unlikely that all of it would be benign.

It began to rain when they pushed off, the silent motor backing the simple but sleek craft out into navigable water. The drizzle freshened and cooled the air. Unlike the ocean, it did not smell or taste of alcohol.

That meant, Tellenberg mused, that the alcoholic content of

the local seas arose from a source other than the clouds. Did it dissolve out of ancient deposits? Could one establish an alcohol mine on Quofum? How would one identify and label such a claim? A host of possibilities crossed his mind in rapid succession, many of them more frivolous than scientific.

Off in the distance thunder boomed, hinting at heavier precipitation to come. A touch on a console unfurled the boat's stiffened plastic roof. Seated at the controls, N'kosi swung the bow around and headed the craft upstream, accelerating modestly as he did so. Erupting from the water in advance of the boat's prow, a flurry of winged white worms scattered, as if the silvery surface had suddenly been embossed with ivory.

"Beautiful morning." Haviti leaned out slightly to look at the sky, which had begun to weep more heavily.

Eyeing his fellow scientist's supple form as she turned and twisted slightly to scan the clouds, Tellenberg decided that he could not have agreed more. On the shore off to their left, something like a garbage heap fashioned of fragments of dark blue glass hastened to flatten itself against the earth, minimizing its silhouette to potential predators. Nearby, what at first glance appeared to be half a dozen tall narrow huts abruptly rose up on lanky, polelike legs and ambled off into the brush.

What a world, an energized Tellenberg found himself thinking. Not only did it flaunt life in tremendous variety, but life-forms that appeared to follow multiple patterns of development. Employing elementary cladistics he tried to construct a relationship between the long-legged hut-things and the blue glass blob, between the spikers and the stick-jellies, and failed. Even the makeup of the dense forest was suspect. Some growths were clearly composed of familiar complex carbohydrates, but the appearance of others suggested a silicate rather than a carbon base, while a great deal of the understory and brush was derived from a combination of sources, many of which defied casual visual identification. The place was a botanist's wonderland.

As if that was not enough, they had not one but three native sentient species to study. Reputations were going to be made here, he was confident. Quofum might have proven to be a bit of a puzzle to astronomers, but that peculiar conundrum had now been resolved. It might boast an unreal ecosystem, but there was nothing mysterious about the world itself. It was as solid and bona fide as any other world. Privately he wondered at the unique astrophysical distortions that had so often hidden it from detection. A particularly dense and localized dark nebula had to be responsible, he decided, or perhaps some new kind of astronomical distortion yet to be determined.

Not his specialty. What mattered was that Quofum now stood revealed in all its fecund glory, just waiting for a fortunate few to unlock its apparent treasure trove of biological secrets. Not even a week had elapsed and they had already begun, had already started to fill information files with reams of entirely new and unexpected data. Soon they would be able to add details about and descriptions of sentient species to the explosively expanding compendium, starting with the fuzzies.

Boylan had not been happy to see them go. As expedition commander there was nothing to prevent him from accompanying the scientific team, but he knew he would only have taken up space on the boat. Someone had to remain and look after the camp. As he stated on more than one occasion he would have preferred to see his colleagues conduct their studies close to camp, where they would have remained under the protection of the camp and the shuttle's defenses. Underneath his gruff exterior and behind his curt personality the captain was an old mothering hen, a smiling Tellenberg reflected. He would never dare voice such an analogy to the captain's face, of course. Not if he wanted to retain his own facial features in their present familiar configuration.

Even Araza had come to the river's edge to wish them well, in his terse, soft-spoken way. Tellenberg recalled watching both men standing side by side on the bank as they waved the science team on its way.

"Sample all the biota you want!" the captain had yelled after them as soon as N'kosi had started the boat upriver. "Just don't let it sample *you!*"

Better to have a competent, crotchety, irritating, unsociable leader and a skilled accomplice who hardly ever spoke looking after things than a couple of cheerful, companionable idiots, Tellenberg knew.

While the excitement and sense of expectation on the boat was palpable, it was not universal. Though the current was lazy and there was little or nothing in the way of white water, Valnadireb remained resolutely in the center of the craft, as far away from the sturdy gunwales as possible. Observing the thranx's discomfort, N'kosi quietly edged over to port and began pushing back and forth on the side of the boat in an attempt to impart a little extra rocking motion. Only a dirty look from Haviti stopped him. A little sheepishly, he returned to overseeing the control panel. He wasn't having much luck rocking the highly stable inflatable anyway.

Tellenberg had to admit that their thranx colleague was doing an admirable job of dealing with a state of affairs that would have reduced the less stoic and resolved among his kind to shrinking piles of quivering chitin. Not only did Valnadireb stand upright (albeit on all sixes) with his eyes surveying the opposing shores, he even managed to make his share of field observations, taking notes on his recorder while deliberately ignoring the occasional splash that came over the bow.

The only time he evinced any visible fear was on the occasions when one of his counterparts hit a control that turned the sides and bottom of the boat from opaque to transparent, allowing for the study of the riverine flora and fauna directly beneath them. In the absence of visible ribs or a keel, the transformation made it appear as if they were standing or sitting on a particular stiff piece of water. Conscious of their companion's discomfort at such moments, Tellenberg and the others minimized their use of the pertinent option.

There was an abundance of biota to study anyway, without gazing down into the watery depths. Just as it did in the vicinity of the camp, the alien forest grew down to the water's edge. Seasonal flow must stay relatively steady, Tellenberg decided, since the opposing banks showed little evidence of periodic flooding. Much of the flora lining the shore was large and sturdy, evidence that it had been growing in place for a long time.

If the vegetation was a riot of conflicting patterns, plans, and configurations, the fauna they observed as the craft plowed smoothly upstream verged on the chaotic. As overwhelmed as his colleagues, Tellenberg tried to get a scientific rope around one small part of the local animal life by concentrating his attention on the Quofumian inhabitants of the rose-hued sky.

There were what appeared to be many birdlike creatures, though even with his magnifying lenses flipped down it was difficult to distinguish details among the profusion of fast-moving fliers. Some sported beaks and feathers. But even among these almost-familiar shapes there were discrepancies that spoke of biological bedlam. What did a seemingly skillful flier need with a leathery tail that was twice its own length? Why did some fliers soar on two wings while others boasted four, or six? While many had developed bisymmetrically, others were trisymmetrical, or quadri, or worse. Some displayed limbs and appendages and appurtenances that appeared to have sprouted according to no discernible pattern whatsoever, as if their maturation had been guided by cancer rather than genes.

There were wings with feathers, wings with hair, wings made of leathery membrane, and wings of diaphanous transparency. Propulsion was provided not only by flapping wings and gliding on wings but by spiral lifters and jetlike nozzles, by altering internal temperatures between body parts, and by inflation of others. The more he saw of the native fauna the more Tellenberg found himself thinking of it not as an ecosystem but as a circus.

A logical corollary would be to look for an external influence as the source of rampant mutation. The only problem was that preliminary observations had revealed none. Quofum's star was comfortingly Sol-like. It rained no surfeit of damaging radiation onto the planet's surface. Nor had instruments located any identifiable internal source. What then, he found himself wondering, was the cause of what they were seeing? Could they simply put Quofum down as one of the most biologically diverse worlds yet visited by humanxkind and leave it at that?

They could not, he knew, because it was not the planet's diversity that kept nagging at him. It was the seeming lack of organic relationship between so many of the life-forms, both plant and animal, that they continued to encounter. For example, it was not unreasonable to record several dozen different species of reedlike growths colonizing the river's watery shallows. What was unsettling was to discover that some of them were built up of cellulose, others of silicon, still others of biosulfates. And this developmental disparity among the flora was nothing compared to what he had seen occupying the sky and the land.

Dazzled by the unending parade of exotic life-forms, they passed the rest of the day wholly occupied in making individual and collective observations. Having failed by sundown to resight the group of fuzzies first encountered by Haviti and N'kosi, they settled down to spend the night cruising the middle of the river. While Tellenberg reported back to Boylan, N'kosi turned the craft's controls over to its unpretentious AI. The automatics would keep the boat properly positioned, keeping it away from shore against any shift in current or sudden rise in water level. They would thus be able to sleep secure in the knowledge that they would not drift ashore and expose themselves to any marauding terrestrial carnivores. As for anything that might rise out of the deep or come swimming toward them, the boat's integrated security systems would either deal with any such threat on its own or wake them with ample time to confront and analyze it themselves.

Inflatable sleepers (flat and rectangular for the humans, narrow and slightly rounded for Valnadireb) provided comfortable platforms for a night's rest. Despite these beckoning temptations, everyone was reluctant to turn in for the night. With the disappearance of the sun and in the absence of a moon, a vast and varied multitude of night-dwellers soon took wing in the star-filled alien sky. They constituted, Tellenberg immediately determined, an entirely new and astounding biota that was if anything even more exceptional and perplexing than the fauna he and his colleagues had studied during the day. As he busied himself with his recorder, which automatically adjusted for the greatly reduced light, his fascination and unease continued to expand in equal measure.

While his eyes were drawn to the fluorescent and phosphorescent creatures that darted along the shoreline, or winked in and out among the trees, his mind was fascinated by the glowing growths themselves. Within the boundaries of the Commonwealth, plant life that fluoresced was hardly unknown, but it usually restricted itself to one class of flora. Fungi, for example, or the siliceous crystalline sprays of Prism.

Not here. So much light emanated from the forest fringe that Tellenberg guessed it would be possible to wander those alien woods without any artificial light at all. The biological quandary he found himself confronting did not involve a lack of naturally generated light but rather a surfeit of it.

A thicket of ten-meter-high bamboolike shoots alternately flashed a deep red, then purple. Nearby, a cluster of flowers with weirdly twisted petals flared bright yellow, their internal luminescence flashing in sequence from petal to petal as if their internal lights were chasing each other around the outside of the flower. Gnarled scrub that during the day would have defined inconspicuousness pulsed with soft pink, then green light. The tips of grasslike ground cover twinkled like a billion blue stars. Some otherwise florid florals remained perfectly dark, choosing to bask in the radiance of their neighbors.

Or perhaps to hide among it, he thought as he let his recorder run. Flashier plant life might draw the attention of nocturnal herbivores away from tastier growths that did not phosphoresce at all. Maybe the fluorescence was the luciferaselike equivalent of the bright colors worn by certain toxic Terran fauna, warning prospective predators that their potential prey was poisonous, treacherous, or both. For a xenologist, to see what amounted to the blanket application of luminous protective coloration was startling. Or possibly he was ruminating in the wrong direction. Perhaps all the rampant floral luminosity had another purpose entirely, one that could only be properly divined by patient research in the lab. For example, carnivorous plant life might use such internal lights to attract prey.

Whatever the function, the shimmering forest certainly made for a spectacular journey upriver. Reflected lights danced off the water as the boat cleaved a steady path to the northeast.

Flecks of deep crimson like windblown bloodstains swooped and darted through the night air just aft of the stern, surfing the disturbed air that trailed in the boat's wake as they sought even smaller arboreal prey. One time something like a blue blanket soared past, blocking out the stars as it glided silently downriver. An increasingly drowsy Tellenberg estimated that its wingspan was at least twice that of the shuttle's length. On shore, unseen animal life squealed and meeped, whistled and sang and hooted, the startling multiplicity of voices forming a perfect choral counterpoint to the sea of dancing floral colors.

One by one even the most dedicated among them retired to their respective sleeping platforms. When N'kosi had finally had enough, he too retired, after checking to make sure that the craft's internal AI understood its instructions. It would wake them if the boat was threatened or if anything of exceptional merit manifested itself. Defining the latter meant radically expanding the AI's definition of "exceptional." Though they revised the definition several times during the night, the AI still woke them on two different occasions.

Tellenberg had always been able to sleep soundly. In this he was luckier than any of his colleagues. Much to the simultaneous admiration and consternation of his companions he even managed to sleep through the boat AI's two uncertain and unnecessary alarms.

So it was not surprising that he should finally be awakened by half a cup of purified river water that N'kosi, with great precision and considerable satisfaction, trickled onto his face. He sat up sputtering.

"Hey, what's the . . . ?"

Valnadireb cut him off with a suitable four-armed gesture. "I have seen dead people more easily stirred. We are all jealous. How do you do it?"

Sitting up on his sleeping platform, Tellenberg wiped water from his face and muttered, "Do what?"

"Sleep through anything. Sleep through forest screams, sleep through lights that burn with the brilliance of unwanted urban advertisements, sleep through alerts sounded by the boat."

Tellenberg looked around uneasily. "I slept through an alarm?"

"Two." N'kosi was now preparing a hot drink in the same cup that had been used to douse his colleague. "Remarkable."

Tellenberg was apologetic. "I've always been able to sleep anywhere, even out in the field." He grinned shyly. "I have a clean conscience, I guess."

"Or none." Valnadireb turned away, pivoting on all four trulegs and both foothands. While Tellenberg noted that the thranx's supporting limbs did not dig quite so deeply into the deck as when they had first boarded the craft, neither were they completely relaxed. Not even the redoubtable Valnadireb could completely ignore the fact that he still had water underfoot, even if he was separated from it by the bottom of the boat.

It was less than an hour later that Haviti, perched attractively

if professionally in the observation seat in the bow, called back to
N'kosi to reduce speed. Relaxing casually in the command chair
behind the weatherproof console, her fellow xenologist moved
to comply as Tellenberg and Valnadireb rushed to the bow.

"Take it slow," she called back. Obedient to N'kosi's touch,
the craft decelerated until it was barely making headway against
the current.

It took only a moment to share Haviti's vision and to see
what had impelled her to direct N'kosi to reduce their speed.
Actually, Tellenberg heard it before he saw it. Valnadireb was
standing so close to him that the thranx's natural perfume was
nearly overwhelming. Instead of being held vertically, both of
the insectoid xenologist's antennae were inclined forward, in
the direction of the nearest bank.

Off to starboard, the forest was thinning rapidly. As the boat
came around a bend in the river, the level of the noise they had
been hearing suddenly rose tenfold in both volume and complexity. The sound was terrible. It was as if some maniacal music
maker had decided that instead of mixing rhythms and melodies
he would attempt to merge recordings of riots from half a dozen
worlds—none of them populated by humans. The shrill, frantic
cacophony threatened to give everyone on board including Valnadireb a severe headache. That concern was forgotten as soon as
they got their first look at the source of the uproar.

There was a war in progress.

It was a limited war; limited by the number of participants as
well as the primitive nature of the weapons they were employing. But a war nonetheless, with potentially grave and lethal
consequences for all who were involved. A village was on fire.
Actually, that was too sophisticated a definition for the community under siege, Tellenberg decided. It was more a cluster of

slapdash huts crudely thrown together out of fallen leaves and scavenged wood. Still, it was home to those who were presently under attack.

Even from the center of the river it was not difficult to sort out the combatants. The community was being defended by stick-jellies acting in concert with groups of fuzzies. Assailing them were lines of spikers. As if the odds did not already seem stacked against the defenders, the spikers had allies of their own. To the astonishment of the scientists, these comprised yet a fourth sentient species, as unrelated to the previously discovered three as the stick-jellies and the spikers were to humans and thranx.

Averaging about a meter in height and almost as broad, these hard-shelled newcomers advanced slowly on twin muscular pseudopods. The stone axes they wielded at the ends of their short, stubby arms had very little reach. On the other hand, their armored bodies were impervious to the spears of the stick-jellies.

The fuzzies had better luck against them. Rounded stones accelerated by throwing slings were capable of cracking the outer carapaces of the hardshells. Stone-headed clubs were able to bash in less heavily armored skulls. Meanwhile the stick-jellies showed surprising determination and agility in battling the spikers. Such confrontations looked uneven, until N'kosi pointed out that stones cast by the spikers simply slid off or lodged harmlessly in the stick-jellies' bodies while spear thrusts had to strike a vital spot to do any damage at all. Relying on first impressions in combat, Tellenberg realized, was as dangerous and foolish as doing so in science.

So preoccupied with the intense fighting were the combatants that they failed to notice the boatload of aliens that had by now halted in the middle of the river. Meanwhile more and more of the primitive shelters were going up in flames. On board the boat each of the scientists looked on in fascination, their recorders automatically preserving multiple accounts of the native confrontation. Except for an occasional whisper, no one on board said a word. Nor did they stop to wonder why they were whispering.

It looked bad for the defenders of the village. Then, just when it seemed as if one more push by the attackers would overrun the community completely, the defenders counterattacked. From the woods to the north, a small horde of fuzzies erupted to pounce on the attackers' flank. Taken completely by surprise and believing themselves on the verge of total victory, the spikers and hardshells suddenly found themselves assailed on two fronts. While stones rained down on the attackers, the stick-jellies rallied to hold the ground in the middle of the village, using the surviving structures to split and isolate their attackers' lines.

For the first time since they had come upon the battle, N'kosi raised his voice above a murmur. It prompted a collective clearing of throats from all on board. "Our first evidence that at least one of the species displaying sentience is capable of concocting advanced tactics."

"I don't know that I would call them advanced." Valnadireb was recording with a handheld unit in addition to the automatic that was mounted atop the right side of his b-thorax. "Although hardly my specialty, it would seem an obvious maneuver."

"To someone developed enough to understand the concept of maneuvering, yes." Haviti was still sitting in the bow. Her legs hung over the side of the boat. Not one to tell others how to comport themselves out in the field, Tellenberg kept his thoughts to himself while hoping that nothing lurking in the water found those dangling offworld limbs worthy of a nibble.

"Tactics and maneuvers might have nothing to do with it," she continued. "The newly arrived combatants might be allies arriving from another village off to the north, or members of a returning hunting party. Advanced strategy and subterfuge might not enter into the present circumstances." She gestured with her own handheld. "What appears premeditated on the battlefield might be nothing more than fortuitous coincidence."

Valnadireb gestured understandingly. "There's one way to find out. Talk to some of the natives and ask them."

"In good time," Haviti replied. "First we have to see who survives."

The tide of battle had definitely turned in favor of the defenders. Assailed from two sides, whether by design or accident, the spikers and the hardshells fell back. Unfortunately for them, that meant retreating to the river. Regrouping, they made a stand there, bunching together and packing themselves tight so that their organic armor presented a solid wall to any attackers. Stones fell on them like hail.

Three times the defenders of the village rushed their tormentors. Each time the assault was repelled with loss of life on both sides. On the third occasion, so ferocious and forceful was the charge of the stick-jellies and fuzzies that some of the spikers and hardshells were pushed off the sandy shore and into the water. This produced two new and interesting facts about sentient native life-forms. Hardshells could float, if not exactly swim. Spikers could do neither.

No wonder they were defending themselves so vigorously, Tellenberg realized as he continued to observe the ongoing mêlée. Preliminary cursory observation revealed that a spiker sank faster than a thranx wearing a lead-lined backpack.

Just when it seemed as if the defense of the village was going to turn into a complete slaughter of its assailants, the defenders backed off. Their number had also been considerably reduced and they continued to suffer casualties. Both sides were exhausted; physically, in numbers, and resource-wise. With their original stockpiles of throwing stones depleted, fuzzies and spikers alike were reduced to scavenging suitable rocks from where they lay on the field of battle. Even the discordant sounds and weird alien cries of battle had given way to an excess of heavy breathing interspersed with only occasional outbursts of passion or defiance.

Slowly and carefully the surviving spikers and hardshells began working their way southward, maintaining a rudimentary defensive formation as they did so. A few of the most energetic defenders followed them, slinging the intermittent stone, throwing the occasional sharpened stick. Once the ongoing battle moved back into the dense vegetation, the pursuing defenders' advantage in numbers was reduced. The chase broke off and the remaining attackers were allowed to disappear into the brush.

In their wake, noncombatant stick-jellies and fuzzies worked together in a cooperative effort to put out the fires that continued to consume the surviving huts. Water carried from the river in crude pots and tightly woven baskets was thrown on the crackling flames. Native intelligence had not risen to the point where someone thought to organize a simple bucket brigade.

Limited in quantity though it was, there was fire-suppressant equipment on the boat that could have put out the remaining blazes in a couple of minutes. Looking over at N'kosi, Tellenberg saw that his colleague was thinking the same thing. He swallowed, his throat unexpectedly dry.

"We can't," he muttered. "We can't interfere."

"I know." N'kosi summoned up a wan smile. "Contact regulations. We can only observe."

Fortunately, there was no fuzzy or stick-jelly equivalent of human children running screaming through the flaming village, no limbless thranx larvae squirming helplessly on the ground. Had that been the case, a sympathetic Tellenberg might have found himself hard-pressed not to interfere in the fight with technologically advanced gear a good deal more proactive than just fire-suppressant equipment.

Take a step back, he told himself. For all they knew the brutal assault that had been mounted by the spikers and the hardshells was payback for some earlier, even worse offense that had been committed by the fuzzies and the stick-jellies. For a second time he found himself reflecting on the unsuitability of relying on first impressions.

Odd. The boat seemed to be pitching slightly under his feet. Cruising down the middle of the river with the current due aft there was no reason for a sudden swing in stability. If any of his colleagues noticed the subtle pitching they did not remark on it. A moment later he chanced to glance around. As soon as he did so the reason for the rocking became immediately apparent.

Having drifted downstream silent and unseen while fleeing the aftermath of the battle for the village, three hardshells were struggling to clamber into the boat.

Scientific detachment tends to fall rapidly by the wayside when a croaking, dark-eyed, angry alien suddenly appears within arm's length brandishing a lethal weapon in one's face. To their credit, none of the researchers panicked. All of them had spent time on other worlds; some inhabited by primitive sentients, others not. Perhaps because his kind lived under interminable threat of attack from their traditional enemies the AAnn, Valnadireb was first to draw his sidearm. Up on the bow, Haviti followed him in close order despite the awkwardness of her position.

By the time a slightly rattled but responsive Tellenberg and N'kosi had joined them in taking aim at the intruders, the latter had halted their attempt to climb aboard. Maybe they expected the strange floating object to be full of loathsome stick-jellies and stone-wielding fuzzies. The sight of three soft-bodied, multicolored bipeds and one very large golden-eyed arthropod must have been as unsettling to them as their sudden appearance was to the occupants of the boat. Whatever the reason, it was sufficient to halt potentially lethal stone axes in midswing. Following this first confrontation, formal first contact between the official representatives of the Humanx Commonwealth and the indigenous hard-shelled natives of Quofum progressed swiftly and not at all according to preferred protocol.

Emerging from the state of shock into which sight of the creatures on board the floating vehicle had sent it, the hardshell nearest Tellenberg took one step forward and one roundhouse swipe with the axe it gripped in its right pseudopod. Stepping easily back out of range of the powerful but short-reached swing, Tellenberg uttered a startled "Hey!" and promptly tripped over a supply canister that was lying on the deck. Both actions set the other pair of hardshells in motion.

Deciding that this was not the appropriate time to consult the applicable portion of the relevant file, N'kosi proceeded to drill the advancing hardshell directly between its dark, pupilless eyes. Toppling forward and dropping the axe, it struck the deck with a resounding thump. Observing this, the other hardshells reconfirmed the principle that primitiveness was not equal to stupidity by turning and throwing themselves (their physiology rendering them incapable of jumping) overboard. Rushing to the slightly flexible gunwale, Haviti and N'kosi made sure the pair of would-be boarders continued to drift away as Valnadireb rushed to help Tellenberg stand.

"I'm fine, I'm fine." Embarrassed by his gaucherie, Tellenberg stepped away from the thranx.

Valnadireb looked his friend over. "You sure? From where I was standing I couldn't see if it hit you or not."

Tellenberg gave an irritable shake of his head. "It missed me. They have short swings. The only damage is to my dignity."

The thranx responded with a whistle of sympathy. "What scientist in the field holds on to that for more than a day?"

"Well, this is just great." Having seen off the intruders, Haviti returned to the center of the craft and slumped down onto the top of a half-full storage purifier that was busily rendering river water safe for humanx consumption. "Less than a week we've been here and not only have we managed to bungle contact with all four native sentient species, but we may have made outright enemies of at least one."

"We don't know that." Valnadireb preferred to view the circumstances, as well as the corpse of the dead hardshell, in a more positive light. "Our initial contacts were brief and inconclusive, it is true, but except for that which occurred between myself, Tiare, and the fuzzies, nothing resembling open hostility ensued." Both truhands indicated the alien body lying in the center of the boat. "Until now, of course. While regrettable, this incident may have no lasting effects. Even if the two hardshells who returned to the river survive the attentions of patrolling fuzzies and stick-jellies, by the time they return to their own people they may remember very little of this particular encounter. Even if they do, it is very likely that their story will not be believed. Such generalized ag-

gression may be unexceptional among their kind and in no wise a
clarion call to wider hostilities. We know nothing of their culture."

"We know that they like to fight stick-jellies and fuzzies,"
N'kosi countered. He gestured at the lumpy form lying motionless on the deck. "If nothing else, we have acquired our first
specimen of a second of the four dominant social species."

Having recovered fully from his embarrassing fall, Tellenberg
had moved to the starboard gunwale and was studying the efforts
of the surviving fuzzies and stick-jellies to put out the raging fires
that had been set by their assailants. Despite the fragmented nature of the attempt, sheer determination and persistence found
them having some success.

You had to admire them, he mused. You also had to admire
the ruthlessness and fighting abilities of the spikers and the
hardshells.

"What makes you think there are four?" He put the question
to the thranx without taking his gaze from the dying conflagra-
tion on shore.

Pivoting on all six legs, Valnadireb came close. "We have encountered four. We have documented four. Do you have some
reason, Esra, to dispute these findings?"

"No, no." Turning, he looked down into the thranx's jewel-
like, gold-hued, crimson-banded compound eyes. "What I meant
was, how do we know there aren't more?" Raising his gaze, he
met the curious stares of his other colleagues.

Haviti wrinkled her nose. "How could there be more than
four separate and distinct sentient species on one world?"

Tellenberg shrugged. "Eight is no more improbable a number to encounter than four. Or ten. Or twenty. From an evolutionary standpoint, my friends, and aside from its astronomical

peculiarities, this world is seriously out of whack. I'll find a way to render that in proper biological terminology once we're back in camp."

No one argued with him. It was possible, even likely, that similar thoughts had occurred to them independently. Tellenberg was just the first to give voice to the scientifically tantalizing. That did not stop them, nor mitigate their eagerness, as they set about dissecting the dead hardshell on the way downriver—it having been mutually agreed that for the immediate future formal second contact with the fuzzies and the stick-jellies would best be deferred.

Among the many characteristics of sentient culture that the history of xenology had determined to be universal was the axiom that irrespective of species, a people who had just suffered massive death and destruction was rarely in the mood to sit down for a friendly chat no matter how benign or innocent the intentions of prospective third-party visitors.

5

Though marred by the inescapable memories of the intra-indigenous carnage they had witnessed earlier in the day, night on the river once again brought forth a farrago of alien beauty and diversity. If anything, nocturnal life-forms appeared in even greater variety than they had the night before.

Sweeping low over the glassy surface of the river, membranous-winged fliers trailed glowing tail-tips in the water. These fireflylike lights caught the attention of feeding water-dwellers, who were promptly snapped up by the next flier in line. In this cooperative feeding frenzy, a carnivore's success depended not only on its own skills but equally on those of the fellow flock member gliding and tail-fishing in front of it. As the flock soared silently downriver, Tellenberg saw that a pair of fliers in the lead would ascend, slow down, and take up the position at the rear. By rotating leaders in this fashion the flock assured that every member of the group got the opportunity to feed.

Lights shined over the side of the boat revealed a cluster of large bubbles rising from below. Each contained a small struggling arthropod or frantically signaling silicate life-form. Imprisoned on the surface within their globular containers, they drifted with the current until the school of striped cephalopodian creatures that had thus entrapped them ascended. One by one the caging bubbles were popped and their wriggling contents consumed.

The river seemed to boast almost as many new methods of predation as there were predators to demonstrate them and prey to fulfill the necessary destinies. Occupying the seat in the bow, N'kosi occasionally dipped a collecting net into the water. This straightforward method of securing specimens was as effective as it was ancient. Working carefully so as not to damage them, the xenologist would transfer the frequently fluorescing samples of local aquatic life-forms into the portable holding tank that was secured just aft of his position. In the morning, they would transfer the tank to the lab. There, the hundreds of specimens they had collected could be better preserved and studied.

Upon leaving the arena of aboriginal conflict, Tellenberg had taken his own turn with net and siphon. Now he sat on the port side of the boat, mulling strange stars and the electric panoply of lambent alien life-forms that filled the night sky and the surreal forest beneath. So preoccupied was he that he did not even bother to check if his cap-mounted recorder was operating.

A shape idled over alongside him. Its tone reflected concern.

"Still thinking about this afternoon's butchery?"

Given the evenness of her voice, Haviti might as well have been describing the presentation of some dull academic paper at a scientific conference. Tellenberg felt her attitude stemmed from a need to keep herself emotionally divorced from what after all had been fairly bloodthirsty proceedings. He completely understood because he felt exactly the same way.

"Yes and no," he murmured. Lit only by the distant faint light of stars that pointed back to the familiar spatial realm of the Commonwealth and by the nighttime running lights that were embedded in the fabric of the boat, the rounded curves of her face reflected her Polynesian ancestry. Muted as it was, the craft's interior illumination still picked up the highlights of her smile.

"Well, that's settled," she quipped.

He shifted his position on the bench that emerged from the inner wall, turning toward her and away from the glittering alien cavalcade parading through the forest beyond. "I was thinking about the natives, but not especially in relation to the internecine battle we witnessed. It's something else. The same thing has been bothering me ever since we set down and first began to make contact with them."

"Aspects of one particular species troubling you?" she inquired.

Quofum had no moon, he mused, until Tiare Haviti had arrived. He pushed the thought aside. "Aspects of all four of them have been troubling me. In fact," he went on, warming to the subject now that he had a knowledgeable and responsive audience, "I'd be surprised if the same conundrum hasn't been bothering you, too. And N'kosi, and Valnadireb as well."

"Maybe it has." Sitting back, she drew up one leg and clasped both hands around her knee. "But I can't confirm or deny it until you've told me what it is you're talking about."

He sat up straighter. "Alright, look. We've been here less than a week. In that time we've encountered not one, not two, but four distinct sentient native species living almost side by side.

My knowledge of such things isn't absolute, but I'm pretty sure that's unprecedented."

"I think it is, too. That's what's troubling you?"

"Partly." He glanced back out at the river as something the size of a crocodile briefly broke the surface before submerging once more. Resembling a kinked tree trunk, it displayed one eye on the back of each of its segments. From the quick look he could not tell if it was a single creature or several that were linked front to back.

"What's really troubling me, Tiare, what's been bothering me ever since we began standardized exploration of this place, is not that there is too much of everything. Earth itself is famous for its species diversity. But everything on Earth is related in some way to everything else. You can use evolutionary principles, cladistics, and other means and methods to link worms to whales." Raising an arm, he waved at the shimmering alien spectacle on shore.

"Instead of relationships here, I see chaos. Just when I think I might have confirmed two or three species that relate to one another, something completely fantastic comes ambling or slithering or soaring or swimming along that bears absolutely no relationship to anything that's ambled or slithered or whatevered before it. We have carbon-based life-forms living alongside silicate-based life-forms living next to sulfate-based life-forms living among organisms whose biology we haven't had time to even guess at. It's evolution gone amuck. Pure biological anarchy." He paused to catch his breath.

"And the natives only take it to an extreme. It's absurd enough that we encounter four different intelligent native species in less than a week. But I think I could deal with that, intellectually, if they bore some relation to one another." He leaned toward her. "You tell me, Tiare. Am I overwrought, or worse? Has this place overwhelmed my ability to make rational scientific assessments? Do you see any biological, evolutionary relationship between, say, the spikers and the fuzzies? Not to mention the stick-jellies and the semi-aquatic hardshells. Am I *missing* something here?"

His earnestness was palpable. She was not taken aback, perhaps because, as he suspected, she had considered similar conclusions independently. As he waited, she inhaled deeply and slid her foot off the bench.

"I'd be lying, Esra, if I said that something along the same line hadn't occurred to me."

He rolled his eyes skyward. "Thanks be to Herschel. I was starting to question my ability to look at all this objectively."

Standing up, she turned to look out at river and forest. "How could anyone with even a limited scientific education not wonder how sentients like the stick-jellies could evolve alongside and, presumably, simultaneous with the spikers? The xenological record is consistent. One intelligent species evolves and spreads out to dominate a world. On very rare occasions two may appear more or less simultaneously, usually on opposite sides of a planet. In the case of a world like Horseye, that the natives all call Tslamaina, you might get three." She turned back to him.

"But the three native species that inhabit Horseye can all be traced back to a common ancestry. Anyone can study the breakdown of a Tsla and see its biological relationship to the other species, the Mai and the Na."

He nodded, idly brushing something like a gilded snowflake off his right forearm. It took wing and fluttered off into the night, a golden speck adrift in the starlight. "I defy anyone to find a close structural relationship between a spiker and a stick-jelly. Or even a hardshell and a fuzzy."

She considered. "Well, we have a dead hardshell to work with now, and spiker corpses aplenty back at camp. If we can find an authorized way to obtain specimens of representatives of the other two sentient species, we can do some serious dissection and evaluation. Even with the inadequate equipment we have, making a comparison on that level should prove relatively quick and easy."

He offered a thin smile in return. "And what if there is no relationship to be found? How do we explain the simultaneous evolution of four distinct, unrelated alien species on one world?"

It was silent on the boat. From his position behind the control console, Valnadireb's voice reached them. "Myself, I regret that I have no brilliant explication to propose."

Haviti turned toward him. "You were listening."

Both the thranx's words and multiple arm gestures were unapologetic. "It's a small boat. Anyway, I concur with everything you have both been saying. While I am as reluctant as you to venture generalizations based on less than a week's observations, I have to agree with Esra that according to what we have seen thus far, the biology of this planet makes no sense whatsoever. Based on preliminary observations, the four sentient species we have encountered might as well have come from four different planets."

Speaking from the seat in the bow, N'kosi proceeded to contribute his unsolicited opinion. On such a small craft it was clearly impossible to have a private conversation, Tellenberg concluded.

"Interesting notion, Val. Maybe one worth exploring further," the forward-seated xenologist commented.

Leaning to her right, Haviti looked toward him and past Tellenberg. "You're not suggesting that the local sentients did not evolve here, but were imported from elsewhere?"

Spinning in the seat, N'kosi brought his legs around so that they were once again inside the boat. In the dim light, he was almost a silhouette against the moonless night. "Why not? It makes as much sense as anything else. If initial, rational explanations for an illogical phenomena prove unsatisfactory, one has to consider contemplating secondary, irrational ones."

"Could what we are seeing represent some kind of experiment? One whose causes and rationale we cannot yet begin to fathom?" Valnadireb's jewel-like eyes glistened. Twin sensory metronomes, his feathery antennae bobbed slowly back and forth as he spoke. "Four primitive sentient species are brought here from other locations and allowed to develop on their own, even to the point of engaging in serious combat. To what purpose? Some kind of experiment? For research?"

"We can't simply disregard such possibilities out of hand just because they strain credulity." N'kosi was warming to his hypothesis. "Especially in light of a better explanation." Reaching up, he swatted at something that blushed maroon. His palm struck it squarely, sending it fluttering broken-winged into the water. Within seconds it had been gobbled up by what looked like a triangle of linked-together transparent spheres lined with diamonds. The brief glimpse it allowed was insufficient to identify the predator as protein, glass, or gas-based. N'kosi shook his head. Formal classification of Quofum's fauna demanded the interpretative skills not of a von Humboldt, a

Darwin, or a Russell, but of Lewis Carroll working in concert with Salvador Dalí.

Straightening, Haviti rested both hands on the edge of the gunwale and stared at the alien forest sliding past. Organically generated lights of all colors and patterns blinked madly on and off, dancing among trees and growths that were deserving of other names, some that the visitors would be forced to invent. The sight put her in mind of a city whose nighttime energy sources and society had been completely fractured. Though her tone was naturally and unavoidably sultry, her speech was fortified with confidence that bespoke a scientist who had been awarded several degrees from multiple sources.

"For the moment and for the purposes of discussion only, suppose we grant N'kosi's hyperfictional hypothesis a modicum of credibility. Where does it take us if we dare to carry it to its logical extreme?"

Valnadireb's bare feet made scraping sounds on the deck as he shifted his stance, rising up on all four trulegs. During the preceding days he had gained enough confidence to occasionally let go of the deck with his foothands.

"In that case, the inescapable conclusion is both striking and appalling. If the four sentient types we have encountered are presumed to be introduced species, then it follows that they may not be alone." Truhands and foothands joined in gesturing at the passing shore. "There may be others, floral as well as faunal."

"Which means," Haviti went on, "that a great many of the life-forms we have observed and recorded, and not just the sentients, may not be native to this world."

"Or," N'kosi murmured as he took the premise to its inexorable end, "none of them are." He waved a hand at the water.

"As I suggested, we may be recording the results of an experiment."

"The inhabitants of a zoo," Valnadireb put in.

"More like a circus," Tellenberg finished.

Once again silence descended on the boat as each of the scientists sank back into his or her own thoughts. Around them, the object of their intense meditation sang and swam, flew and squawked, crawled and clashed, and sought cover from their fellow inhabitants.

If the biota of Quofum was not natural but introduced, Tellenberg found himself thinking furiously, had it been done casually? Or, as N'kosi proposed, with some purpose in mind? And if purpose, what? The latter implied a higher intelligence that was a master not only of biology but of improvisation. But if there was a purpose to species introduction on such a massive and inexplicable scale, why allow so many and such divergent life-forms to evolve and mature? Why not pursue a single chosen line, to some unknown, unimaginable end? The whole approach, exceedingly theoretical as it was, struck him as scattershot and futile, a waste of time and considerable resources. It was as if God were having a mental breakdown while making the world.

Perhaps more than one originating intellect was involved. Maybe N'kosi's imagined experiment was more of a contest. He thought of the games he had played as a child and still engaged in, albeit rarely. Had he and his companions inadvertently stepped into some kind of bio-evolutionary game being played by unknown intelligences? If so, assuming they were monitoring their experiment or game or ongoing work or whatever it might be, how would they react to the presence of uninvited eyewitnesses? Peering up at the night sky and the alien stars, he was suddenly even more uncomfortable than usual.

Of course, he reminded himself firmly, all this was still nothing more than outrageous speculation. Like any thoughtful scientist, N'kosi had proffered a radical explanation in the absence of a more sensible one. The latter, based on the drastic but not untenable notion of radical evolution occurring under extraordinary and as yet undefined circumstances, was still the best extant explanation for everything they had seen. They had only been on Quofum for a few days. Wild tangents such as direct offworld intervention by an unknown intelligence might be proposed and discussed, but it was far too early in the game to accept them as anything more than impulsive conjecture.

Evidence. It was time to amass some hard, cold evidence. To date they had spent nearly all their time out in the field. Now it was time to sit down in the lab, to dissect a serious number of specimens in the search for links between species and types, and to let the camp's AI engage in some fundamental extrapolation and sequence-crunching. In short, it was time to buckle down to the kind of time-intensive, repetitive, methodical, frequently boring work that constituted the greater preponderance of real science.

His line of thought changed to something else entirely when Haviti moved closer to him. It changed again, and not for the better this time, when she pointed to the west.

"Is that cloud moving?"

He squinted. His night vision had never been the best. Flipping down his visor, he joined her in studying the expanding phenomenon.

"It's moving, but I'm not so sure it's a cloud."

"It is not." Valnadireb's huge compound eyes needed no artificial assistance to discern the true nature of the star-muting shadow. "It's alive, and it is coming this way."

More than the mood was broken as for the second time that day the four scientists unlimbered their sidearms. There was nothing to indicate that the dark mass would prove to be hostile, but its sheer size dictated caution. Better to be prepared than to be caught off guard and forced into making life-or-death decisions at the last moment.

As it turned out, the decision to take up arms proved prudent.

The sound of the onrushing shadow was surprising. A whispery hum, it was anything but threatening. That did not prevent N'kosi, ever the enthusiastic researcher, from letting out a yelp of surprise when the first of the gently parachuting larvae spiraled down to land on his arm. Half again as long as the scientist's extended limb and nearly as wide, the larva was almost paper-thin. On contact with his forearm it lay there light as a leaf, allowing him to examine it closely. The pale, translucent form weighed next to nothing. A single black dot at one end hinted at the location of a very primitive eyespot.

"It's like tissue." As he addressed his colleagues, N'kosi raised his arm slowly up and down. "I don't see any indication of . . ."

He grunted in pain as the larva contracted sharply around his forearm. Shrinking and tightening with frightening speed, it was transformed from a ten-centimeter-wide strip of pale protein into a swiftly shrinking tourniquet. Setting aside his pistol, N'kosi used his free hand to try and pull it off. Not only did the "flimsy" material fail to break, it burned his clutching fingers on contact.

"Get it off!" he yelled to his companions. Already the now wirelike strip was cutting off the flow of blood to his forearm and hand and threatening to slice right through his protective shirtsleeve into his flesh.

Haviti and Tellenberg fumbled for the knives contained in their field multitools. By the time either of them could get a blade out, an alert Valnadireb had clipped the shrunken larva in half. Using both foothands and truhands, he pulled it apart. The caustic fluid the migrating alien maggot secreted might sear human skin, but it barely left a mark on the thranx's much tougher chitinous exoskeleton.

"Thanks, Val." A grimacing N'kosi was rubbing his arm, stimulating the flow of blood to his throbbing hand.

They had no time to commiserate or study the dead creature now lying on the deck, because as the dozen or so enormous soaring night fliers continued passing overhead, blotting out the sky, their teeming progeny drifted downward like slow rain. Each of the nearly silent gliders released dozens, hundreds of the deceptively innocuous larvae from a line of multiple ventral cloaca. These floated downward or were carried off by gentle breezes like so much shredded tissue paper. The quartet of edgy scientists could only look on and admire the highly efficient means the creatures employed for spreading their spawn.

The larvae's translucence allowed them to blend in with their surroundings, making it hard for potential hosts to separate them from forest and river surroundings. During the day, bright sunlight would have reflected off the ghostly protoplasm. At night the larvae were nearly invisible. They made no revealing noises, emitted no identifying sounds as they drifted downward. Their slow, gradual descent, disturbed only by the occasional draft, enhanced the stealth of the mass seeding. Outspread in parachute mode, their insubstantiality assured that their landing on a potential host would usually go unnoticed. Until they began to contract, by which time it would be too late for the hapless host to do anything about it.

Soaring noiselessly off to the east the adults continued on their migratory way, having sown the night behind them with silent horror. The horde of twisting, fluttering parasites descending in their wake landed everywhere: in the forest, on the water, on the glistening river-cast beaches. The researchers counted their good fortune as they clustered together in the center of the boat. The folding roof that was designed to protect them from the weather was a hundred percent effective in keeping the down-drifting larvae off their heads. Whenever the wind threatened to blow one of the creatures underneath, it was quickly knocked down with whatever heavy object was at hand.

At first they tried crushing the writhing, crinkling brood underfoot. One such attempt by Tellenberg was sufficient to show the inefficacy of that approach. The larva in question dodged his descending boot and curled around his ankle with horrid speed. For a second time, Valnadireb's dexterous fingers were called upon to remove a constricting larva from one of his human associate's more vulnerable limbs. Thereafter they took no more chances. Standing back-to-back and utilizing a pair of beamers taken from stores and set on low, they fried each successive gossamer intruder.

They did not relax or let down their guard even when it seemed that they had cruised clear of the last of the parasitic cloud. Tellenberg found that he was swallowing repeatedly and unnecessarily. He kept imagining what it would feel like to have one of the constricting creatures land softly on the back of his neck. This was one species where dead specimens would have to suffice for study not out of necessity but by choice and mutual agreement. Even with Valnadireb's assistance, the live larvae were too treacherous to handle.

In the wake of the gliders' passing, horrifying sounds began to resound from the forest. At first there were only one or two. As more and more of the larvae touched down and found hosts, the cries and shrieks of those organisms who had been successfully parasitized rose shockingly above the familiar din of otherwise healthy forest-dwellers. After a while this too died out. For a quarter of an hour or so the alien woods were unnervingly silent. Then, gradually, customary night sounds returned, until both sides of the river once more echoed to the bleat and wail of the thousands of unknown creatures who had managed to survive the ghastly seeding.

N'kosi was sitting on a bench studying the first larva that had landed on the boat. Or rather, on him. Ripped in half by the helpful Valnadireb, it lay stretched out immobile between his hands, a pair of thin strands of dully glistening protoplasmic thread.

"What do you suppose the next stage is?" Reaching down, Haviti ran an inquisitive forefinger along the middle part of the lifeless young. Dead, it no longer secreted its protective caustic liquid.

A nonscientist would have turned away or eyed the slender corpse uneasily. Despite having been attacked, N'kosi was all curiosity. "Maybe once it has secured a purchase on the prospective host, it burrows in and feeds."

"Not too deeply, or too much," Tellenberg commented astutely. "A smart parasite doesn't kill its host right away. The successful ones are always good stewards of their food supply."

"You saw how quickly and powerfully it contracts." Haviti straightened. "Maybe the whole animal burrows in, the way an assassin uses piano wire."

Tellenberg gaped at her. "What do you know about assassins and piano wire?"

She smiled back at him. "When I'm relaxing in my off-time, I watch a lot of cheap tridee productions. One does not live by assimilating scientific papers alone, you know."

He wanted to add something witty, but not in general company.

Instead, he rose. "Well, we may not have any live specimens, but we've got plenty of fried ones." He busied himself helping Valnadireb gather dead larvae from the deck. Those too badly burned by the beamers were dumped over the side, to the great delight of a trailing swarm of aquatic scavengers.

One of the latter, he noted almost absently, was some kind of floating plant with multiple orifices. He shook his head. The variety of life-forms thriving on this world was exceeded only by the mystery of their origins.

Despite everyone's pretense at scientific detachment, the rain of parasitic larvae had unsettled all of them to the point where it was decided that the boat's automatic defense mechanisms notwithstanding, a watch would be mounted for the rest of the night. A lucky Tellenberg took the first. Settling himself behind the control console, he watched while his companions bedded down for the night; the humans on their traveling inflatable cots, Valnadireb on his simple raised pad. A flash of jealousy shot through Tellenberg as he noted the proximity of N'kosi's bed to Haviti's.

He was being silly, he chided himself. No matter what he felt toward Tiare he had never expressed those feelings. Such desire remained wholly private, and likely would continue to do so until they neared the expedition's end. Articulating his feelings here and now, while they were thrown together out in the field with no way of really avoiding one another, could impact the quality of her work as well as his. Worse, she might respond negatively. He shuddered inwardly. She might even laugh.

Upon further consideration of the alternatives, he decided he would rather endure the attentions of one of the parasitic larvae.

6

The wretched condenser was acting up again. It had to be the condenser, Boylan figured. Not only because the system that delivered water to the different segments of the camp had already failed once, but because the supply was gravity-fed and there was little else that could go wrong with it. Spun like spider silk from a central silicate core, the simple and straightforward network of pipes had no seams, joints, or connectors. All the components were brand-new. Since the pipe material hardened on contact with air, it was unlikely there were any leaks.

It did not matter whether he activated dispensers in the living area, the lab, or outside. They all came up dry. Every time he said "cold water" or "hot water" to a spigot, it responded with an apology instead of the requested liquid. A part designed and manufactured to be as trouble-free as a water spigot could not be self-analytical. It could not provide a breakdown of the trouble. In the final analysis, it appeared, there were still some problems that required the attention of humans.

There was also the fact that the condenser had already failed once before, right after the science team had departed on their expedition upriver. The brief reports Boylan had received suggested that this had gone even better than expected, though in ways none had foreseen. While curious to learn the details of the outing, it was not his priority. As captain of the ship and nominal commander of the expedition, his job was to expedite the work of the researchers without coddling them. That meant ensuring suitable working conditions. The lack of a reliable water supply could hardly be counted among these.

The first time the condenser had broken down Araza had fixed it immediately. Precedent suggested that the latest problem, if it involved a similar failure, would be simple to fix. This time Boylan would supervise the repair work himself. Araza was a good workman and a solid technician, but he was not perfect. Even with the help of automatons and integrated construction servors, whipping the newly erected camp into working order and maintaining it was a full-time job for two men. In his haste to move on to the next project it was possible that Araza had overlooked something, had not quite finished the repair work properly, or had simply left it incomplete and had forgotten to return to complete the job.

Whatever the cause, this time the condenser would be fixed permanently. Boylan would see to that. Araza was like a lot of workmen the captain had known. Wholly competent but easily distracted. You had to keep on top of such people. For their own good. Every once in a while they needed to be chewed out. It inspired them to better work. The trick was to admonish without generating resentment. This was something at which Boylan had had plenty of practice. He was very good at it.

He did not have to go looking for the technician. Araza answered promptly when the captain buzzed him. The miniaturized communit clipped to Boylan's right ear served as both pickup and speaker.

"Water condenser again," he snapped. "Got to be condenser. There's nothing coming out of any of the pipes."

"Irrigation also?" Araza was a master of the terse interrogatory.

"I haven't checked it for leaks, but I don't see why that part of system should be any different. We know it can't be vapor problem." On this part of Quofum, at least, the air was saturated with moisture. With that kind of spongy atmosphere to draw upon, even a partially functioning condenser should have been able to provide plenty of water to all parts of the camp.

"I will check Irrigation," Araza replied. "If it is dry also, I will get right on the condenser."

Boylan was not in the mood for delays. "I told you, there no reason to check Irrigation. I'm heading up to the installation. Meet me there."

There was a pause at the other end. "I would really like to run a system's check on Irrigation first."

"Condenser installation," Boylan snapped in his best no-nonsense tone. "Now." He shut down the commlink.

Maybe he was being too rough on Araza, he mused as he headed for the life-support wing of the camp. Give him his due: the tech did work hard. But he had on more than one occasion demonstrated a proclivity for overanalysis, for wasting time on checking that which had already been noted and dismissed. Even if water was flowing to Irrigation, the condenser's condition still needed to be checked and its status determined before they could rule it out as the cause of the shortage. He knew from experience that every so often it was important, even in small ways, to remind others who was in charge. Perhaps the occasion of the loss of flow to the camp was not the best time to make the point, but it was already done. He smiled thinly to himself. Araza was tough. The man would survive another brief bout of criticism.

When Boylan surmounted the roof of the third and south-ernmost wing of the camp he found the tech already hard at work on the condenser. Seeing the captain, Araza waved. Boy-lan, who had ascended via a different set of steps, responded with a brisk gesture of his own. While rising to little more than a single story in height, the top of the gently arching snap-together roof sections offered a pleasant change of view from that available at ground level. As he made his way across the dimpled gray-green surface toward the roof-mounted condens-ing unit and the waiting technician, Boylan reflected on what the expedition had accomplished thus far.

There was reason to be proud. With minimal staff, they had erected a small but complete camp. Preliminary contact had been made with not one but with an unprecedented four species of native sentients. The planet had proven to be both a biologi-cal mine and an evolutionary minefield of new genotypes. When the official report of the expedition was filed upon their return home, the science team would be showered with honors. As for himself, he could look forward to a significant promotion within the civil service ranks as well as the approval and admiration of his peers.

Assuming, of course, he and his people didn't die of thirst first.

Despite the ongoing condenser problems, that likelihood was sufficiently improbable as to verge on the impossible. After all, the pink-tinged sky gave up rain periodically and there was a sizable river nearby. Both sources could be drawn upon in an emergency. However, purer, safer water for drinking, bathing, and scientific work was to be had by extracting it directly from the atmosphere, so it would be better to fix the condenser.

Kneeling on the rooftop, Araza had his repair kit spread out to one side and several dissembled components of the big, boxy condenser unit carefully placed elsewhere, well within reach and where they would not be likely to slide off the roof.

"How it coming?" In a pinch, Boylan could probably have performed the necessary repairs himself. Modern scientific equipment was designed to self-diagnose. Repairs usually involved simple module replacement. But he would have been the first to admit that Araza could do the work better, and faster.

"Same problem as last time," the tech told him. "This is the second antibacterial third-stage purifier that has failed on us." His voice was accompanied by a slight reverb since he spoke while his head and upper body were inside the condenser's protective shell. "I have run checks. The preliminary indication is that the module in question is overpowered. As a temporary fix and until I can run tests on the remaining replacements, I am putting in a bypass via a reduction circuit. This will lower the power to the third-stage purifier while allowing it to continue to function normally." Scooting backward on hands and knees, he straightened and used a cloth to wipe perspiration from his forehead.

Araza was considerably taller than the captain, slim and muscular as a marathon runner. His shirt and shorts were soaked with sweat. Working on the ground was hot, making repairs on the roof hotter still. There was no breeze this morning.

"How long?" Boylan inquired.

The technician considered. "Five more minutes. Ten at the most."

"Then we have water?"

The taller man smiled thinly. At times it was impossible to tell what the man was thinking, Boylan knew. Not that he cared. All that mattered was that the tech did the necessary work.

"Then we will have water," Araza assured him. Kneeling again, he picked up a tool and thrust his torso into the open condenser housing.

Bending over to peer inside, Boylan rested one hand on the lip of the opening. "You know," he essayed conversationally, "if you'd fixed this right the first time you wouldn't be stuck up here now, sweating away the morning."

"The problem could not be anticipated." Araza spoke while continuing to work, his voice emerging slightly distorted from the depths of the condenser. "It is very uncharacteristic for such simple modules to fail. An official note of complaint to the manufacturer would not be out of order."

"Record it," Boylan replied testily. "I'll second and sign it." Raising his gaze, he squinted at the sky through his tinted visor. "We just lucky we set up camp in a wet forest and not in a desert." Shifting his stance, he leaned back against the unit and folded his hands over his belly. "Of course, we set up in desert, then air-con fails, or something similar. Is first unwritten rule of exploration." He concluded the observation by drawing the sidearm he always wore at his waist. "Another rule is that indigenous life-forms will have no fear of humans or thranx. Like for example, the ones that are having a go at me right now."

Araza quickly scrambled backward out of the unit. His own weapon lay close at hand among the rest of the tools. As Boylan crouched down nearby, using the square mass of the condenser unit for cover, both men took aim at this latest manifestation of predatory Quofumian wildlife. It was not, the captain reflected as he sighted carefully over the back of his pistol, that the outrageous diversity of native life was atypically hostile. It was simply that with so many life-forms running amuck in the sky and river and forest where they had chosen to set down, a certain proportion were bound to be carnivorous. Carnivores are intrinsically curious. When presented with something entirely new, the only way for them to find out if it is good to eat is to taste it.

Declining to be tasted, he and Araza fired almost simultaneously.

The nearest of the half dozen or so toothy arboreals diving toward the roof of the building flew apart in a shower of alien bone, guts, and what more than anything else resembled an exploded ball of yellow twine. For an instant, a small portion of sky was stained darker than its usual pink. Now missing most of the body to which they had formerly been attached, membranous wings flapped and fluttered to the ground, coming to rest in the circular clearing that had been sheared around the camp's three interlocking living modules.

The explosive demonstration had a salubrious effect on the rest of the plummeting feral flock. While they had no idea what had caused the sudden disintegration of their leader, collective prudence declared that hovering in the immediate vicinity of the attacking matriarch's noisy and messy demise might prove unhealthy. Banking sharply, they whirled and fled back toward the trees from which they had emerged.

Rising, a satisfied Boylan walked to the edge of the roof to stare down at the shattered corpse of the aerial predator he had shot. Unraveling on impact, the peculiar cluster of stringy organic material reached halfway from the mangled body to the inner edge of the camp's charged perimeter. Araza had come up alongside him. Despite his quiet, phlegmatic nature, the technician could be an inadvertently uneasy presence. There were times when he seemed to appear out of nowhere, making not a sound. Haviti had once stated that he didn't walk—he floated. His tread could be as subdued as his voice.

The captain pointed. "See all that stringlike material? I wonder at its function."

"Not for me to say." Nevertheless, a curious Araza leaned forward and looked down to examine the carcass. "Some kind of internal support, perhaps. Sinewy integuments, tendons—N'kosi will know. Or Haviti."

"Yes, Haviti will know," Boylan murmured. "Quite a woman, that."

The tech shrugged his lean shoulders. "Too smart for me. Sometimes when I listen to her it makes my head hurt."

While he could have continued the chat, Boylan decided not to. In the course of the journey out from the Commonwealth he, like the rest of the team, had learned that pretty much any kind of conversation seemed to make Araza's head hurt. Though he was not in any way overtly antisocial, the technician managed to make it clear without having to come out and say so that he preferred the company of his tools and manuals to that of other humans. Or thranx, for that matter. This insight upset no one. Boylan also cherished his privacy. And as he had just reiterated, there was little Araza had to contribute to casual conversation among four experienced and knowledgeable researchers.

Anyway, it was not banter Boylan wanted from the team's technician. It was water.

Araza was as good as his word. Discounting the time he had been forced to pause in his work to help drive off the attacking aerial carnivores, final replacement of the failed filter unit had taken less than ten minutes. It took only a few more to replace the exterior panel on the condenser and secure it in place.

"Finished," he declared as he began to pack up his tools.

"I hope so." Boylan grunted. "The perimeter has been solid, but I want to get rest of the lab equipment unpacked and shelled in. Be a nice welcome back for our friends. With all they have seen, they will be wanting to dive right into follow-up studies, I think. It will be nice for them to find all equipment on-line and functioning when they return."

"I will get right on it." Araza started toward the steps he had used to climb up onto the roof. They were embedded in the side of the building. "It is what I was doing when the water pressure went down."

"Disappeared, you mean. We don't want it happen again."

"I think it will be all right now." As he started down the side of the building, the technician looked back up at him. "I promise. If I have to ask you to help me with the condenser again, I will shoot myself first."

Boylan was quietly startled. It was the tech's first attempt to make a joke that the captain could recall. A good sign, certainly. Not that he expected the placidly dour Araza to suddenly metamorphose into the expedition's comic relief. The very idea was itself amusing. No one, he told himself as he retraced his own steps across the roof while keeping a wary eye out for the return of any winged predators, appreciated the hygienic benefits of shared merriment more than he did. Even if others did tend to say that Nicholai Boylan was apt to confuse disdain with humor. What nonsense! True, he could be stern, but that was only out of concern for the safety of his companions, those whose well-being had been entrusted to his care. There was that old joke about barbarian cream pie, for example, which he felt he told as well as anyone.

He chuckled aloud to himself as he turned and made his way down the steps that were integrated into the side of the laboratory building.

He did not need to retire to a central communications station to contact the scientific team. There was no central communications station because it was unnecessary. Every member of the expedition carried with them one or more compact communits that were capable of multiple functions. Besides the ability to carry out complex field analysis, conduct full and detailed on-the-spot medical evaluation of an injured member, and perform various other tasks, each unit was capable of serving as a full-scale, fully featured communications center. The camp had no need of a separate room, or even a separate console, devoted to communications.

Out in the field a team member so equipped could even contact any developed world in the Commonwealth. Of course, once the communication in question had been relayed from communit to shuttle to mother ship and then via narrow space-minus beam, the time delay involved would be considerable. It would take far longer for the communication to reach its intended destination than one that was boosted by a planet-based beam. But it would get there, eventually.

A striding Boylan placed the call while inspecting the inner border of the camp's defensive perimeter. Though it had proven thankfully more reliable and trouble-free than the water condenser, he made it a point to personally examine it at least twice a day. He wanted no repeat of the spikers' intrusion, nor any surprises by other terrestrial belligerents.

As he paced along the inner barrier something blue, fist-sized, and active came tumbling out of the nearest undergrowth. Taking an evasive, zigzag path, it approached the boundary. Contracting its entire body, it unexpectedly leaped off the ground with the intention of entering the camp compound a meter or so ahead of the captain.

There was a bright flash of light and the singeing stink of ozone. Blackened and smoking, the small body lay on the ground where it had been knocked backward, just outside the perimeter. Boylan paused in his inspection to study the tiny body. A viscous, greenish gunk was leaking from the creature's cracked core. In both directions all along the perimeter could be seen the blackened, crumpled corpses of a wide assortment of unsuspecting Quofumian fauna that had attempted to penetrate the camp perimeter, as well as several examples of mobile native plant forms.

There was no sign that any of the confrontational spikers, either singly or in groups, had attempted to penetrate the enhanced perimeter subsequent to their initial failed assault on the camp. One could have tried and been fried, Boylan reflected, and the body hauled away by its surviving companions. But since that first attack there had been no alarms. The latter were programmed to alert the camp's inhabitants only if the perimeter was breached. If they had been set to go off every time an attempt was made, just based on what he was seeing now in the course of his casual inspection, the ringing inside the buildings would have been continuous.

There was an additional benefit to be gained from the lethal fence line. It was generating an abundance of specimens for the scientists to study, a collection that required minimal gathering activity. Admittedly, most of the samples thus unintentionally acquired were not in the best of condition. But as a supplement to the researchers' fieldwork they would still be welcomed.

He lingered a moment to study something the size of a large

dog. It had six legs, though the shock of its demise had splintered two of them. Lying on its side he could not tell which was the front end, which the back, or in the case of this particular woodland denizen if such regional designations even applied.

He was quite pleased. Every aspect of the fence line appeared to be in working order. One reason less to chew out Araza. As Boylan resumed his walk, he acknowledged the delayed response to his call.

"Tellenberg here, Nicholai." The scientist knew it was Boylan calling back because every one of the communits in use by the team had its own signature. Besides which, the researcher could see the captain on his own unit's screen, just as Boylan could see Tellenberg. Neither man adjusted his device to produce a full three-dimensional image. Each already knew what the back of the other man's head looked like. Calling forth full fidelity was an unnecessary waste of power. He might have chosen differently, Boylan mused, if he were talking with Haviti.

"Everything is okay?" Boylan inquired. "Everything is good with you and the others?"

"Everything is good, yes." Of the four researchers, it was Tellenberg who could manage the best imitation of the captain's gruff tone. "Mother," he finished.

"That's right, make fun of Nicholai. I am only responsible for camp, for success of this mission, and for your continued health and safety. I have no responsibilities and I can relax all day and watch bad tridee recordings. Not like you, who have arduous responsibility of spending a few hours each day collecting butterflies."

"Some of the 'butterflies' around here bite," Tellenberg told him.

Boylan's concern was immediate and real. "Someone has

been bitten? Already I see that on this world it could prove difficult to defend against so many possible dangers, small as well as large."

"No, no." The scientist hastened to correct him. "As reported, we've had a few run-ins with some of the simpler local life-forms. You know how it is. Very typical for a planet where the predatory fauna has no reason to fear offworlders. Such attacks just enable us to add to our collections."

Striding along the inside of the fence line, Boylan came across another heap of dead wildlife. "Without even being directed to do so, the camp is also adding to your collections. Or to dinner. I will leave to your expertise the requisite categorizations."

"Sounds appetizing," Tellenberg riposted. The image on the captain's screen shifted as the scientist turned his own comm-unit away from his face. "What do the rest of you think?"

With Tellenberg's vit pickup now pointed in their direction, Boylan could see the other members of the group scattered throughout the boat. From the seat at the control console, N'kosi responded with a rude gesture. Nearby, Valnadireb also responded with a gesture. The thranx utilized all four hands, rendering actions as complex as they were unintelligible.

Sitting on the narrow bench that was an integral part of the hull and ran around the inside of the boat, Haviti just smiled. "I don't mind eating a few specimens—after they've been catalogued. Or if we have duplicates. If the food prep's analyzer says something is edible, I'm game to try it. Local forage is always a nice change from dehydrates and synthetics. You never know when you might bite into something exceptional."

"Like a new flavor," commented N'kosi. "How often in one's lifetime do you get to experience a new flavor?"

Upon reaching the gate, Boylan completed his circuit of the

camp's interior safety perimeter. More than satisfied, he pivoted on his heel and headed back toward the domed, climate-controlled entry module.

"A patentable discovery like that would repay all costs of expedition," he pointed out via his communit.

Tellenberg was apologetic. "I'm afraid all we have so far are hundreds of unprecedented discoveries and thousands of new species to be placed in an absurdly large number of Quofum-specific phyla. Alas, no new flavors."

Reaching the entrance to the outer lock, Boylan had to pause for a second while Security read his bioprofile. The door then slid aside to admit him. An invigorating blast of cool air greeted his arrival.

"We must make do then with your pitiful vast scientific discoveries. When will I be able to see some of them for myself?" Waiting for a reply, he could clearly hear Tellenberg consulting with N'kosi and the others.

"Even with occasional stops to collect, we should be back at the river landing sometime tomorrow morning," the scientist told him. "Before lunch, certainly. Assuming the boat doesn't give us any trouble."

"Boat is self-maintaining." Boylan stepped through the inner doorway and into the module that had been fitted out as the expedition's living quarters. "Not like camp, where I have to do so much work by myself with only personality-deprived half-mute technician to assist. See you tomorrow morning, then."

"Don't eat anything we wouldn't eat," Tellenberg directed him by way of signing off.

The captain clipped his communit back onto his service belt. He was pretty fortunate, he knew. On previous expeditions he had found himself forced to operate in the company of researchers whose notion of uncontrolled hilarity was to alter recordings of alien zygotes and pass the results off as genuine. All too many of them could consider humor only in the abstract. To Boylan, anyone who could not laugh when one of a team's members slipped and fell in a pool of alien excrement was not worthy of the extra help and companionship that were so vital to an expedition's success.

Who said he had no sense of humor?

Tellenberg slipped his communit back into its weatherproof holder. The device itself was also completely weatherproof, which meant that the holder was somewhat superfluous, but he was a firm believer in the efficacy of redundant systems—especially out in the field. He smiled to himself. Boylan's attitude toward the science team bordered on the schizophrenic. On the one hand the captain professed little interest in the researchers so long as they did their jobs and did not violate accepted Commonwealth standards for carrying out fieldwork. On the other, he could be as solicitous as a brooding hen. He would never admit to such concern, of course. It would never square with the macho image he sought to project.

Something bumped the underside of the boat. Hard. Hard enough to jolt his attention as well as his backside. Thoughts of the captain were abandoned as he turned to look back at N'kosi.

Having nearly been knocked out of his seat by the unexpected impact, the other xenologist had grabbed the bar that ran around the control console. He hung on with one hand as he checked the instruments. Nearby, Haviti was picking herself up off the deck. She appeared unhurt. Valnadireb helped her up. The thranx had been standing on all six legs and had not fallen. None of the four scientists felt the need to say "What the hell?"

An intent N'kosi was studying readouts. "Hull integrity intact," he announced immediately. Tellenberg assumed he meant both hulls, since the boat had two. "Systems status unchanged. Minor course deviation corrected." Glancing up, his gaze met Tellenberg's. "What did we hit? Depth scanners indicate we still have ten meters of water under us."

Haviti was leaning over the port side. A strange expression had come over her face as she looked back at her colleagues. "You mean 'who.'"

It was truly amazing, Tellenberg marveled as he rushed to the side of the boat, how one small world could contain such a vast wealth of implications.

There were two—no, three of the massive creatures. They lolled on their backs, or at least on their dorsal sides since it was impossible to truthfully identify a front or back, and lazily regarded the boat and its occupants. More than a little dazed, the four researchers gazed back at the beings who had come up under the boat. There was no way of telling if the contact had been intentional or accidental. None of the alien trio appeared to be injured. As the scientists looked on, the three rolled and dipped in the water, easily keeping pace with the boat.

It occurred to the three humans that they ought to be operating their recorders. Fortunately, Valnadireb had never taken his off. It had been monitoring the encounter from the moment of collision.

As he was fumbling to position his own ear-mounted unit, Tellenberg's fingers dropped away from the device. He had been overcome by the sudden realization of what they were seeing.

A moment fraught with implications as profound as they were unexpected. A glance would have shown that his companions had been equally affected. One by one they checked their individual documenting instrumentation.

The nearest of the three aquatic organisms had disappeared, having submerged fully. The other two continued to loll on the surface. It was evident they were as interested in the exotic creatures on board the strange floating object as those terrestrial beings were in them.

Formed of lustrous, glassy protoplasm, each of the alien pair was a good four meters long. Their central bulges were approximately the same in diameter. Both fore and aft ends tapered to a stub, at the end of which was an obvious eye. Two eyes, one at each end. Remarkable, Tellenberg found himself thinking. Not only could he and his colleagues not tell the creatures' dorsal side from the ventral, they could not tell front from back. The organisms' design was fantastic, absurd, outrageous. A biological joke. He did not rule out the possibility that each of them was actually two individuals joined tail to tail, perhaps for purposes of ongoing reproduction.

But if that was the case, how to explain only one pair of waving appendages protruding from the central bulge? If each organism was comprised of two individuals joined together, would each separately be equipped with only one limb? And why not? he challenged himself. Each would have only one eye. One limb, one eye—but that was not what was most astonishing about the translucent shapes. Mere physiological aberrations were not what had him struck dumb.

What mattered was not whether the creature he was looking at was controlled by a single brain or two. What rendered him speechless was the unmistakable fact that both sets of waving limbs were semaphoring an intricate series of gestures in the direction of the boat. When Valnadireb responded by attempting to mimic the pseudopodal signaling as best he could, the two aquatic beings promptly reacted by gesturing in kind.

Standing at the railing, Haviti called forth a series of ancestral arm movements. Drawn from formal dance moves handed down through her family, they were languorous and serpentine. The creatures in the water imitated them beautifully. They then proceeded to follow this display with a succession of simple twists and turns of their flexible limbs. Tellenberg joined his friends in trying his hand at mimicry. The alien gestures grew more complicated. When the humans' and thranx's attempts at imitation failed, the water slugs simplified their efforts and repeated them until those on board got the movements right.

This gesticulating exchange continued until dusk. At that point the river-dwellers gestured their farewell and dove. N'kosi spotted all three of them swimming back upriver in the wake of the boat. As the interior of the vessel's hull began to glow softly, providing illumination in response to the fading daylight, three of its passengers gathered near the stern. It being Haviti's turn to handle the controls, she participated from where she sat behind the console.

N'kosi spoke up first, voicing the conclusion they had all already reached independently.

"No mouths. No visible or audible means of modulating air. Instruments found nothing unusual in the way of electrical discharge. No nonvocal vibrations of any kind were detected, subsonic or otherwise." Using his right hand he brushed sweat from his forehead. "Communication was strictly via gestures."

"A certain minimal amount of body language may also be involved," Haviti declared from her position behind the console.

"We can't say that all that twisting and rolling was not involved."

"Physical punctuation." Tellenberg was shaking his head in disbelief. "I guess none of us ought to be surprised. We'd already agreed that the biology of this world was insane."

In the dim light Valnadireb's feathery antennae bobbed forward. "So now we are faced with the reality of a fifth indigenous sentient race. As if intended to drive us mad, it bears even less evolutionary relationship to the four other intelligence species we have previously encountered than any of them do to one another."

"They could be related to the stick-jellies." N'kosi's half-hearted conjecture sounded feeble even to him. Whether comprised of possibly mating pairs or bizarrely designed individuals, the dexterously gesticulating water slugs were like nothing else the team had encountered so far.

Tellenberg let out a quiet sigh. "I wonder what we'll come across tomorrow. Artistic air bags? Literary forminifera? Intelligent rocks?"

"Now you're being silly," Haviti chided him.

He looked back sharply. "Am I? Am I the only one who thinks we've stumbled onto some vast cosmic joke?" Spreading his arms, he gestured at the nearest shore, sliding past in silhouette. The sounds that emanated from its trees and bushes and other as yet undefined growing things were epidemic with aural absurdities.

"The more we learn about this world, the more unarguable it becomes that what we're encountering here is not natural. Biology and evolution simply don't work this way. The Commonwealth consists of dozens of habitable worlds whose biota have been studied, catalogued, and researched in depth, plus dozens of others that have at least been cursorily surveyed. Some of them are home to flora and fauna more outrageous than imaginable. But all of it, everywhere, regardless of whether it's carbon- or silicon-based, regardless of whether it's fueled by oxy-nitro or methane, liquid or dissolved sulfates, reactive organic hydroxides or reverse protein electrophoresis, follows certain laws." Rising, he moved to starboard and leaned his hands on the rail as he stared at the dark, raucous, unfathomable Quofumian forest.

"Mushrooms do not evolve from starfish. Gorillas do not arise from liverworts. Birds do not develop from sequoias."

"Thranx do not develop from tegath," Valnadireb put in solemnly, to fully emphasize the point.

Tellenberg turned back to his colleagues. "So what do we have here? External intervention for purposes of amusement, as was suggested earlier? A globular zoo whose keepers we have yet to contact? The hand of a deity, albeit a mighty capricious one? Or am I missing a conclusion that should be obvious?"

"I hope so," muttered Haviti. "Anarchy is bad for biology. It complicates the classifying of reports."

"Something unique is going on here." Pulling a drink tube from a storage container, N'kosi popped the top, waited a few seconds for the contents to cool, and swallowed thirstily. Lightly smacking his lips, he turned to study the slowly passing forest. "Maybe we aren't coming up with the right explanation because we simply don't possess the proper reference points. If what we're encountering lies outside the body of accepted biological knowledge, perhaps we have to find a way to step outside existing wisdom in order to explain it."

"A neat trick." Taking the tube from his friend, Tellenberg chugged down the rest of the contents. "When you figure out how to do it, please let me know."

"You'll be among the first." N'kosi smiled.

"We could all get drunk," Haviti suggested. "My ancestors recommended kava. I think the camp's synthesizer could manage the necessary molecular chains."

"Comforting, if not enlightening." Tellenberg tried to imagine the brilliant and insightful Haviti stumbling around the camp dining area stone blotto. Half the vision was appealing, the other half oddly unsettling. Having no idea how he might cope with such a reality he put it resolutely out of his mind. Faced with an entire world of unreality, he really had no time for personal adjuncts.

Other drink tubes were brought out and their contents sipped or chugged after first being heated or chilled, depending on individual thirst preferences. Food joined fluids in being consumed as the boat continued its way downstream. As they proceeded they were serenaded by flanking forest and star-filled sky and even gurgling, burbling river with a chorus of sounds as riotous and lunatic as the organisms that must be generating them. Others might have found the nocturnal refrain vaguely disturbing. To the quartet of slightly giddy researchers drunk on speculation it was an auditory carnival marred only by the lack of time available for study and their inability to identify the source of each and every shriek, scream, squeal, and screech.

There had to be an explanation, Tellenberg mused furiously as he gnawed on his rehydrated food wrap. There had to be a conjoining link. It couldn't all be random. Nature was diverse. She could be passionate, even wildly eccentric. But she was never, not ever, arbitrary. It was the same on every world humanxkind had ever explored. Until now. Until Quofum.

Tilting back his head, he peered out from beneath the craft's protective canopy. The stars were different from those viewable on the world of his birth. But they were still stars. The spaces between them were filled with a largely understood quotient of particles and energy. Natural laws were in place, even if some still remained to be discovered and quantified. The clock that was the universe ticked onward.

Where, in that vast panoply of organized matter, was the key to the irrational world on which they had landed?

7

It was no slight to Araza that Boylan was unwilling to take his word for it that the condenser was once again in full working order. The captain no more trusted his own observations than he did those of his technician. For Boylan, proof of accomplishment resided in reality, not words.

He had visited all three main modules plus checking on Irrigation and had spoken to dozens of separate spigots before he was satisfied that the camp's water delivery system was functioning properly once again. A casual observer might have deemed such behavior obsessive. Boylan would not have bridled at the designation. Alone on an alien world parsecs from the nearest help, obsessiveness might prove detrimental to social interaction, but it might also save the lives of those who thought they were being treated with condescension.

Better to have lots of running water, he felt, than a few cozy friendships.

The afternoon wound down without incident. That is, if one

discounted the attacks made by three entirely new and totally unrelated species of flying predators, the several efforts by terrestrial organisms of varying size and strength to frontally breach the charged perimeter, and at least one attempt to burrow beneath it. The latter two did not escape the lethal effects of the fence. As for the aerial carnivores, their repeated and misguided efforts to penetrate the convex plexalloy and nanofiber roof of the compound gained them nothing more than broken teeth, split talons, and bruised egos. At its worst, the banging and scratching they caused was no more than distracting.

Have to get together with Araza to rig up some kind of motion-activated fright lights or something, Boylan decided. It wouldn't do to have large predators continuously slamming into and banging off the roofs. If nothing else, the constant clamor would disrupt work inside the lab module.

A mist-laden evening was clothing the surrounding forest in gray gossamer when he finally found time to check the main storage bay for gear that might be used to improvise the crude equivalent of an alien scarecrow. Located at the rear of the lab module, the large chamber contained equipment and supplies that had been brought down via the shuttle but had yet to be sorted out and put in its proper place. There was no lock or security seal on the door. No one would steal supplies to which they already had legitimate access, and no natives could get in. So Boylan was more than a little surprised to find the small room a mess.

Everything should have been sorted by department, individual researcher, predetermined experiment, and stacked neatly on the floor or placed on the integrated shelving that protruded from the module's inner wall. What he found instead were opened cartons with their contents exposed to the air, smaller

containers piled haphazardly in one corner, boxes of supplies
that had been accessed but not resealed, a jumble of organic
materials marked FRAGILE that ought not to have been stacked
at all, and loose bits and pieces that should have been returned
to their original packing instead of being left where they had
been unpacked. There was no getting around it: the storage
room was a disaster area. It had not been one when the science
team had departed upriver. Therefore the scientists could not be
responsible for the storeroom's current intolerable condition.
And since he himself had not visited it for days, the only possibility remaining was . . .

"*Araza!*"

Boylan could have raised the tech on his communit, could
have located him in an instant, but he wanted to confront his
subordinate in person and without warning. How could someone charged with maintaining the camp treat a critical portion
of its supplies so cavalierly? While carrying out assigned tasks
with reasonable efficiency, Araza had always been somewhat indifferent to orders. But until now there had been no reason for
Boylan to accuse him of abject carelessness. Handling vital materials and important equipment in such a slipshod fashion not
only threatened to ruin important experiments before they
could be run, it posed a danger to far more significant stores
such as medicinal supplies.

He found the technician in the dining area, eating his evening
meal. Araza looked up as the captain entered. If the tech noticed
anything amiss, it did not affect his appetite. After an acknowl-
edging glance and nod, he looked away and returned to his food.

With exaggerated deliberation, Boylan sat down in the seat
opposite, on the other side of the thin but sturdy table. "Enjoy-
ing your supper?"

Araza forked up another mouthful, chewed, swallowed, shifted his attention to the side dish of reconstituted pasta with its improvised alfredo sauce. "Yes, thanks." When this reply produced no response, he added politely, "Aren't you going to eat?"

"In due course." Boylan leaned back in his chair. "I don't like eat until after I've assured myself that everything is done for the day and that camp is in optimal run condition for following morning."

The next forkload paused halfway to the technician's mouth. "Isn't it?"

"Not quite. Not exactly." The captain's stare was, if not exactly murderous, at least accusatory. "There a certain storage room whose contents could use modicum of professional attention. In fact, if I did not know better, from looking at it just now I would think it had been vandalized."

Araza unhurriedly put down his fork, picked up a hand wipe, cleaned his fingers, and set the soiled wipe aside for recycling. "The camp perimeter is intact. Nothing has been inside that could do such a thing."

"I know." Sarcasm and satisfaction in equal measure now poisoned Boylan's tone. "That reality would seem to lead us to an incontestable conclusion: that present condition of storeroom in question is responsibility of someone already inside perimeter. Pardon if I exclude myself."

For the first time Araza appeared to show a reaction beyond mere annoyance. "With the scientific team away, the contents of the storeroom are not presently being utilized." He hesitated. "I realize that there is some disarray."

"'Disarray'?" Boylan eyed the technician in mock disbelief. "You mean, as if everything in room had been sucked into a black hole only to be spit out again?"

Pushing his plate aside, Araza started to rise. "Since it upsets you so much, I will stack and organize everything in the morning."

"Sit—down," Boylan growled tersely.

For an instant Araza appeared to freeze. His expression did not change. Only after a noticeable pause did he finally comply and resume his seat. Boylan was neither intimidated nor slowed. "I want it fixed now. I want everything back in its proper place, on its indicated shelf, with appropriate labels and spacing. Tonight."

Unruffled as ever, Araza eyed his superior. "Why? I will have everything back in place before the researchers return. Right now there is no one else to see the room except you and I."

"Well, 'I' want it put right tonight." Boylan smiled thinly. "I'll sleep a lot better knowing that the necessary work has already been done. It benefits both of us. You will have a lighter workload tomorrow. We'll both need the rest. The team will have crates and bottles full of specimens to be unloaded, brought to camp, and stored."

"Tonight." Araza checked his chronometer.

"Tonight," Boylan told him. "Now would be good time to start." Again the smile. "So that you don't forget."

"All right. You are correct, Captain Boylan. If I get everything that needs to be done out of the way tonight, the workload tomorrow will be lighter."

"That's the spirit!" Pleased with the result of their little confrontation, Boylan rose. "You don't have to rush off. Just get on it soon."

"No." Pushing back his chair, Araza stood and stepped away from the table. "I have finished my meal. Perhaps when I have performed the remainder of this evening's work I will pause for a drink and something else to eat, and to take time to relax. You know that I am not much of a dessert person."

"Me, I love the sweets too much." Patting his stomach as he headed toward the food prep unit, Boylan started around the table. "If I'm still up, I'll join you for that drink."

"There should be time," Araza murmured as he walked away, heading in the direction of the lab module.

Boylan had finished his main courses and was scooping up last of the cupuraçu sundae from a self-chilling bowl when the technician returned. The captain frowned.

"That was quick. I know you can work fast when you want to, Salvador, but that was too fast. Surely you haven't finished the job yet?"

"No." Araza's voice was even softer than usual. Not like that of a man dead, but like that of one for whom the other half of a conversation had little meaning. "I have only prepared myself to do the work."

"Well, damn it then—and damn you, too, man!" Boylan pushed the empty bowl toward the center of the table and wiped his mouth with a cloth. "Is this some kind of joke? Did you think I wasn't being serious when I told you to clean up the storeroom *tonight*?"

"I do not think this is some kind of joke," the technician replied evenly. "Before I can think of doing the work you specified, one other matter must be dealt with first."

Boylan's sarcasm was in full flower. "Wonderful! What is it this time? You have dirty underwear that need emergency cleaning? There is chapter in a book you need to finish reading? Serious ear wax buildup that desperately need attention, perhaps?"

Unexpectedly, Araza smiled. There was no humor in it. "You

have a voice, Nicholai Boylan, that is deserving of both respect and contempt. It serves you well in your chosen profession. It is to be regretted that your ability to manipulate timbre and words is not matched by an equal skill with numbers."

What's going on here? Boylan wondered to himself. Something was not right. Most obviously, something had gifted the normally taciturn technician with uncharacteristic articulateness. What had suddenly inspired in him the power of speech? And not just minimally comprehensible speech, either. Then there were his eyes. Normally distant or disinterested, they had acquired a new and disturbingly intense focus that had not been there before. It was as if during the transition from dinner to dessert the tech had suddenly become a different person.

Or was it possible, the captain mused, that this was the real Araza, and the persona of shambling, competent, minimally communicative technician they had known all along was the false one? If that was the case, then what was he dealing with here? In the absence of information it was no disgrace to plead ignorance.

"I don't know what you talking about, Salvador. But I do know that I don't like you attitude."

"Only the guilty find detachment threatening." Araza's gaze bored into the captain's.

In the course of a long career Boylan had been compelled to stare down many men, some women, and not a few aliens. It was therefore hard for him to admit to himself how badly the mechanic was unsettling him.

"Do you recall," Araza continued, "a loan of some sixty thousand credits, advanced to you by one Char-pesh Hambilah-ah-Salaam, in the city of Barragath, on Thalia Major?"

The captain blinked. Corroded bits of memory bestirred

themselves and linked together to form coherent thoughts. "Good God, that was twelve years ago!"

Araza nodded once. "Your recollection is correct. A ship captain and expedition commander is required to have some small command of figures. Therefore you should be able to roughly calculate the interest that has accrued."

Boylan gaped. He started to laugh, stopped when he saw that the technician was dead serious. "I can't believe this. A minor but still important scientific expedition, with much at stake and already a great many new discoveries made, and I am expected to take the time to explain a prehistoric personal fiscal misunderstanding to mission technician? I don't know how you know about this or what misleading and outright wrong tales you have been told, but is no concern of yours. Especially not now, not here, on this world and in this place." Slowly, he pushed his chair back from the table. The last remnants of his sundae formed a streaky puddle in the bottom of the serving bowl.

"It is a concern of mine, Nicholai Boylan, as I have been charged with extracting recompense." Araza stared solemnly across at the captain.

Now Boylan did laugh. How could he not? The situation was so preposterous, so outrageously absurd. "A bill collector! Someone go to trouble of engaging a highly competent, if often slothful technician to collect an outdated credit advance while in the course of an expedition to a new and potential hazardous habitable world. It beggar belief."

It was plain that the man standing on the other side of the table did not see the same humor in the situation. "The loan is not outdated. There is no statute of limitations on the payback of monetary advances from this particular source."

Boylan took a deep breath. "You have been misinformed, my friend. Misinformed and deceived. When it was made, no time limit for repayment was placed on that old loan. Not by Hambilah-ah-Salaam nor by his associates nor by their company. It will be repaid, I imagine, in due course."

"Twelve years." Araza's gaze had not wavered. It occurred to Boylan that the technician seemed to have stopped blinking. An unusual and curious skill. "Plus interest. Due on demand. Due now." The faintest of smiles reappeared to mar an otherwise fixed expression. "Tonight."

"Now?" The captain had moved beyond laughter. He was starting to get angry. He had an expedition to supervise, four eager and excited scientists returning to camp in the morning, hostile flora and fauna to deal with, several species of belligerent native sentients to somehow simultaneously study and keep at arm's length, and—no time for this.

"There are details involving this financial transaction of which you are obviously ignorant. Maybe I'll discuss its history with you tomorrow. Or next week. When I can find the time. There is no time now. We both have much to do." Rising, he glared across the intervening table at his obdurate subordinate. "I have a responsibility to my team and to the Commonwealth."

"You have a responsibility to your creditors." Araza was quietly implacable.

Leaning forward, Boylan rested his fists on the table. "You not listening to me, Salvador. Pay attention. *I have no time for this now*. Leave it alone. Get back to you real job. Clean up that storeroom."

"You refuse to settle your account?"

Straightening, the captain turned his hands palm upward and cast his eyes ceilingward. "Oh, sure, I settle it. I send space-minus communication now, to Wolophon III, which passes details to Cmkk, which transfers information to maybe Balthazaar, which coordinates deposit of necessary credit on Thalia Major." Lowering his gaze, he glowered across at the placid technician. "Is no problem because I have nothing else to occupy my time right now." His tone changed from cantankerous to the kind one would use when addressing a child.

"Firstly, no guarantee from this place and location that initial communication would successfully make contact. Secondly, is waste of expedition resources. Thirdly, is illegal to utilize mission equipment for personal matters. And lastly, according to terms agreed upon when original loan was made, time to pay back is incumbent on my ability to do so. That is presently inadequate."

"You should have saved your money," Araza told him. Unlike Boylan, there was not a hint of scorn in the technician's voice.

"Even if I had it, I would not be bothering with such a thing now. Not here, not in this place. In case you not noticed, I have other responsibilities."

"Your responsibility is to your long-patient creditors. You have been in a position to make payback on numerous occasions during the past twelve years." Araza was quietly implacable. "You have not paid."

The captain shrugged, unconcerned. "Time passes. Things happen. The load will be repaid. Eventually."

" 'Eventually' is insufficiently unambiguous for my clients. You will pay now."

Though he was not really worried, Boylan casually let his right hand slip toward his waist. Along with a varied assortment of other gear, it held his holstered sidearm. If he could not make the technician see reason, he would have to force it upon him.

A week or two spent locked up in his room should give him sufficient time for reflection. He had delivered his demand and found the response wanting. That would be the end of it. When the expedition returned to Commonwealth space, Araza could communicate that information to whoever had hired him. If his stubbornness proved to be unrelenting, the expedition would simply have to get along without his abilities. Boylan didn't think it would come to that. The withholding of food, for example, was usually enough to convince the recalcitrant to cooperate.

"Even if an effective means of doing so existed," he told the intent technician in an attempt to put an end to the charade, "I couldn't pay off loan now. I don't have the credit."

Digesting this response, Araza nodded comprehendingly. "Very well. If that is your concluding word on the matter. I have been charged with extracting recompense. I will do so now."

Boylan's fingers furtively undid the snap on his sidearm's holster. "Don't threaten me, Salvador. Not to my face. Not in my own camp."

Reaching up, the technician fingered the top of the seal that ran down the front of his jumpsuit. The captain tensed, but Araza was only unsealing his jumpsuit. No hidden weapon revealed itself as the tech slipped the seal all the way down to the crotch of his clothing. The green-and-beige camouflage worksuit fell away from slender shoulders. Beneath, in place of the usual lightweight underwear, the technician was clad in a light-absorbing jet-black skinsuit of a type Boylan did not immediately recognize. Encircling it at the waist was a black belt festooned with gleaming, highly miniaturized gear whose functions were unfamiliar and subject to multiple interpretation. The belt buckle . . . the buckle . . .

Boylan froze. His breath caught in his throat. Though it was pleasantly warm in the dining area, a chill ran up and through his entire body as if his spine had suddenly been flash-frozen in a slab of glacial ice. Only his right leg stayed warm, because it was down that limb the trickle of tepid urine from his voided bladder curled.

The buckle that secured the black belt at the technician's waist had been faceted from a single artificially enhanced, specially treated crystal of vanadanite. The bright orange-red stone was inset with a gold skull and crossbones. As if that was not conclusive identification enough, the technician proceeded to doff his work cap. Instead of his shaven skull, a second head covering was revealed beneath the hat. This was a black skullcap inlaid with signs, insignia, and cryptic script that had been laid in with crimson foil.

There was no longer any doubt as to Salvador Araza's true profession. The revelation was only further confirmed when he reached up and calmly peeled off first one and then the other prosthetic eyebrow.

The Qwarm favored full-body depilation lest even a single stray hair betray their presence or get in the way of their work. That work, as it had been practiced ever since the clan had been established hundreds of years earlier, ran the gamut of a great many disreputable but tolerated specialties. Bill collecting could be counted among these. Assassination was another.

Boylan was badly shaken by the disclosure, but he was not paralyzed. The hand that had been sliding toward his sidearm and had unlatched its holster now drew the weapon and fired. His stocky build notwithstanding, the captain could move fast when he needed to. Deceptively fast. The tiny but deadly shells his weapon fired sped straight toward the somber-faced specter standing before him. Unfortunately, by the time they reached the point of contact, their target was no longer there.

Boylan looked around wildly as smoke rose from the holes the double shot had blown in the module's interior wall. Araza had vanished. As the captain crouched next to the table, gripping the sidearm tightly, the technician's voice drifted up to him from somewhere down the corridor.

"There is neither need nor sense in making this difficult, Nicholai Boylan. I have told you that I am charged with exacting recompense. If my employer cannot have your money, then he must have your life."

"I *told* you!" Boylan was trying to look every which way at once. "I don't have the money! I need more time." He was breathing faster than he had in years and his heart was pounding so hard it threatened to punch its way out his chest. "I will have substantial credits waiting for me when this expedition returns. First thing, I will transfer them to whatever account you specify." Despite his fear, he tried his best to sound conspiratorially convivial. "That need not even be your bedamned employer's account." Even as he spoke he was edging stealthily toward the hallway opposite the one from which Araza's calm voice emerged.

"I am Qwarm," the unseen technician told him. The corridor imbued his voice with a slight reverberation. "A Qwarm cannot be bribed. In any event, I have some knowledge of what someone in your position in charge of an expedition on this scale is likely to be paid. The amount would not cover the interest owed, much less a satisfactory portion of the principal."

"I told you." Boylan's stressed response was half entreaty, half curse. "I need more time!"

"You have had twelve years." Had the tech's voice moved?

Boylan couldn't tell. He was almost to the hallway entrance. Araza continued patiently. "Not only my employer but any legitimate Commonwealth bank or credit monitoring facility would consider that you have already been granted an excess of leniency."

"Banks don't hire assassins to extract revenge. Not because they're any more compassionate than the people who are paying you, but because they know that a dead creditor is a complete write-off." The captain found himself with a clear line into the hallway.

"You should have dealt with a bank," Araza's voice informed him coldly. "I have been advised that my client is prepared, albeit with due reluctance, to consider Nicholai Boylan fully amortized."

Accompanied by a barely perceptible hum, a neat hole half a centimeter in diameter appeared in the wall slightly above and to the left of Boylan's head. The edges of the puncture were perfectly smooth. No smoke rose from the perforation, no heat radiated from its edges. It had been made by one of the Qwarm's preferred weapons: a sonic stiletto. Shaped sound had blown a hole in the tough nanofiber material. Boylan knew it would have no difficulty punching an equally perfect hole in his head.

Pulling the communit from his duty belt, he made sure its locator was turned off. Then he whirled and raced down the corridor. As he ran he did not look back. Doing so would only slow him, however marginally, and might result in his not seeing something on the floor and tripping over it. Looking back under such circumstances was a waste of time. He would not see a sonic burst coming. As for Araza, if he was near enough to observe the captain's desperate flight, then Boylan knew he was already as good as dead. As long as he could not see the Qwarm, could not hear him, and nothing spanged through his skull or his torso, the captain thought he had a chance.

A slim chance, to be sure, but he had survived near-death encounters on other worlds. As long as his brain functioned, there was hope. If he could just reach the shuttle he could safely lock himself inside. Then he would be the one in a position to make demands. Of course, Araza would recognize that as well. The shuttle was the one place where his quarry could find safety. That knowledge would persuade the Qwarm to go there first, to prevent the captain from engineering exactly that kind of escape. Realizing this and knowing that he could not best or get past the professional assassin in an open fight, Boylan had opted for an alternative strategy.

If he could get outside before his pursuer brought him down, the captain planned on switching off the security perimeter. The Quofumian forest would be his equalizer. Salvador Araza might be comfortably at home within civilized surroundings and a master of humanx culture, but he arguably knew even less about this world than did Boylan. Out in the teeming, volatile, unpredictable alien jungle the Qwarm would find himself only one more predator among hundreds. True, one of the latter might as easily decide to make a casual meal of the fleeing captain. In that event Boylan felt he would be no worse off than if he tried to stand his ground inside the camp. But there was also the possibility that Araza might become a meal for some wandering carnivore first.

Of course, the Qwarm could simply choose to remain inside the camp, comfortable within its confines and at ease with its amenities. Boylan did not think Araza would resort to such idleness. Such inaction would be very un-Qwarm-like. Having held his true identity in check for so long, the captain doubted a professional like the technician would be content to sit back and wait for circumstances to favor him. Naturally proactive, he was unlikely to sit on his butt and wait for his target to wander in and surrender.

He might also realize, as Boylan had, that if the captain could get to the river first he might through truth or trickery be able to inveigle the members of the science team on his behalf. While the researchers were untrained in matters of interhuman conflict, they knew how to conceal themselves in the forest (in order to better observe animals) and how to defend themselves with the sidearms they carried as part of their standard field issue. A Qwarm was still a Qwarm; impressive, well trained, and thorough. But on Quofum, Araza was operating on unfamiliar ground, and five guns against one would be an improvement in the odds sufficient to give even a professional killer pause.

Once outside the last module Boylan could instruct his comm-unit to disarm the perimeter fence. That way he would not be confined to exiting via the gate. He could vanish into the woods in any direction. Within the forest he would have to deal with the fantastic array of local life-forms. It was night outside, too. Were the spikers active after sundown? Boylan hoped so. He was ready to take his chances with hostile natives of any species so long as the cocksure Araza was forced to do the same. They would see which man was better prepared, both mentally and otherwise, to survive under such conditions.

He hesitated at the module's emergency doorway, but only for an instant. Knowing how fast a Qwarm could move, he understood that the one currency he could not afford to squander was time. Easing the barrier open, he held his sidearm out in front of him as he emerged. In the absence of moon, phosphorescent flora and fauna, stars, and the subdued perimeter lights provided just enough illumination for him to make out his surroundings. His eyes struggled to adjust. There was movement visible, but only on the far side of the barrier, within the deep woods.

Putting his lips close to his communit he hastily whispered the command for cutting power to the security perimeter. Given that there were defense issues involved, it took more than a moment to set up the correct sequence. He was halfway across the flat open space that had been cleared between the camp buildings and the fence line before he had the command string in place. After that, it was only a matter of murmuring a code word to set everything in motion.

He waited until the last possible moment. Once the security barrier went down Araza would immediately connect it with Boylan's absence. Unless the technician was a complete fool he would just as quickly divine the fleeing captain's intentions—and the Qwarm did not train fools. But in the absence of a locator signal from the captain's communit the tech would have the entire perimeter to check, by which time Boylan expected to be deep within the forest. Once inside he would follow an erratic, unpredictable, zigzag course toward the river. He did not for a moment doubt that Araza, like all of his clan, was an excellent tracker. But this was not a Commonwealth world. There would be arbitrary distractions. If Boylan was lucky one of them might even prove fatal to his pursuer, or at least slow him down.

He approached the nearest perimeter relay post. Crouching low, he muttered the word that would initiate the disabling sequence. Seconds later the activation telltales on the inside of the post changed from red to green. It meant that the power to the perimeter was down. It could mean nothing else. Still . . .

Ah well, he told himself. If something was amiss and the barrier was still active, he would not live long enough to wonder at the cause of his mistake. Straightening, he started forward. He was across the line in a second.

And still breathing.

The wall of low alien scrub that occupied the space between the perimeter and the forest proper was less than a meter wide. Once among the towering, twisted, frequently hallucinogenic growths, he had to force himself to slow down, to move forward purposefully and steadily but under control. Having successfully made it this far, the last thing he wanted was to make so much noise that it ended up drawing Araza's attention.

As soon as he had gone a hundred meters or so he promptly did something unthinkable. He put his communit down on the ground, and left it.

After his sidearm it was the most useful piece of gear he had with him. But he could not take the chance that a professional as skilled and experienced as Araza might not have a way of tracking such an instrument, even with its locator signal turned off. If so, let him find it here, and then contemplate the possibilities. The captain grinned mirthlessly at the image of a bemused Araza standing over the abandoned communit, scanning the dense forest while trying to decide which way his quarry had gone. Under such circumstances would the technician still come after him? Or might he have second thoughts? It would all depend on his dedication to his job. Without actually seeing and recording a corpse, he could not provide incontestable proof that he had fulfilled his assignment.

Made necessary by the need to leave as little in the way of a trail as possible, the erratic stumble through the jungle took hours. How many, Boylan could not have said. His communit lay somewhere behind him and his thoughts were focused elsewhere. He only knew that eventually he reached the river, "eventually" being a unit of time that was firmly nonspecific.

There was no sign yet of the boat and the scientific team. It was still pitch-dark out and too early. The captain could tell that much even without his communit or a wrist chronometer. He would find a good spot; one where he could settle down in comparative comfort while still having a good view of the river. Already he was putting together the speech he would deliver to the members of the team. It would be simultaneously con-trolled and impassioned. He would not beg for their aid. He would describe the situation in such a way that they would con-clude they had no choice but to help him. Then they would caucus. Boylan was good at strategizing. Araza was a Qwarm. But there would be five of them.

He was almost relaxed when something like a giant bee buzzed his left ear and tore it off.

Pain screaming through the side of his head, he still had enough presence of mind to roll and raise his weapon as he fell. In the forest of the night, something shrieked. His shot had struck home.

Unfortunately, it had struck home in the heart of something plump, furry, and multilimbed. In aiming at movement, he had neglected to pause long enough to evaluate shape. A second, more subdued buzz blew a hole completely through his gun arm, at the elbow. Whimpering, he dropped the weapon, clutched at his injured arm, and started scrabbling desperately among the thick waterfront ground cover for the fallen sidearm.

A shape stepped out of the darkness. Clad as it was all in black, it was difficult to make out more than a silhouette. A glimmer of starlight penetrated the forest canopy just enough to

reflect slightly off the enigmatic and intimidating designs embossed on the black skullcap.

"I have been waiting for you, Nicholai Boylan. I knew you
would come here, in search of allies."

Grimacing in pain, the captain stammered a reply while sur-
reptitiously using only his eyes to search for his dropped
weapon. "What—what if I had made for the shuttle?"

"I secured its airlock with a personal security code before I
came this way. It was not difficult to find the place where you
had left the boundaries of the camp and entered the woods.
You are not a narrow man, Boylan. You break a wide trail, and
you make many tracks."

Something metallic lying on the moist earth picked up a
glint of phosphorescent fungal light: his weapon. Could he get
to it? And if he managed to snatch it up in his good hand would
he have time to aim and fire? Or at least to fire? *You're wasting
time*, he admonished himself.

"I am compelled to extract recompense." Araza gestured in
the direction of the captain's injured arm. "Consider that a
down payment." The hand gripping the phonic stiletto rose
slowly. "This is principal."

Boylan made a wild dive for his sidearm. His fingers wrapped
around it. Unfortunately, it was at that same moment that neural connectivity between arm, hand, fingers, and brain was terminated.

8

It would have been a sincere understatement to say that the returning science team was in good spirits. Unbridled exuberance would have been nearer the mark. Every collection tank and container on the boat was full. They would need the transporters to move some of the heavier specimens, including the dead hardshell, back to camp. Individual recording units contained hours and hours of cross-referenceable tridee footage of native flora and fauna—not to mention the rough-and-rowdy battle for the village of the fuzzies. They had encountered and recorded contact with a fifth intelligent indigenous species. All this in the space of a few days.

Was ever a first contact team blessed with such a wealth of discovery? Tellenberg mused as the boat began to turn in toward shore. If they departed Quofum tomorrow, they would take back with them samples and data enough to keep an entire block of a Commonwealth science center busy for years simply dissecting, analyzing, and classifying. They had come to this world in hopes of settling a few basic astronomical, geological, and biological questions. Among the scientific staff it was hoped that a few worthy papers might result from the low-key expedition. Now it appeared that reputations might be made.

His personal professional prospects had been equally enhanced by the discoveries of the previous days. He could hardly wait to get back to the camp and start working on the material they had amassed. If they never again went out into the field before the scheduled date for departure, none of them would be lacking for work.

In his mind's eye he envisioned what they could reasonably look forward to: awards, promotions, publishing opportunities, the approbation of their peers, perhaps even a modicum of social notoriety. He didn't know about his colleagues, but as for himself he was more than ready to cash in on a personal appearance or two. It would make up for all the repetitive lectures he'd had to record or deliver in person over the years during which time the greatest reward he had received had been occasional polite applause or the rare intelligent question from someone standing out in a youthful audience.

As the sturdy vessel neared the bank there was no need for anyone to go into the bow, no ropes to be cast ashore to tie to trees. Accelerating, Haviti drove the boat forward until the glutinous shoreline mud gripped it firmly. A touch of another control sent a pair of gripper units shooting outward at opposite angles. As soon as these gained a purchase on sufficiently rooted riverine growths, a beep sounded on the control console to indicate that the little vessel was secured to the shore.

Another control unfolded the ramp that was built into the bow. Extending forward and out over the mud, it set down and locked into position on the same patch of relatively dry ground they had used for disembarking days before. Tellenberg recognized the spot from the presence of several empty food containers they had left behind that were only halfway through the initial stages of accelerated biodegradation.

They took only the lightest and most unique bits of their collection in their backpacks. They would return later with Araza and a pair of transporters to recover the remainder. Hermetically sealed in tough containers on board the boat, the rest of the specimens would be safe from any marauding scavengers. Nevertheless, Tellenberg knew he and his companions would worry about the well-being of what they had accumulated until it was safely back inside the camp's laboratory module. While scavengers could not see or smell the carefully packed examples of local life-forms, should they happen to come across the moored craft, curious indigenes such as the stick-jellies or others might try to pry open the containers.

The team had shouldered their packs and were preparing to head inland when Valnadireb unexpectedly blocked the way. "My apologies, all of you, but I detect a very distinctive smell that I fear demands further investigation."

"'Demands'?" A bemused expression came over N'kosi's face. "That's a pretty strong way of putting it, Val."

"It is a pretty strong odor. One that I wish I did not detect. I may be mistaken as to its nature. I hope that I am."

Even in the absence of the usual punctuating hand gestures there was a grimness to the thranx's tone that none of them could miss. As the xenologist from Willowane followed his antennae into the undergrowth, his colleagues trailed behind him. Away from the boat landing the rich, pungent panoply of exotic forest smells grew thick; all moist loam and alien dung and ripely decomposing things. So too did the specific odor that had attracted Valnadireb's attention.

They did not have to go far. The body lay sprawled very close to the landing. It was lying facedown in a mass of meter-wide growths that featured pale red leaves alternating with nubby yellow tendrils. Coiling tightly back upon themselves, the latter drew in protectively as the vibrations generated by advancing footsteps hinted at the approach of large, possibly herbivorous visitors.

Catching sight of the corpse N'kosi uttered an inarticulate sound from the back of his throat. Valnadireb's mandibles clicked twice to express his dismay. Haviti bent to push aside the broad, flat leaves that partially concealed the captain. In the course of doing so she uncovered, among other things, Boylan's left hand. As soon as they were exposed to the light the small horde of translucent, disk-sized arthropods that were swarming the revealed flesh scattered into the undergrowth. They had eaten all the flesh up the wrist.

Disdaining the use of advanced monitoring equipment Tellenberg knelt next to the motionless form and checked it for a pulse. There was none. He checked for a heartbeat and was not rewarded. By this time N'kosi had his communit out and set on Medical. Holding it a few centimeters above the captain's torso he passed it slowly back and forth. A couple of minutes of this was sufficient to give him the answer he didn't want.

"He's dead. Been dead for a while, too."

"Couldn't have been dead too long." Haviti stared at the body that the Quofumian forest had already started to claim. "We haven't been gone that long." She indicated the hand that had been picked clean by the swarm of tiny scavengers. The bones gleamed whitely in the diffuse light of the understory. "That's horrible, but it's not a fatal wound."

To Tellenberg the skeletal appendage sticking out of the dead man's wrist looked unreal, like a gag toy that had been temporarily attached to the captain's real body. Despite the results of his perfunctory examination and N'kosi's scan, he half expected the indefatigable captain to sit up, detach the exposed bones, and screw his real hand back into his wrist. A fine joke that would be on all of them.

Except no one was laughing. Boylan was not going to get up, and there was no other real hand lying in wait in the bushes.

"We must try to determine the cause of fatality." Valnadireb was using both truhands to probe and prod at the corpse's lower torso.

"Here, look at this." Kneeling on the opposite side of the cadaver from Tellenberg, Haviti was pushing at the hair on the back of the dead man's head. For once utterly indifferent to his fellow xenologist's physical appearance, Tellenberg joined her in searching.

What they found was a small hole. Some of the captain's hair had fallen down to cover it. Years of fieldwork had sharpened Haviti's vision.

"Let's turn him over," she suggested solemnly.

Working together, they rolled the heavy body onto its back. As there was no hair to cover it, they saw the matching hole in Boylan's forehead immediately. Small and perfectly round, it went all the way through skin, brain, and bone. A lot of blood, and other things, had leaked out, staining the captain's face and the upper portion of his jumpsuit. Though Tellenberg was an experienced researcher who out in the field had examined and collected a great many disagreeable dead and dismembered specimens, he still found himself glad that Boylan's eyes were closed.

Raising his gaze, he scanned what he could see of the surrounding alien forest. "Spikers? Or the hardshells? Or maybe something else? First we encounter two wary indigenous intelligences, then four, then five. Who's to say there aren't more?"

"Not me." Bending low over Boylan, Haviti was using a field scope to inspect the wound closely. "I can't see too far in—need lab equipment for that—but from what I can tell the ossial perforation is perfectly round and smooth-sided. Turn him again." Tellenberg and N'kosi helped her roll the body. A quick evaluation of the exit wound found her sitting back and nodding.

"Front to back it's a perfect match. Pretty hard to envision a spiker making a wound like that with a crude spear."

"We only know the native weapons we've seen," Tellenberg pointed out reasonably. "We know nothing of those unknown to us." He eyed the corpse. "Still, I tend to agree with your assessment, Tiare. To cause an injury like that with primitive technology you'd almost have to hold him down and drive a metal spike through his head." There was no hesitation, no quaver in the xenologist's voice as he delivered his opinion. He was used to dissection. The captain, in his own involuntary way, had become a specimen. A specimen of just what, they did not yet know.

Actively studying the surrounding foliage, Valnadireb opined, "Perhaps Boylan was killed by some kind of large local predator. The fauna of the Commonwealth includes many very large carnivores equipped with teeth and jaws of sufficient penetrating power to make such a deep wound. My homeworld alone counts several such among its inhabitants."

Haviti looked thoughtful. "So does mine. Deadly meat-eaters

even still roam parts of Earth itself—albeit only in parks and reserves." She indicated the body. "But if it was a predator, one would expect the entrance wound to be larger than the exit, or vice versa, since killing teeth and talons usually taper to a point. I'm not ruling out an exception, though." She gestured at the surrounding undergrowth. "Especially not on this world, where biological exceptions seem to be the rule."

Tellenberg looked around uneasily, unable to keep from wondering what might be lurking just beyond their range of vision and hearing while contemplating its next move. If something local, sentient or otherwise, had killed Boylan and left, there was no telling when it might come back.

"There's something else to take into account." With his right foot, N'kosi nudged the dead man's left boot. "One would think that a predator expending enough energy to make a kill would at least taste its prey. Even an animal defending young is likely to take an exploratory bite out of something it has slain. Except for the hand that was gnawed away by those small scavenging arthropods, the corpse is untouched."

"We're thinking like biologists." N'kosi joined his fellow humans in taking a close look at the deceased captain. "Maybe we should be thinking like psychologists."

Tellenberg blinked at his colleague. "You're saying that maybe Boylan killed himself?"

"That makes no sense," Valnadireb injected.

N'kosi looked back at him. "Maybe not to a thranx. Captain Boylan always struck me as a little high-strung. Like any expedition commander he was under a lot of pressure." He eyed his companions. "Who's to say how seriously it affected him? We only knew the public man. He could have been under stress from all kinds of private demons."

"I dunno." Straightening, Tellenberg found himself staring in the direction of the camp. "Sure, he bitched and yelled a lot. I even encountered him muttering to himself a number of times. But those aren't exactly signs of a suicidal psychosis." He eyed N'kosi. "I know, I know—public versus private man. But still, did he ever strike you as likely to go over the edge?"

N'kosi chewed his lower lip. "No. He always struck me as logical and rational, if a bit prone to hysteria at times. I'm just putting forward another hypothesis. The man's dead and we don't know how or why. We have an event. I'm looking for a cause."

"I do not think we can count self-death among the possibilities." Valnadireb had settled back on his four trulegs, his foothands and truhands folded in front of him. "The fatal wound suffered by the captain is not consistent with the type of weapon he favored. An explosive shell would not leave such a neat, clean puncture. It would not leave a head."

"He could have taken another device from stores," N'kosi argued.

"There's one other possibility." Haviti also rose. "Maybe—maybe he and Salvador had a fight. They were always arguing. At least, the captain was. Even when he answered back, Salvador was always soft-voiced."

"I wouldn't call it arguing," Tellenberg corrected her. "You need at least two to have an argument. Boylan was always bawling him out for some reason or another. I never saw Araza yell back."

She met his gaze evenly. "There you have it. Potential for repressed anger. Only strengthens my point."

Tellenberg spread his arms. His tone reflected his disbelief. "Come on, Tiare. There's always tension between superiors and subordinates. And yes, sometimes it can build to the point where it leads to more than verbal confrontation. I can almost envision a frustrated Salvador taking a swing at Boylan. But murder?" He indicated their surroundings. "And if so, even if we countenance it just for purposes of discussion, why here? If Araza wanted to kill Nicholai, why not murder him in his sleep?"

"I don't know," she muttered, "since I don't spend any time myself plotting imaginary homicides. What I do know is that Val makes a good point about weapons." Crouching again, this time near the captain's waist, Haviti checked the holster on his service belt. It took only a moment to learn what she wanted to know. "Empty," she declared, looking up at each of them in turn.

Tellenberg's lips tightened. "Irrespective of cause of death, that makes no sense at all. No matter what the circumstances, Boylan wouldn't have left camp without a gun. Hell, he always wore one when he was *inside* the perimeter." Turning, he started hunting through the undergrowth, shoving aside oversized leaves and thinner strands of other organic material of uncertain composition. His companions joined him.

His hunch proved correct. Valnadireb found the discarded sidearm lying in the mud. Picking it up in a foothand, the thranx xenologist transferred the weapon to a truhand and showed it to his companions. One chitinous digit tapped a readout on the side of the device.

"This holds ten rounds. Assuming it was fully loaded as usual, several are recorded as having been fired." He stowed the recovered weapon in his backpack. "In camp we can access the weapon's recorder to see what he was firing at."

After fumbling through the dead man's service belt, Tellenberg let out a puzzled sigh and stood. "There's no communit. I'd sooner be stuck out here without a weapon than without a communit. This really makes no sense."

"An active communit puts out a locator signal." Haviti nodded in the direction of camp. "If Boylan was afraid of being tracked, he might have left his behind."

"You mean, if Araza was after him?" N'kosi joined her in looking eastward. "If that's the case, it didn't do him any good."

"We could find out all the answers," Tellenberg put in, "if we could ask him."

"Can't ask him." Haviti withdrew her own unit. "Can ask someone else who might have some answers."

Tellenberg put a hand on her arm. "What if you're right?" he murmured.

She met his gaze. "You mean about Boylan and Araza having a fight? Look, Esra—there are certain things we can do. We can stand here hypothesizing 'til the end of time, or we can move forward with this. The captain's death may have a depressing but perfectly reasonable explanation. I grant you that murder might be one of them. But it's only one among several. One way or another, under one set of conditions or another, we have to get back to camp. That means confronting Salvador—unless our initial suspicions were correct and this is somehow the work of one or more groups of natives or some as yet unknown predator. If that's the case, then Araza will be even more anxious to hear from us than we are to talk to him."

N'kosi swallowed. "And if there *was* some kind of altercation and Salvador followed Boylan out here and killed him?"

Her reply was as hard as her gaze. "Then we might be able to ascertain that by asking the right questions and analyzing Araza's answers, which would be a hell of a lot better than walking right up to him and putting the matter to his face, don't you think?"

They spent several minutes debating their options. As these

were limited, the discussion was concluded fairly quickly. It was agreed that they should contact the technician via communit.

"You talk to him," Tellenberg told her.

Haviti blinked. "Me? Why me? Why not you, or even Val?"

Despite the seriousness of the situation Tellenberg almost smiled. "When he replies he'll be thinking of you. Somehow I think that's likely to be more reassuring than if he's thinking of me, or Mosi, or Val."

"That's not a very scientific rationale, Esra."

It was definitely not the right place or time to smile. "No, Tiare, it's not. But it's realistic."

She hesitated. Seeing that all three of her colleagues were in agreement, she shook her head once and addressed the communit, instructing it to alert Araza.

As it turned out it did not matter whether she was chosen to try to talk to him, or Tellenberg, or even Valnadireb. It did not matter because no matter what method she employed, whether verbal or via wholly electronic input, the expedition's technician did not answer.

"Maybe something's wrong with your unit," Tellenberg suggested after several attempts at contact had failed.

She shook her head. "It shows full functionality. Still . . ." She extended a hand.

He lent her his device. The results were exactly the same.

"This isn't good. Not good at all." N'kosi had tried to reach Araza on his own unit. "I can't even raise his emergency locator. At least the camp's separate module beacons all respond."

"Same here." Haviti handed Tellenberg's device back to him. "It suggests that his unit has been knocked out of action. Or turned off."

"Why would he turn off his communit?"

"Maybe he doesn't want to be located," a somber-faced N'kosi ventured. "Or maybe he's just not in a talkative mood."

None of the possible explanations were pleasant to contemplate, Tellenberg knew, although it was encouraging that the individual camp beacons were functioning. At this point, any sign of normality was welcome.

"Could the spikers have attacked the camp, chased Boylan out here, and killed Araza?" N'kosi wondered. "How would they get through the perimeter?"

"That still wouldn't explain the precision of Boylan's injuries," Haviti pointed out, "or how he came to be out here, this far away from camp, without his communit. Unless of course there's still more to this world than we can envision, and we're being stalked by something unimaginable. Until we have some answers we have to proceed with the utmost caution." She took a deep breath. "But proceed we must. We can't just stay here and wait for explanations to come to us."

Tellenberg nodded agreement. "All right—we go back to camp. But carefully. We scope things out as best we can before trying to enter. Assuming we make it safely back inside the perimeter, we look for Salvador." He caught Haviti staring at him. "At the same time we don't reject any worst-case scenarios no matter how convivial any greeting we may receive." He eyed the rest of his companions. "Tiare's right. We can't risk making or disregarding any assumptions until we get some answers." Reaching down, he tapped the holster that was attached to his own service belt. "And we go in with weapons activated."

"Activated—or activated and drawn?" Valnadireb's compound eyes and feathery antennae were aimed in Tellenberg's direction.

The xenologist looked at Haviti, who in turn eyed the thranx.

"No," she declared firmly. "I don't think that's a good idea. We don't know Boylan's state of mind before he died. By the same token, we don't know what kind of pressure Araza may be under. I agree with Esra. We have to be ready to defend ourselves from anything—or anyone. But we don't want to be unnecessarily provocative, either. We have no idea of the true nature of things."

Tellenberg nodded agreement. "No matter what the circumstances we should be alright if we just keep our heads and act sensibly. Something bad has happened. We don't know the cause but we're going to find out. And if it should turn out that Araza is in some way responsible for this blanket silence from camp and for the captain's death, well . . ." He met the gaze of each of his colleagues in turn. "We're not military people, but we've all had to handle weapons in the field. We know how to shoot to defend ourselves. And there are four of us." This time he slapped instead of tapped his belt holster.

"If it comes to it, four experienced field operatives should be able to handle one disturbed repair technician."

9

There was no disagreement about leaving the body of the captain behind. Everyone was of the same mind that it was too heavy and that under the circumstances, given the uncertainty with which they were presently faced, it was a burden they could not safely manage. They could come back for it later, with a transporter, and bring it back to camp.

Besides, Tellenberg found himself thinking gravely as he followed N'kosi back toward the waiting boat, Boylan would not mind.

There was some discussion concerning the hard-won collection of specimens. "Look," N'kosi told his colleagues, "if the captain was killed by natives, or by some as yet unknown local life-form, or if despite the illogic of it he actually did commit suicide, we're going to feel awfully foolish if we come back here only to find that other natives or fauna have damaged or knocked overboard everything we've worked so hard to accumulate."

"Maybe I'm wrong, Mosi," Haviti retorted, "but right now I could care less about specimen preservation. Call my scientific dedication into question if you want, but the most important thing we have to do right now is try to find out what happened to Boylan—and what's going on at the camp. Should the worst-case scenario you describe eventuate, we can always acquire more specimens." She turned from him to Tellenberg and Valnadireb. "Our most pressing need is to find out why Araza's not answering his communit."

Tellenberg's tone was apologetic. "Tiare's right, Mosi. No-body'd miss the collection we've put together over the last several days more than I, but that's not really important right now."

N'kosi turned to the sole nonhuman member of the expedition. "Val?"

"I must agree with Esra and Tiare. The specimens are all dead. Captain Boylan is dead. We, on the other hand, are still alive. Ensure the latter first, deal with the deceased afterward."

"All right then." But as they started off back toward camp along the crude trail they had hacked out of the alien forest several days earlier, N'kosi could not keep from casting more than one regretful glance back in the direction of the grounded boat and its un-paralleled cargo of recently accumulated native life-forms.

While making their way through the forest they stayed on maximum alert, though for what they did not know. An attack by Quofumian aborigines, perhaps, or an assault by some previously unknown local predator. A growing unease gnawed at the back of everyone's mind at the continued silence from the camp. Why wasn't Araza answering? Even if he chose silence, his comm-unit would keep advising him of the repeated attempts by his colleagues to make contact. There was still another possible explanation. He might be dead, too.

"If there was a fight," Tellenberg murmured as he pushed aside a softly mewing knot of vines, "and Salvador killed Boylan, maybe the captain managed to shoot him. We know that Boylan got off three rounds. Maybe he wounded Salvador fatally." He gestured over his shoulder. "Araza might be lying back there in the bushes just like the captain. Maybe we didn't look hard enough."

N'kosi glanced up at his friend. "We have to come back to the river for our specimens. If Salvador's not in the camp, it would lend credence to that idea. Maybe we'll find other indicators of what's happened. Bloodstains, destruction of property." He brightened. "The internal security system should have recorded any trouble."

"Good thought, Mosi." Having been raised on and lived most of his life on typically tropical thranx worlds, Valnadireb was more comfortable in their present surroundings than any of his human companions. "That's the first thing we should do."

It was such a good idea, in fact, that Tellenberg tried to access the camp's security system via his communit. He failed, but felt it was worth the few minutes it took to make the effort. While a fair number of the camp's systems could be remotely contacted and controlled, Security was not among them. Allowing remote access to Security would open that security to the possibility of being breached or otherwise compromised. Security that could be accessed externally was by definition no longer secure. Still, pondering the possibility gave him something to do. For a few moments it had the benefit of taking his mind off their present gloomy situation.

Soon they were approaching the main gate at the camp's perimeter and there was no more time to waste on hopeful diversions.

From the edge of the forest fronting the barrier nothing appeared amiss. A quick check with a communit indicated that the defensive perimeter was active and fully charged. Beyond, the three completed modules and the entrance dome stood as the team had left them; undamaged and apparently otherwise untouched. Within the expansive cleared grounds enclosed by the perimeter fence, nothing moved.

Concealed in the undergrowth, Tellenberg leaned to his left and whispered to Haviti, "Try and raise Araza one more time."

She proceeded to do so, both verbally and via a series of electronic signals. None of them produced any response. The xenologist considered her colleagues.

"He's dead, his communit is broken, and he's not near the central communications console; he's alive but choosing not to respond; he's alive but not near a working communit; he could be severely injured and unable to reply; or we're simply overlooking something."

"Too many possibilities." Having drawn his sidearm in spite of his companions' concerns, Valnadireb held the distinctively thranx weapon securely with his right foothand and truhand. "None of them fill me with hope. Let us proceed cautiously and be ready for anything—most especially that which we do not expect and cannot predict."

The main gate, at least, responded immediately and welcomingly to their verbal request for admission. There was no solid barrier to push aside. The space between two designated relay posts simply deactivated. Despite the indicators on both having switched from red to green, Tellenberg still found himself stepping through the gap a touch more briskly than was necessary. He felt better once he and his friends were all safely inside the perimeter.

With the gate reactivated behind them they headed quickly for the front entrance. The doorway there responded as efficiently as had the perimeter gate. Inside the dome everything was as they remembered having left it. Like discarded skins, biohazard suits hung neatly on the main clothes rack off to the right. Supplies, some of them still half unpacked, filled storage shelves off to the left while sealed containers lay stacked on the floor where they had been unloaded. The absence of any indicators of violence was almost as disturbing as if they had found blood on the floor and damage to the interior.

The integrity of their individual quarters had not been violated. Even the dining area was unaffected, with the exception of one overturned chair that hardly constituted a significant disturbance. In their haste no one noticed the slightly blurred interior panel where part of one wall had automatically repaired itself.

Finding themselves in the galley area, they took a break from their inspection long enough to eat. Barely heated food was downed quickly, with no thought given to proper digestion. Everyone was still far too nervous and uneasy to relax, even at the dining table.

"What now?" N'kosi's words filtered out around the edges of the sandwich that filled most of his mouth. He was swallowing without hardly bothering to chew.

"Security." Haviti was seated next to him. "I suggest starting with the morning we left and running back all internal recordings first. If they don't show anything we can move on to the tridee from the external pickups."

"That may be premature."

Both of them turned. Tellenberg looked across the table. Behind N'kosi and Haviti, Valnadireb was straddling his narrow bench. A truhand held food while a foothand clutched a spiral-spouted thranx drinking vessel. Another truhand was holding his communit. The xenologist was concentrating on the instrument and not his food.

"I thought that while I was eating I would set my unit to run an activity scan. It picked up a lot of the kind of noise I expected: autosystems cycling, security monitoring, water purification in progress, lights and other proximity-activated equipment going on and off in response to our presence. There is one set of readings, however, that demands more detailed scrutiny."

Haviti put down her cup of kava derivative. "Where's the activity? In the lab? Outside the perimeter?"

Slipping off his bench, Valnadireb set his unfinished food and drink aside. "Indications are that multiple systems are being cycled within the shuttle."

There was a flurry of movement as the four scientists hurriedly finished or set aside the rest of their food. As they raced back toward the main entrance N'kosi suggested anew that they draw their weapons. Again he was voted down.

"Not a good idea. As Val said, premature." Haviti turned a corner. "If it's Salvador, and I can't imagine that the shuttle is cycling the systems in question by itself, we don't know what kind of shape he's in. Physically *or* mentally. He could be injured, he could be panicky, he could be frightened." She glanced over at Tellenberg.

"Besides, as Esra pointed out, there are four of us and only one of him. When we get there, let's make sure we stay spread out. Not so much that it looks like a deliberate tactic, but enough so that if Salvador exhibits tendencies toward the homicidal he'll have to choose one of four separate directions in which to aim."

"That's encouraging," Tellenberg commented dryly.

She threw him an unblinking, no-nonsense look. "Just being careful, Esra. That's what you do in the field when you find yourself confronting fauna that might present unknown dangers."

He did not reply. Despite his sardonic comment, he had been thinking along exactly the same lines.

Located well away from and behind the established camp, the shuttle had been hidden from view when they had first stepped out of the forest. Their natural and proper inclination had been to investigate the buildings first. Now they found themselves slowing as they approached the craft. Though only a few external telltales were alight, they were sufficient to verify Valnadireb's finding. A soft but powerful hum emanating from deep within the vessel confirmed it.

Following Haviti's recommendation they spread out. There was no movement outside the craft. The loading ramp was down and deserted. Advancing with caution, Tellenberg and N'kosi started toward it. A voice stopped them.

"You are looking for me, I suppose."

From where they were standing everyone whirled simultaneously to gaze in the direction of the calm, familiar accent. Emerging from the nearby portable workshed, Salvador Araza came toward them. Though Tellenberg's fingers twitched anxiously he did not reach for his sidearm. Not because he realized that the phonic stiletto that hung loosely from the fingers of the technician's right hand could be raised and aimed before the xenologist could draw his own weapon. Instead, he was stunned into inaction and an immediate response was forestalled by the unexpected spectacle of the tech's attire. The sight of the dark garb had an equally immobilizing effect on the xenologist's companions.

Recognition was as immediate as it was disbelieving. What Araza was wearing was as distinctive as the uniform of a Church peaceforcer, though inexpressibly less welcome. The foil-inscribed skullcap, the black jumpsuit, the distinctive and unmistakably hostile belt buckle were as well known to the four xenologists as to any casually well-informed citizen of the Commonwealth. Clearly, Araza no longer felt any need to hide his true identity or principal occupation. One could study to become a technician. To become a Qwarm, one had to be born or adopted into the secretive clan. His present appearance not only redefined him, it silently and simultaneously addressed most of their questions as to how the captain came to meet his untimely and unexpected end.

Most, but not all.

Haviti's right hand kept fluttering back and forth, back and forth, like a timid bird unable to decide where to perch, as it hovered indecisively in the vicinity of the field sidearm she wore holstered at her waist.

"We found Boylan. You killed him." It was not a question. "Why?"

As Araza approached the loading ramp Tellenberg and N'kosi slowly backed away. They did not take their eyes off their fellow expedition member.

"Nicholai Boylan was a good captain and a hard worker." The Qwarm's words were grudgingly complimentary. "If he had worked as hard at paying off the debts he had accumulated as he did at managing this mission, I would not be here. He would even now be safely inside his living quarters, probably raving and ranting about some perceived trivial oversight, and you would now

be speaking to a different specialist. Someone for whom technical repair and maintenance was his or her only profession."

Off to his left, one of Valnadireb's foothands had edged close
to his own weapon. Araza barely looked in his direction, but the
brief narrow-eyed glance was enough to persuade the thranx to
let his four-fingered hand slide away from the gun.

"I was able to obtain the tech position on this unpretentious
expedition through means and manipulations that need not concern you. My clan has many contacts. Had this been a major first
contact voyage to an important new world, personnel screening
would doubtless have been more vigorous. The true nature of
my real occupation might have been discovered, or at least suspected. That it was not is a credit to those among my peers who
have devoted themselves to the less visible but no less important facets of our profession."

N'kosi's fingers continued to feather the air in the vicinity of
his pistol. "If you were hired to kill Boylan—"

Araza interrupted the xenologist. "I was hired to give him
one last chance to pay what he owed. And failing that, yes, to
extract recompense in full. The only thing those who contracted
for my services abhor worse than nonpayment of a debt is the
flaunting of such nonpayment. It makes them look bad. It
makes them look stupid. It tends to encourage others to default.
This is bad for any business."

"I didn't see anything that would lead someone to believe
Boylan was flaunting something like that," Haviti remarked. "He
certainly never mentioned it."

The Qwarm turned toward her. "Why should he? There
was no reason for him to bring it up to any of you, his crew. Be
assured that he did allude to it, repeatedly, in other places and
times where circumstances assured that his injudicious loquacity

would get back to those to whom he owed the money. They felt chafed. Laughter had been induced at their expense." Araza straightened slightly, almost as if he was coming to attention in the presence of his unseen employers. "Safer to shoot at such people, better to beat them, than to make them the butt of cheap jokes. They do not take kindly to such embarrassment."

N'kosi tried again. "If you were hired to kill Boylan, why did you wait as long as you did? Why didn't you just shoot him on the ship, while he slept? Or as soon as we arrived on Quofum? Here, you could have made it look like an accident."

Araza's voice never changed, never altered, from its cool, calm, utterly collected tone. "I did not kill him on the ship because the vessel was new to me and I wished to be confident of its confines and secure in my knowledge of its functions. I did not kill him as soon as we arrived because—as surprising as this may sound to you—I was initially more interested in what might be learned here. There is always profit to be gained from new discoveries." One hand gestured at the surrounding forest.

"There is clearly money to be made from this extremely strange world. A great deal of valuable information has already been uploaded to storage on the ship. It will provide the clan with a welcome bonus in addition to what they have already been paid for the specific task I was assigned to carry out here."

N'kosi stepped reflexively forward. "That information belongs to Science Central and to every citizen of the Commonwealth."

"A noble sentiment, and one that does you proud." Araza smiled thinly at the protesting xenologist. "Sadly, yet another government promise that must perforce go unfulfilled."

Haviti went cold. They had to do something, to act, and quickly. Someone had to make the first move while the opportunity to do so still presented itself. Moving slowly and carefully, she determined to draw her weapon and shoot. All those years spent buried in studies and academics, she mused apprehensively. If only she'd had some military training. Should she try to pull her sidearm quickly and fire? Or would her chances be improved by working as slowly and inconspicuously as possible? Perhaps one of her colleagues would do something to draw more of Araza's attention. In trying to decide how best to proceed and what to do next, she ended up doing nothing.

It was to N'kosi's credit that his voice did not crack as he asked the question that was on everyone's mind. "Are you going to kill us, now?"

"Not at all." This time the smile that accompanied the Qwarm's response was slightly wider. It was almost, but not quite, genuine. "I was hired to extract recompense from Nicholai Boylan: not from any of you. Through no fault of your own you have become unfortunate accessories to an awkward set of circumstances.

"However, it must be obvious to each of you that I cannot allow you to return with me." He raised a hand to forestall N'kosi's reply. "There are no promises that would suffice, no assurances you can possibly give that one or all of you would not eventually decide to convey to the authorities a full or partial accounting of what has transpired here, thereby placing myself individually and my clan collectively at risk of prosecution.

"By the same token, I must take steps to ensure that you are not rescued and thus placed in a position to give such damning information. This can be done without murder. As integrated identifying factors make it virtually impossible to adequately disguise and therefore resell a Commonwealth government starship, once the *Dampier* has been stripped and gutted of all useful equipment and stores and its AI has been suitably disabled, removed, or reprogrammed, the vessel's shell will be placed in a suitable orbit to be discovered by the authorities. Finding it thus scavenged and abandoned, they will assume that you, its crew, either participated in its demise or were lost while defending it. With the craft being rediscovered within the borders of the Commonwealth, there will be no logical reason for the authorities to assume that anyone remains here on Quofum. Therefore, no relief or rescue mission will be mounted.

"I am honestly sorry. You have been redefined, for want of a better description, as collateral loss."

Tellenberg spoke up. "Do you really think you can make it back to the Commonwealth and to a habitable world all by yourself?"

Araza turned to confront the xenologist. "Do you really think I would have accepted this assignment and come all this way without confidence in my ability to do exactly that? While there are exceptional occasions on which a Qwarm will consent to a suicidal mission, this is not one of them. You know as well as I do, Esra Tellenberg, that a modern KK-drive vessel is operated and navigated by its AI, and that an organic presence such as Captain Boylan is required only for supervisorial purposes. Interstellar space-plus navigation being what it is, no human or thranx or representative of any other organic species is capable of the mental contortions necessary to effectively fly such incredibly complex craft. Only a machine can do that. I assure you that the one controlling the vessel that brought us to this world will respond to my commands and requests as readily as it did to those of the recently deceased Mr. Boylan." His smile vanished.

"It will be especially responsive under 'crisis' conditions. The crisis in this instance being my need to return to orbit around a certain world without being observed by Commonwealth Science Central while doing so." He turned back toward the boarding ramp.

"I would have left yesterday after concluding my work here, but there was some minor trouble with the shuttle. I thought it better to make certain everything was working at maximum efficiency before departing. I was just about to be on my way when you arrived, thereby avoiding any need for this present discussion." He eyed them all in turn, lizard-quick, without spending more than a second or two appraising each of them individually.

"Perhaps this way is better. I, of course, feel no remorse at carrying out my assignment, but I shall take some satisfaction in knowing that I was not obliged to perform any unnecessary additional murder. The Qwarm pride themselves on efficiency and an absence of untidiness."

" 'Untidiness'?" N'kosi gaped at him. "If you leave us here and allow the empty ship to be found back in the Commonwealth then you're killing us as surely as if you put a hole through each of our heads, just like you did to Boylan! What about the hostile natives? We've barely been here a week and they've already succeeded in penetrating the compound once. Even if you leave us alive, sooner or later they're likely to slaughter us."

Araza shrugged indifferently. "Maybe you can join the alliance of the stick-jellies and fuzzies against the spikers and the hardshells. That's assuming the stick-jellies and the fuzzies don't try to kill you, too." Turning away from him, he started up the ramp.

An increasingly desperate Haviti took a couple of steps forward. "You can't do this, Salvador! You can't abandon us here with no means of getting back or expecting relief. It isn't *civilized*!"

Partway up the ramp he paused to look back at her. "Every civilization redefines itself, Ms. Haviti. The Greeks thought the tribes of the British Isles uncivilized. Later, the British thought the Hindus uncivilized. The American tribe believed those of Islamic faith to be uncivilized. When the thranx first encountered humans, they believed us to be uncivilized. Today we know that all the so-called nations of primitive one-world Earth were nothing more than glorified tribes, as barbaric and uncivilized as all the various other smaller tribes who preceded them. The only difference was that their huts were bigger. They fought and warred among themselves over such inconsequentialities as personal faith and combustible hydrocarbons, over the accumulation of simple metals, and even the percentage of melanin some people carried within their skin. Every sentient being contains within themselves their own individual standards and definition of what it means to be civilized. Frequently that definition excludes everyone in the universe except themselves." Once more he turned away.

"Many disagree with the standards held by the Qwarm—but at least we are consistent."

As she listened to him her hand continued to hover in the vicinity of her sidearm. For a split second it drew close, only to fall away. She slowly raised her fingers toward the seal, but despite her desperation and determination she could not bring herself to shift them the few final millimeters necessary to unseal it and draw the waiting weapon within. She screamed silently, cursing herself for drowning in a mixture of indecision and cowardice. She was convinced she could see him watching her out of the corner of one eye as he mounted the ramp.

Similarly convinced that the Qwarm was concentrating on the only female member of the team, Tellenberg reached down and drew his sidearm.

He was neither as slow nor as clumsy as one might have thought. It did not matter. A black blur, Araza spun, raised his own compact weapon, and fired.

The coherent sonic burst struck Tellenberg above the bridge of his nose and directly between the eyes. Such accuracy with such a small weapon over such a distance was remarkable. None of those in a position to observe it ventured a comment, however—unless one discounted the flurry of shocked obscenities and Haviti's scream.

As Tellenberg stumbled backward a couple of steps, blood began to flow copiously from the hole in front and the hole in the rear of his skull. Unlike Boylan his eyes never closed, not even when the xenologist toppled over onto his back.

From holding his arm out straight as an arrow, Araza slowly lowered it back to his side. "A pity. That annuls a portion of the satisfaction that only a moment ago I said I was feeling about not having to kill any of you outright."

Having as thorough an awareness of what certain humans were capable of (and perhaps more than most of them), Valnadireb had turned and sprinted on all six legs for the protection of the camp's entry module. N'kosi was right behind him. More stunned by the shooting than either of her companions, Haviti had retreated only a couple of steps. Almost as if she had forgotten Araza she kept staring at the prone, profusely bleeding body of her friend and fellow scientist Esra Tellenberg.

The Qwarm, however, had not forgotten her. Shifting his stance slightly, he started to raise the stiletto a second time. He could have killed her effortlessly, with one eye closed and the other half open. As the members of his clan were wont to say, "A Qwarm has no qualms." Instead he exhaled softly, pivoted, and resumed his climb up the boarding ramp. He did not forget her entirely, but neither was he especially concerned that she might try to shoot him in the back. If she had possessed the guts, she would have tried already. By this time he was reasonably certain she would not, could not, do it.

He was a professional, and he knew the signs.

Haviti took a couple of steps toward the body, then stopped. Esra Tellenberg was no more. However brave and well intentioned he had been in life, he could not help them. Looking up at the shuttle entryway she saw that the lock was already beginning to cycle shut behind Araza. If they were going to stop him, if they had any chance of surviving, wasting time keening over the body of a friend was not going to help.

For an instant she considered drawing her sidearm and firing on the shuttle. Designed for travel in both space and atmosphere, resistant to extreme heat, cold, and violent changes in pressure, its hull would not be easy for a simple biofield sidearm to penetrate. Such an assault might also prompt Araza to delay his departure for the moment or two it would be required for him to deal with her.

It struck her forcefully that in that event she would be confronting the certified assassin alone. Turning, she ran as hard as she could for the nearest modules.

Valnadireb and N'kosi were where she expected to find them: in communications central. Though it sounded impressive, CC was little more than a couple of self-contained consoles linked together. They could not stop Araza, but maybe they could stop the shuttle. Ideally, they would have taken control of the mother ship's AI. All communications with the main vessel, however, had to be relayed through the shuttle. In answer to her breathless query, N'kosi announced glumly that the everefficient Araza had already blocked that channel of contact.

That meant they had to find another way to somehow prevent the shuttle from lifting off—and quickly.

"Can we interface with the shuttle's AI?" She fought to slow her breathing.

"I don't know, I don't know." A harried N'kosi was trying to make sense of the camp communications system's more arcane possibilities. Like her and the equally anxious Valnadireb, he was a field xenologist. It was not necessary for him to understand the inner intricacies of such devices. Only how to use them.

Pushing past his clearly overwhelmed colleague, Valnadireb addressed the console's aural pickup. "Shuttle is not to lift off! This is an emergency override. Shuttle *Hyla* is not to lift off. *Confirm!*"

It was a worthy effort. When in doubt as to which command to recite, an admiring and hopeful Haviti reflected, try shouting. The response from the console, however, was disheartening.

"I am under direct crew command. Preparations for orbital return have commenced. Emergency override can only be initiated from on board."

That route was also closed to them, Haviti realized with a sinking dread. Araza had restricted all commands to crew already on board. To himself. They could not verbally countermand his instructions from within the camp. Leaning forward and resting her hands on the lower edge of the console, she tried to divine the purpose of each individual control, the meaning of every lambent telltale.

There had to be something they could do. Some switch that could be thrown, some order that could be given, some override that could be engaged. There *had* to be!

Outside, the escalating whine of the shuttle's engine rose to a howl, stimulating a symphony of shrieks from the depths of the surrounding Quofumian forest. Flocks of flying things exploded from the treetops while arboreal hallucinations and taxonomic nightmares hastened to flee in all directions. With stately aerodynamic grace the shuttle rose vertically on its landing pads, folded those mechanical limbs into its belly, and accelerated into the pink sky. From within the camp's science module Tiare Haviti, Moselstrom N'kosi, and Val of the hive Na, clan Dir, family Eb, could do nothing more than watch via instruments as the shuttle vanished beyond the clouds.

It was gone. The Qwarm Salvador Araza was gone. Their colleague Esra Tellenberg was dead.

And they were assuredly, unarguably, indisputably stuck.

10

Araza felt no remorse. Not a tinge, not a touch, not an iota. If he regretted anything at all it was that as a curious man he felt it a shame that so much new scientific knowledge had to be left behind. It did not have to be so. He could have remained, taken his time, and one by one terminated each of the three remaining scientists, after which he could at his leisure have stuffed the shuttle with even more recorded information in addition to a choice assortment of carefully preserved specimens.

Personal penchant, however, was not the province of a Qwarm. He had not been taken into service to participate in scientific research. Engaging him as a member of the crew had not been easy. More experienced technicians with longer résumés had been available and had been nominated for the position. It had taken a good deal of work on the part of the clan's administrative arm to secure the appointment for him.

He was a fully qualified tech, of course, or he would never have succeeded in concealing his true nature for the duration of the outbound voyage. No one on board had suspected that his true specialty lay in an area as utterly alien to them as the world for which they were headed.

No, that wasn't entirely true, he told himself as he relaxed in the shuttle's command chair and occasionally glanced at the instrumentation. There were times, instances, when Boylan had shown some suspicion. But the captain had put his tech's occasional failings and slowness to finish assignments down to the kind of individual imperfection often found in his subordinates. Araza's subterfuge had never been challenged.

In the end, it was a failing of Boylan's and not of Araza's that was responsible for the man's death. The Qwarm did not know the names of those to whom the recently demised captain owed money. It was not necessary for him to know in order to carry out his assignment. All that he needed to know was contained in the formal clan briefing that he had committed to memory long before he joined the *Dampier*'s crew.

Now it was over. He had completed his task successfully and in such a way that it could not be traced back to him. As for the *Dampier*, it would be stripped and then placed in a stable orbit around a suitable planet. Eventually it would be found, investigated, and discovered to be a missing Commonwealth Science vessel. Finding the empty survey vessel in orbit around a Commonwealth world would lead investigators to believe that she had either been scavenged and abandoned by a renegade crew or diverted from her assignment by others. There would be nothing explicit to implicate the Qwarm.

The absence of the crew would be remarked upon and for a short while would provide fodder for jaded media. Perhaps a reward would be announced for information leading to their exposure. The attention of the greater Commonwealth public being always brief and forever submerged in a continuous, never-ending stream of reportage of disasters, scandals, gossip, and actual straightforward news, the matter would soon be forgotten. Commonwealth Science Central would take charge of its recovered vessel, continue to muse on the fate of its crew, debate the alternatives of group desertion or disaster, and move on. As would Salvador Araza. As would the Clan Qwarm.

All that remained was for him to report back in to his seniors. They would then convey the pertinent information to those who had hired the clan's services. A final payment would be made. Though it was not a matter of great importance to him, Araza knew there would be a sizable bonus payable to him personally.

He felt quite calm and outright good about the outcome of his assignment. The obligation had been appropriately discharged, he had not been harmed, and he had been compelled to slay only one potential witness. While unable ever to return to civilization, the remaining three he had managed to avoid killing outright might still live out their modest remaining lifetimes on a world that was, if not particularly hospitable, at least supportive of humanx life. If they watched their collective step and rationed their resources, they might not only survive but be able to continue their work—albeit in the knowledge that the results were unlikely ever to be seen by another human or thranx until long after the last of them was dead. Continuing with their research would give them something to focus on besides simply surviving. Araza hoped so. He was a technician and a professional, not a sadist.

Of course, in the absence of any hope of rescue they might also go mad. It was immaterial to him. Despite his superficial and calculated efforts at conviviality while in their company, now that he was on his way home it was of no import to him whether the trio of scientists he had abandoned lived or died. Genuine sociability was a luxury he could not afford. A Qwarm made friends with someone they had been assigned to kill only if it would facilitate their work.

Once outside Quofum's atmosphere he could no longer locate by sight the river delta where the camp had been established. He could not even tell for certain on which of several continents it was located. The camp, like his former shipmates, had already receded into memory. All that remained now was for him to return home, make his report, and embark on a well-earned and richly deserved holiday. The life of a clan member was not all blood and death-dealing. It was perfectly possible for those whose business was murder to relax and enjoy life— provided they were psychologically well adjusted. Araza was secure in the knowledge that he fell into the latter category. Though a more complex mission to plan and organize than most, the Quofumian assignment had been comparatively undemanding to carry out.

He busied himself in mentally preparing for the journey homeward as the shuttle docked with the *Dampier*. Once back on board, he took the time to enjoy a meal and a shower before paying a visit to the bridge. No alarming telltales greeted his arrival. Any last promises, pleading, cursing, screaming, or other attempted communications from the surface would have had to be relayed through the shuttle's system. Since the shuttle was now here instead of there, such contact was no longer possible. Anyway, he had shut off the shuttle's ground receiver as soon as he had boarded the transfer craft. His last words to his former shipmates had truly been his last words.

As a safety measure in the event that its designated captain became incapacitated (Araza allowed himself a slight inward smile at the thought—despite their profession the Qwarm were not entirely devoid of humor), the ship had been programmed to respond to any of its passengers. Araza now took it upon himself to issue commands.

"You wish to return to point of origin?" The AI was designed to query any instructions it found equivocal.

"I do. Promptly and without detour, maintaining communications silence throughout." Sitting back in the command chair, Araza spoke easily and without hesitation. He had rehearsed this encounter and its possible variations long before the ship had even left for Quofum. Anticipating the current exchange had been as much a part of his preparations for the mission as planning how and where he might confront Boylan.

The AI entered into a pause that might charitably have been described as contemplative. "I do not detect the presence of Captain Boylan or any member of the official scientific team."

"They are presently engaged in active research on the surface below. Much of importance has been discovered. I have been instructed to file a report in person and return with needed additional personnel and supplies."

"I could do that without you," the ship responded.

"AIs can file reports, but they suffer when it comes to conveying emotion and other unquantifiable components necessary to persuade." Well rehearsed in the potential objections an AI might raise to a request for departure, Araza didn't miss a beat in his replies.

"That is true," the ship conceded. "Why are you doing this and not Captain Boylan?"

"Captain Boylan's organizational expertise is required below. As the camp is now up and running smoothly, the presence of a repair and construction technician is temporarily expendable. Captain Boylan's presence is not."

A long pause followed. "I, of course, cannot confirm this assessment because I cannot at present raise any member of the scientific team."

Araza found himself nodding in agreement. The ship would easily be able to establish such individual contacts and verify the veracity of the technician's claims—so long as the shuttle and its advanced communications system was present at the camp and in a position to relay such requests onward. The *Hyla*'s present location within the mother ship's cargo bay presented the main AI with a dilemma. It could send the shuttle back down on automatics and subsequently utilize its integrated systems to contact one or more members of the crew in an attempt to confirm Araza's statements. But that would mean countermanding a directive from an authorized member of that same team—Araza.

Finding no reason to do this, encountering no objections from below, and determining from the last time it had the opportunity to do so that all components of the recently established surface camp were functioning normally, it finally replied, "Departure as per request in five minutes."

Araza leaned back and smiled contentedly. It was all over now but the trip homeward, the filing of his official report, and the collecting of kudos for a job well done. As the ship readied itself around him he retired to his cabin. Along the way he passed the entrances to those living quarters that had been occupied by the members of the science team. Their silence did not in any way impinge upon or trouble his conscience.

It took the ship the better part of a day to boost outsystem in normal space. It could have made the changeover to space-plus much sooner, but Araza was in no hurry and was curious to examine the system's other worlds. Once beyond the last gas giant he issued the necessary final commands.

"Preparing for changeover," the ship promptly responded.

Comfortably ensconced in his own cabin, Araza tensed slightly. No matter how many times an individual underwent the shift from space normal to space-plus, one could never be sure how one's innards would react. He waited. It would all be over within a minute or two and then he would be on his way homeward at a velocity outside and beyond that available to travelers in normal space. After a few minutes of waiting, he relaxed. It had been the smoothest changeover he had ever experienced. He waited for the expected corroboration from the ship.

It was soon forthcoming, but it was not at all what he expected to hear.

"There is a problem."

A frown drew Araza's brows downward. "A problem? What kind of problem?"

Though not programmed to overtly express confusion, the AI managed to convey it anyway. "I am currently experiencing a navigational quandary." While that confession was unsettling, it was nothing compared to the feeling that shot through Araza's gut at the ship's next words. "Ancillary advice is in order and would be appreciated."

What the hell? Using a hand to sweep aside the tridee play he had been viewing, the near-naked Araza left his room and made his way quickly back to the bridge.

There everything seemed normal enough. He untensed slightly. "What's the problem? You said something about 'a navigational quandary'? Be specific." Looking around, he could see nothing visibly amiss. All instruments appeared to be functioning normally. Telltales, projections, and readouts were clear and sharp.

"It is a quandary that is at once both simple and complex," the AI informed him. "I cannot retrace the outward-bound route nor plot a new one because I do not know where I am. My reference points for performing the necessary calculations are gone."

Gone? What the devil was the AI blabbering about? Araza found himself wondering. How could navigational reference points be "gone"?

"What do you mean when you say your 'reference points' for navigation are 'gone'? Are you suffering an unreported mechanical infarction?" He spoke harshly, in the menacing tone of an angry Qwarm addressing another organic sentient rather than a machine. It did not matter. Insensitive vocal inflections had no effect on the ship-mind.

"No. All of my internal systems are functioning normally."

Araza's impatience grew. "Then I don't understand. What's wrong?"

"I can explain fully, though it will take some time and require reference to certain highly advanced mathematical and astrophysical terminology. In the interests of conciseness, I believe it would be useful to begin with simple visuals."

It was as if the interior of the control chamber abruptly turned transparent. That was not the case, of course. What had happened was that Araza now found himself standing in the center of a full spherical projection. This in itself did not in any way upset him. It was a common tool utilized for both professional and entertainment purposes. The shock he experienced was a consequence of what he was seeing, not how it was being shown.

The projection displayed what was outside the ship. Nearby

should have been a small gas giant—the lifeless, outermost world of the system he was in the process of leaving. A bright spot of light would have marked the location of the now-distant local sun. Around this and in all other directions would have been the regional stars and nebulae. Approximately to his right and in the general direction of the galactic edge a brighter, denser swath of stars indicating the position of the Commonwealth within the Orion Arm would have been visible.

There was no small gas giant. There was no local sun, around which orbited Quofum, half a dozen other worlds, and at least two asteroid belts. There was no sign of the local equivalent of a Kuiper Belt. All of these astronomical absences and omissions were unsettling. But what really accelerated his normally precisely controlled heart rate and caused his eyes to widen slightly was what he saw off to his right. Or rather, what he did not see.

The Commonwealth had gone missing.

Or it was at the very least lost. Lost in a sea of stars the likes of which he had seen only in images and recordings. It was as if the ship he was on had in the blink of an eye been shifted nearer to the galactic center, where stars clustered far more closely together than they did out in any of the spiral arms. Swallowing hard, he put the possibility to the ship's AI. The response was cool and controlled, the tone as even as that of a butler announcing that dinner was ready and would he care to attend.

"No. I can identify no stellar configuration in any direction that corresponds to the Shapley Center. Furthermore, my external sensors detect none of the extreme radiation that would be expected were we anywhere in that vicinity."

Bad enough, Araza thought as he fought back rising panic, to have misplaced the Commonwealth. But to lose track of the galactic center meant . . .

"Extend sensor range to maximum. Attempt correlation of present position using all available charts." The ship needed to find a recognizable reference point, he knew. Just one would be sufficient. No matter where they were or how they had come to find themselves here, a single identifiable waypoint that the navigation program could lock on to would be enough to allow them to find their way back into familiar stellar territory. The fact that it was taking the AI long seconds to respond was not encouraging. When the seconds stretched into minutes, Araza found himself on the verge of despair.

Where in the name of O'Morion's matrix *were* they?

"Correlation failure." The ship's voice was maddeningly impassive. "I can locate nothing familiar. Not only within our galaxy, but without and beyond. There is no correlation. I regret to confess that for the first time since my consciousness was activated, I am lost."

Lost. As injurious a four-letter word as could be imagined, especially under present circumstances. It was absurd. It was crazy. The advanced AIs that directed and controlled KK-drive starships did not, could not, become lost. Within their complex electronic guts were buried multiple levels of backup. One recognizable reference point was all they needed to navigate by. Just *one*. Surely, surely, there had to be an identifiable star, or nebula, or other stellar phenomenon within range of its preceptors. He refused to accept the explanation. Or confession. He wracked his brain.

A thought. A possible out. Even a supposedly infallible AI could theoretically suffer from a momentary blackout. "If you cannot locate a standard reference point, search for one that is nonstandard. What about intercepting communications? Try a space-minus scan."

When the response came back in seconds, a little of the fear that had begun to seep into him receded.

"I have detected multiple strata of stressed spectrum that indicate the presence of sentient communication."

Araza was much relieved. Such encrypted transmissions could not be intercepted and read, he knew, but their mere presence was reassuring. "Can you approximate volume?" This far out of the Commonwealth, space-minus resonance would likely be reduced to a few dozen energy strings. While they could not be understood, they could be traced. Doing so might lead the *Dampier* home along a different route than the one it had taken on its outbound journey, but that didn't matter. He was in no hurry.

"Yes," the ship responded. "One moment, please." Reassured, Araza did not begrudge the vessel the inordinate amount of time it was taking to formulate its replies. "I have recorded approximately six million, two hundred thousand, four hundred five individual strings. This is preliminary. I am still compiling." The AI promptly went silent again.

Insane. Araza was beginning to think that was the most likely explanation for what had happened. The ship's AI had gone mad. That did not explain the explosively luminescent astral display outside the forward port, but it went a long way toward illuminating the *Dampier*'s other responses. With an effort, he held his anger in check.

"That is something like ten times the number of space-minus communications strings one would expect to find in the immediate stellar neighborhood of Earth or Hivehom. It is infinitely more than one would expect to encounter anywhere within the Commonwealth, much less in the vicinity of an outlying out-arm world like Quofum."

"I concur. The logical conclusion, therefore, is that we are no longer in the vicinity of the Quofumian system, or Earth or Hivehom, or the Commonwealth."

Gritting his teeth, the Qwarm hissed out the words: "Then—where—are—we?"

"I don't know," the ship replied with maddening and unvarying matter-of-factness. "I told you: I am lost."

"But you just stated that you can detect, or think you can detect, more than six million lines of space-minus communications."

"Yes. I have run every one of them through my system. Not one is recognizable."

Araza's voice was now as flat as that of the AI. "Track one. Any one. The nearest. Integrate it as a temporary waypoint. Take us there." If the AI could not find a way home from their present position, surely it could do so from the immediate vicinity of a communicative hub.

"Complying."

Full changeover, at least, proceeded normally. Even the slight nausea he experienced was welcome as an indication of normality. When the ship emerged back into normal space a day later, Araza forced himself to hold his emotions in check. It was just as well.

They were still lost. The Commonwealth was still absent from the bowl of heaven. Quofum was still missing.

Something else had taken its place, however.

The new star system was as unfamiliar as the galactic surrounds into which the ship had emerged. It was centered on a binary: a normal Sol-type star that was accompanied by a red dwarf companion. Orbiting around the binary in surprisingly stable trajectories were five closely spaced worlds. The innermost was a blackened charred cinder that tracked too close to the larger star to support life. The outermost was an exquisitely striped triple-ringed gas giant.

The inner trio were synthetic.

Dark surfaces of unknown material soaked up the light and energy of both stars. Gaps of oceanic proportions showed where star-going craft of unimaginable proportions entered and departed. Using its preceptors to zoom in on the outermost artificial globe and peer through one such gap, the ship's AI revealed that within the center of the incredible construct was a miniature, bright yellow thermonuclear glow: an artificial sun. It ought to have been too small to maintain its self-sustaining internal reaction. It defied known physics.

Known physics. Confronted with revelation after revelation, with engineering on a scale beyond dreams, Araza slumped into the ship's command chair. Where *was* he?

Quofum. The planet that only occasionally appeared on roving astronomical sensors. The world that seemed to wink in and out of existence. Where did it go when it was not detectable? Did it reside here, in this vast stellar otherness? He had just come from there. And if it was still there, visible and visitable on the edge of the Commonwealth, then did that mean it was no longer here? Wherever "here" was? Or could it exist in two planes of existence at the same time?

He thought furiously. If Quofum was not here now, then maybe it was presently near home, meaning the Commonwealth. In its place he was now here, perhaps where it ought to be. Where was this "wherever" where Quofum normally floated, out of sight and perception of Commonwealth astronomers? Though he was no polymath, Araza considered himself to be a reasonably well-read and well-informed citizen. To the best of his knowledge and experience, no known constructs came close to approaching the scale of the science and engineering he was presently seeing.

Under magnification, lambent lines of force could be seen linking the three artificial worlds. Others lanced out into emptiness, to vanish beyond range of even the ship's deep-space preceptors. Directing the *Dampier* to move closer to one such glistening filament, he saw that it resolved itself into a strand of shimmering plasma. Energy readings of the material of which it was composed were off the ship's charts. Occasionally, glowing green ovoids shot through the center of the strand at impossible speeds, luminous emerald corpuscles in an electric-bright capillary.

His presence so close to the plasma filament must have been observed. A ship approached his. At least, he assumed it was a ship. So did the *Dampier*'s AI, though it was unable to identify the sudden solid manifestation. Another lacking reference point, a dazed Araza told himself. Eyeing the vessel's advance, he started to laugh. The craft was approximately half the size of Earth's moon. He knew it had to be a vessel because his own ship's AI told him so. The amount of power necessary to move such an immense artificial mass was beyond his comprehension. The thought that it might be able to generate energy enough to achieve changeover suggested the ability to manipulate quantities of energy and matter that were beyond his scales of value.

Of course, such manipulation was likely child's play for beings who could construct artificial worlds around artificial mini-stars to power them. No, he was most definitely not in the Commonwealth anymore, nor way out on its fringes in the vicinity of a most peculiar world called Quofum. He had no idea where he was. In that, he was one with his ship's AI. That artificial mind had at least one easily identifiable advantage over his, Araza reflected. It was not likely to go mad.

"Ship! Get away! Pick a destination, any destination! Any waypoint! Just get away from here!"

"Complying."

The colossal craft of unknown origin loomed close, blocking out most of the starfield. Time passed with infuriating sluggishness, like honey dripping from a ladle. Then there was a physical wrench, a gastrointestinal follow-up, and his ship entered changeover.

When it emerged, the giant vessel was nowhere to be seen. Araza breathed a sigh of relief. He had not realized how frightened he had been. Frightened! Him, Salvador Araza, a second-degree Qwarm assassin, frightened. It was scarce to be believed.

"Where are we?" he whispered, wondering even as he heard his own words why he was whispering.

"I don't know," the AI informed him pleasantly.

Araza was neither surprised nor upset. This time he was only numb.

Preceptors showed the triple star system on which the ship had randomly keyed. Light from two of the stars was nearly overwhelmed by the unimaginably bright disc of the third, an immense red giant whose diameter was on the order of Betelgeuse. Unsurprisingly, the system was devoid of planets. In response to Araza's panicked command, the AI had keyed on the brightest system within range of its preceptors. There was no life here, no habitable worlds natural or artificial, no impossibly gigantic starships to dwarf him into insignificance.

He forced himself to eat. A few hastily warmed packets, a small meal. And to drink. When he returned to the bridge and settled once more into the command chair, he discovered that his hands were shaking slightly. He regarded this wholly novel and unprecedented neural response with the same detachment as a scientist studying a new alien life-form.

Scientist. What he would not have given at that moment to hear the voices and see the faces of the researchers he had left behind. Of the two men and one woman he had not killed. But they were on Quofum. And search as it might, the ship's AI could not locate Quofum. That it was here, somewhere in this wherever, Araza was unaccountably certain. But its position had only been plotted from within the Commonwealth. To find it, the ship's navigation system would need the stars of the Commonwealth as reference points. As Araza reviewed his options he sank deeper and deeper into a gathering, deepening depression that threatened to swallow him entirely and drown him in darkness.

"Ship. Take us back to where we just were." He would deal with artificial worlds and moon-sized starships. He had no choice.

"I cannot." As ever, the AI's voice was steady and unvarying. "My reference points for performing the necessary calculations are gone."

Araza's voice rose to a scream. The emphasis was wasted. Volume had no effect on the AI. "What do you mean the reference points are gone? Just go back to where we just were! Run a reverse route!"

"I cannot." The ship was very apologetic. "The reference points for performing the necessary . . ."

Araza sank back into the command chair, not listening to the rest of the AI's generic and unforgiving monotone. If the ship could not get back to where it just was, then it could not possibly have any chance of finding Quofum again. And if it could not find Quofum again . . .

Lost indeed.

The ship drifted, holding position in space, patiently await-
ing its sole passenger's next command. Outside, an immense
star and two much smaller companions blazed. Within the tiny
composite speck of atmosphere-holding matter nearby, a single
organic intelligence emitted minuscule mouth noises while generating liquid heavy with dissolved sodium chloride from its oc-
ular orbits. This went on for quite some time. Then the being in
question began to scream again. This time he did not stop.

There was no one around to hear.

11

They waited out the rest of the day in camp. Haviti chose to cling to the possibility that Araza might have second thoughts about abandoning them and would return, if only to kill them one by one. At least that would give them a chance to fight back and maybe regain control of the shuttle and thus a means of leaving Quofum. She knew it was an absurd thought, an irrational notion. In marooning them, Araza had murdered them as effectively as if he had lined them up against a wall and shot each of them through the head. Come morning she had abandoned the halfhearted hope as thoroughly as the covert Qwarm had abandoned them.

They would not die immediately. As long as they kept up the camp's infrastructure they would not die for a long time. The water purification system would keep them hydrated and its food synthesizer and preparation apparatus would provide them with nourishment. Sanity, she reflected as she strolled listlessly toward the dining area and lounge in search of an undesired but necessary breakfast, would be of greater concern than sustenance.

While waiting out the long night she had tried hard not to think of Esra Tellenberg, and failed. She recalled his many kind words, his common sense, his vibrant intellectual curiosity. Most of all she found herself remembering that to which she had previously paid the least attention. Little touches, a sly turn of phrase, the way she had sometimes caught him looking at her when he thought she was unaware of the attention. It occurred to her now that his interest in her might have been something more than merely that of a respectful fellow researcher.

If he felt that way, he had never expressed such feelings to her. Maybe he had been waiting for the right moment, and that moment had never come. Maybe his occasional comments, sometimes witty, sometimes flat, had been a cover for truer, deeper feelings. Maybe he had held off expressing himself in hopes of receiving some kind of encouraging sign from her. She wished she could ask him. She would never know, now. Esra Tellenberg was dead. As dead as the specimens the team had left on the boat. Swallowing hard, her throat all of a sudden atypically dry, she lengthened her stride. In the long run it didn't really matter. They were all dead.

Her surviving companions were already in the dining area. The look on N'kosi's face was distant and preoccupied. Though their fixed exoskeletons rendered all thranx more or less incapable of facial expression, Valnadireb's slumping stance and the perceptible droop of his antennae were indication enough that he shared his colleague's fatalistic ennui.

She knew she ought to be feeling the same. Inescapable depression had been the rule all yesterday afternoon and on through the night. But now, as she regarded her surviving companions, she felt her mind-set changing. Standing in the dining area, recently unpacked and activated equipment humming efficiently around her, it suddenly seemed gauche to be thinking only of death. She forced confidence into her voice.

"Mosi, how are you coming with the micropreps?"

Waiting for the machine in front of him to finish filling a cup with tea, her fellow xenologist turned to frown at her. "The micropreps? Tiare . . ." His voice trailed away as he struggled to find appropriate words to articulate his thoughts. "We're marooned here. Esra is dead, the shuttle is gone, the ship is gone, and we will never get off this world because as soon as the ship is discovered back home, everyone will assume we're already somewhere here, dead or alive, and no one will bother to come looking for us here."

Bustling past him, she started punching her breakfast request into the food preparation unit. "Then we'll have plenty of time to complete our work."

A hand reached over to gently touch her arm. Its four digits were as hard and slick as plastic, two of them serving the function of opposable thumbs. Turning to her right, she looked down into Valnadireb's jewel-like, red-banded, golden compound eyes.

"I believe I divine your intent, Tiare. It is to be commended. I will do my best to do likewise."

Picking up his cup and its steaming contents, N'kosi added sweetener. "What are you two mumbling about?"

Haviti had a moment before her breakfast was due to appear. "Okay, so we're trapped here. Like the ancient shipwrecked sailors of Earth's seas. We can go fetal and become mentally and physically comatose—or we can fight it. Stay active, immerse ourselves in our work, act like humanx."

N'kosi sipped morosely at his tea. "That might keep us alive awhile longer. It won't get us rescued."

"You're right, the odds aren't exactly the best," she agreed. "But if something happens to us our work will live on. And maybe one day a follow-up expedition will cross the camp's beacon, land here, and find months, years, maybe even decades' worth of important research already completed, catalogued, and stored, just waiting to be uploaded."

" 'Decades.' " N'kosi repeated the word as if it was a particularly evil curse. "Do you really think we can survive here for decades? We've been here for about a week and nearly found ourselves overrun by the natives. A lapse in judgment, a failure of Security, and the spikers or the hardshells are likely to pick us off. If not them, then some local parasite, or predator, or bad weather, or contracted illness."

She met his gaze evenly. "There are still three of us, Mosi. Three healthy, experienced, field-savvy researchers. We have a skimmer and the boat available for local transport and study. We have ample supplies, purifiers and synthesizers, multiple regenerative power, and secure living quarters. Not to mention whatever we can scavenge from our surroundings. As long as we watch our step and look out for each other there's no reason why we can't last for a long, long time. Who knows? Despite what that bastard Qwarm thinks, maybe even until a second contact expedition arrives, even if it takes years and, yes, decades for Science Central to decide to mount one. Meanwhile it would be a waste of a great scientific opportunity if we chose to spend all that time sitting around camp, doing nothing, and waiting to die."

Valnadireb gestured assent. "We have much work to do. Specimens to prepare, recordings to index, camp defenses to strengthen. However, I will not commence such work of my own until one other pressing matter has first been attended to."

She eyed the thranx xenologist uncertainly. "What pressing matter?"

He responded with the soft whistling that was an unmistakable indication of thranx amusement. "Breakfast, of course."

Initial concerns aside and despite having to pause periodically to raise the dejected N'kosi's lagging spirits, the days at the camp gradually fell into a routine that at least initially was comforting in its repetitiveness. It certainly was productive. Sending out such a small team demanded that it be comprised of generalists. Though each of the xenologists had their favored specialty, their expertise necessarily overlapped.

So while N'kosi preferred observing his faunal specimens through an assortment of magnification devices, he was not above helping Valnadireb sort out the thranx's exploding collection of botanicals. Similarly, Valnadireb spent time assisting Haviti in trying to bring some order (and Orders) to the continually expanding list of large animals. They all shared in trying to come up with new ways to contact the local sentients.

Where they threatened to have trouble was with the infrastructure of the camp itself. With the exception of the scientific apparatus, maintenance and upkeep had been the responsibility of Boylan and Araza. With one dead and the other fled, the three scientists spent a good deal of time away from science while devoting themselves to such mundane tasks as making certain the automated waste and recycling gear continued to operate in the efficient self-sanitizing manner promised by its assorted warranties. Equal if not more time was allotted to daily checking and rechecking of the separate systems that supplied the camp with fresh water, scrubbed air, cooled or heated internal atmosphere, food, and all the other components necessary to maintaining a minimal standard of semicivilized living.

While each system was designed to be as self-sustaining as possible, periodic checks were instituted to expose the slightest weak spot. It was critical that minor defects be detected as soon as they occurred. If allowed to become significant, none of the three xenologists possessed the knowledge or ability to fix them.

On the other hand, Haviti reflected one morning as she knelt on the roof of the living quarters module sealing a small leak in one of the condensation collectors, they had plenty of time to get better at such tasks.

Despite the drudgery imposed by having to devote time every day to ensure the continued functioning of the camp's life-support systems, new discoveries were made with giddy frequency. As scientists they found it terribly frustrating to be unable to share their findings with the rest of the Commonwealth and especially with their peers. Someday, Haviti ruminated as she carefully slid yet another tray of unique Quofumian samples into vacuum storage, another expedition would find what she and her friends left behind. The newcomers would marvel at the range of discoveries, at the precision with which they had been documented and logged, and at the skill with which they had been preserved. Her reputation and that of Valnadireb and Moselstrom N'kosi would be ensured.

Better posthumously, she reflected, than not at all.

As she climbed down from the roof, something large enough to cast a sizable shadow momentarily blocked out the sun. Twisting around, she peered upward, relying on the photosensitive lens of her work visor to automatically protect her from the sudden surge in sunlight.

A gravent was passing overhead. N'kosi had named the creature less than a week ago. Another treetop-feeding glider, the
eminent gray had a gaping mouth and multiple, charcoal-hued
wings. Despite its impressive wingspan, its foamlike internal
skeleton allowed it to soar effortlessly on the slightest of
breezes. Dissecting a dead one, she and Valnadireb had discovered its unique internal structure; semirigid despite the absence
of bones, tendons, or ligaments. Young gravents were neither
born live nor hatched from eggs and did not spring from spores
or seeds. Extruded from a special organ located on the underside of the adults, they unfolded their wings and took to the
pink skies of their inimitable homeworld like so much drifting
paste.

The soaring gravents were only one of thousands of unique
and frequently unclassifiable life-forms that she and her companions had encountered in the months since Tellenberg's death
and the Qwarm Araza's departure. From a taxonomic standpoint
they could hardly keep up with the new Orders, much less classify and give names to every new plant and animal. To even
begin to accomplish what was necessary on a world as diverse as
Quofum would require the presence of not three but three
thousand full-time xenologists.

Initially it was hard to tell which of the trio threw themselves into the necessary and beckoning scientific work with the
most enthusiasm. Freed from the need to think about rescue
once they had accepted that as a remote possibility, and also to
preserve their sanity, they focused on their efforts with an enthusiasm that for a time was refreshing. As days became weeks
and as weeks ran into months, this initial fervor faded. They still
did their research, rising every morning to begin work in the lab
module. But despite intermittent efforts at celebration or to rec-

ognize Commonwealth holidays, none of them could avoid the inevitable melancholy that had settled over the camp.

Even the communal meals to which they had hewed religiously for several months had been abandoned in favor of taking individual nourishment. Passing in the corridors, they hardly bothered to acknowledge one another's presence. In lieu of civilized conversation a grunt was now sufficient, or the flick of an eye. Information was still exchanged verbally, but earlier sociability had gradually been replaced by a lackluster courtesy. There simply seemed no reason to spend time engaged in idle chitchat.

As the only two humans on the planet, it was inevitable that Haviti and N'kosi would enter into a relationship. It lasted awhile, provided a diversion, and then did not so much break up as simply perish of its own accord, guilty of the sin of repetition. There was no shouting involved, no accusations, no yelling and screaming. Given their present circumstances, such typical remonstrations would have seemed childish as well as futile. She and the other xenologist remained close friends, if no longer intimate ones.

For a while it left poor Valnadireb lonelier than ever, though not jealous, of course. He took to making unaccompanied collecting excursions into the forest that surrounded the camp. Despite carrying a communit and sidearm, these solo expeditions were inherently dangerous. On one such outing he was attacked by what recordings suggested was a slow-moving carnivore but which on more detailed analysis turned out to be a predatory mobile plant. It would have cost the thranx a foot-hand had not N'kosi and Haviti worked tirelessly in tandem with the camp medunit to stanch the flow of blood and see the severed limb properly reattached. After that, a camp rule was established that no one would work outside the perimeter alone. Like many such rules, it was soon broken and forgotten.

One also had to take extra care while working on or conducting observations from the roof, Haviti reflected as she reentered the living quarters module. Not all indigenous fliers were as inoffensive as the gravent. The atmosphere of Quofum was as filled with predators as was its surface. Her alarm had remained silent while she had been carrying out the necessary maintenance work, however. Though huge, the gravent had posed no threat. It boasted neither fang nor claw and, despite its wingspan, weighed less than she did. Had it come too close, she could have pushed it away easily with one hand.

The three survivors were drifting apart. Knowing that, realizing that, did not make the problem any easier to solve. Perhaps it should not be looked at as a problem, she told herself as she strode into the food prep area to get something cold to drink. Which was safer: seeing less and less of each other, or forcing contact for purposes of sham socialization that might inadvertently lead to acrimony and conflict? They spoke with one another when they wanted to, shared knowledge and new discoveries when they had to, went their separate ways when they grew bored or tired of each other's company.

N'kosi was a good example. On the way to Quofum and for a time after landing, the two of them had been colleagues and good friends. Abandoned, they had eventually become more than just good friends. Now they were friends again. With only three people comprising the totality of their little society, one of them nonhuman, personal interaction was of necessity constrained.

There had been many times when she just wanted to scream. There had been numerous occasions when, locked in her quarters, she had broken down and cried. Neither left her feeling much better. Nowadays . . . As the months continued to pass without any sign or hope of rescue, she was simply becoming more and more numb. If not for the work that had taken on something of a life of its own, she knew there had been days when she would have chosen to sit down on her bed or a chair in the dining area and done her best to stop breathing.

N'kosi was already in the dining area, having worked his way through half a joyless meal. Valnadireb was just coming in. The thranx entered from the opposite direction, from outside. Despite the forest's constant heat and humidity he was not covered in perspiration. For one thing, thranx thrived in heat and humidity. For another, they did not sweat. That did not mean that the insectoid xenologist was buoyant. He was as subdued as both of his human colleagues.

No one said anything. No greetings were exchanged. They had moved beyond that. They had merged to become three parts of a single scientific organism whose individual elements communicated only when it was necessary to ensure mutual survival.

Haviti drew a drink from one of three available dispensing spigots. She did not bother to request the device's name for today's synthesized juice. It was cold and wet, which was all she was interested in.

"I'm going out." Her tone was muted, her words precise. "I'm taking the skimmer. I thought I'd run up the coast a ways. Take a few days, see some totally new territory. I'll keep the onboard monitors running around the clock, of course."

N'kosi spoke without looking up from his meal. Using his fork he rearranged some reconstituted julienned potatoes, to no particular end. "Want company?"

She did not look in his direction. Among the three of them eye contact was no longer necessary or expected. "Not particularly. You can come if you like."

N'kosi hesitated. "I'm finally getting the Order organized for those trees with the crystalline shoots. I think I'll stay here."

She did not reply. There was no need to do so. Having divested himself of his abdomen pack and other field gear, Valnadireb was ambling toward the main food processor. His antennae did not incline in her direction.

"Keep in touch," the thranx told her. "Once in a while, anyway."

"Sure, why not?" she replied impassively. She finished the last of her juice. "I'd do that, of course."

"Of course," he echoed as he punched in a sequence of requests specifying a favored range of nourishment.

When she left the following morning neither of her colleagues came to see her off. What would be the point? She knew they wished her well, just as she wished them well in their own daily research and maintenance duties. That her absence for an unspecified length of time would mean that her portion of the allotted upkeep work would have to be shared between those who remained behind caused no friction. Such responsibilities were minimal. Except for the first of a few small equipment breakdowns that were expected and had been successfully dealt with, the camp largely sustained itself. And if she perished somewhere off to the north, beyond hope of timely help from her companions, well, the inevitability of death was a consequence with which they had all long since made their peace.

She had stocked the skimmer with supplies sufficient for a

couple of weeks. That was about as long as it could travel without a recharge anyway. One week to explore, one week to return. She had no idea what she might see, encounter, or learn. Prior to touchdown, survey from orbit had been pretty minimal— just enough to find a landing site that was safe and interesting. A larger original or follow-up expedition would have been equipped to place relay and reconnaissance satellites in orbit. She and her colleagues had no such ancillary orbital tools to aid them in their work. A minimal first contact team like theirs was designed to get in, perform a quick preliminary survey, and get out. It was not designed to accommodate leisurely or long-range investigations.

The morning of her departure had dawned lightly overcast; a watercolorist's gray wash tinged with pink. Based on what it had learned of local climatological conditions in the limited time since it had being erected on the planet's surface, the camp's meteorological station predicted only a slight chance of light rain along the coast, with the possibility of heavier afternoon showers soaking the interior. She planned her route northward accordingly.

Responding to her commands, the compact, plexalloy-domed vehicle rose high enough to clear the camp's charged perimeter, angled west, and accelerated. As soon as it reached the sea she directed it to turn north and follow the coastline. The low-flying craft's atmospheric scrubbers could not entirely remove the sharp tang of oceanic alcohol from the air inside the skimmer's passenger compartment. She did not particularly mind.

Skimming along just above the wave-caressed beaches she encountered one new species after another. She rarely bothered to pause long enough for the craft's instruments to make proper recordings. Quofum was a nonstop cornucopia of biological riches, a bottomless pit of often seemingly unrelated species that was extensive enough to populate not one but many worlds.

Her reaction to the unending parade was unexpected. Over the course of the preceding months something had happened to her that she could never have predicted. Something that as a young, enthusiastic xenologist she would have bet all she owned would never have come to pass.

She had grown bored with discovery.

That did not mean she ignored the stream of new flora and fauna she encountered. She simply took note of it, species by species, hoped the skimmer's automated recording equipment was doing its job, and moved on. Just being away from the camp for more than a day was a breath of fresh air. The change was mildly rejuvenating, if not exactly exciting.

She lingered for a moment to have a look at the village of the fuzzies. The inhabitants had restored many of the simple structures that had been destroyed in the attack by the combined forces of the spikers and the hardshells. Interestingly, there was no sign of the stick-jellies. It was possible that the latter only sided with the fuzzies in times of warfare and that their alliance did not extend to the more mundane and more time-consuming process of reconstruction. Once her presence was noted, a few clubs and spears were flung in her direction. Those that reached the low-flying skimmer bounced off its composite sides and did no damage. This exhibition of unprovoked hostility did not cause her to judge the natives. As both a scientist and a human being, she knew she did not have enough information to do so. She resumed her journey northward.

Technically the unnecessary exposure of such advanced technology to primitive species was in contravention of Commonwealth contact procedure. Haviti contented herself with the knowledge that the violation was likely to go unremarked upon. Besides, Quofum had not been officially classified. You couldn't break regulations that were not yet in place.

Not that she gave a damn about such things anymore.

The alcohol-flavored sea on her left was alive with as wide-ranging an assortment of seemingly unrelated life-forms as the sky and the land. Quofum was nothing if not endlessly fecund. She and her companions did not lack for divertissements of the biological kind. She would have traded every one of them for a new tridee play, or a new book, or a current news report from even an unimportant outlying world. The continued and likely permanent isolation threatened to drive her and her friends mad.

Take what she thought she was seeing now, for instance. Several days' travel north of the village of the fuzzies and farther inland she began to see high verdant mounds interlaced with straight channels that suggested a jungle-clad city. Directing the skimmer to divert toward them, she flew low and slow over and around several of the overgrown mounds. She felt a surge of excitement, the first of its kind in many weeks. Surely the verdure-clad towers she was circling could not be entirely natural? They were too regular in shape, too severe in silhouette. And there were too many of the channels, which were themselves too straight and precise. While tributaries even on Earth had been known to enter major rivers at perfectly right angles due to quirks of local geology, they tended to have a tapering shape like all good subsidiary streams. The diameter of those below her now were unvarying from one end to the other.

Penetrating onboard instruments soon confirmed her suspicions. The forest-enveloped rises beneath the skimmer were not natural in origin. They had been built, not eroded. In addition to stone there was extensive use of composite paving materials to make surface roads, decorations utilizing various kinds of glass, structures of fabricated ceramic, and most telling of all, sparse but unmistakable use of refined metal.

She circled the area several times. While considerable in size, it would only have qualified as a large town on a developed Commonwealth world. Still, there was no mistaking that it was the first bona fide conurbation they had discovered on Quofum. In size, complexity, and development it was leagues in advance of the village of the fuzzies. In construction and design it was far beyond anything of which the five native sentient species thus far encountered were capable.

Then—who had built it? The omnipresence of the invasive forest combined with the lack of any detectible activity whatso-ever suggested that it had been deserted and unused for a very long time. Strapping on her utility belt and making certain its field sidearm was fully charged, she directed the skimmer to set down in the approximate center of the abandoned city.

Stepping out, she was greeted by the usual flush of moist, overheated, oxygen-rich air. Many of the life-forms she ob-served flying, crawling, slithering, hopping, or walking through the edifice-clinging undergrowth were by now familiar to her. As was typical of excursions anywhere on Quofum, a great many more were not. For once, she did not pause to examine even the most interesting of them. Her cap's integrated instrumentation would automatically make note of them. The resultant record-ings could be studied later.

On this particular morning something more interesting than local wildlife had piqued her curiosity—artificial structures that hinted at the work of a life-form far more advanced than any the expedition had encountered thus far. She did not automatically assume it to be local. The question of how, why, and where Quofum's sentients had arisen remained as undetermined as when Tellenberg had first voiced the conundrum. If anything, this new discovery only added another new piece to an ever-expanding puzzle instead of filling in one of its numerous blanks.

Using a beamer cutter modified for forest work, she cleared brush away from a section of street. That portion of the offended undergrowth that was equipped to do so attempted to fight back, only to be promptly carbonized for its efforts. The avenue her efforts laid bare revealed a surface composed of a dark material that had been lightly roughened. Preliminary analysis showed that it was not hydrocarbon-derived, but neither was it a sophisticated synthetic. A hasty rudimentary field breakdown hinted at some kind of volcanic glass that had been mixed with cellulose.

Very strange blend for a paving material, she thought as she reholstered her analyzer. Which made it perfectly suited to Quofum, where there was furious competition for the title of ultimate strangeness.

Depending on the varying density of the encumbering foliage, she alternately walked or fought her way through the brush to the nearest building. Given the thick overgrowth, it was impossible just from looking at the structure to divine its purpose. It might as easily have been a temple, a storehouse, or an apartment building. The fact that the sides tapered toward the top suggested ancient Terran places of worship. The large hole in the center of the structure, from which dripped the Quofumian equivalent of vines and creepers, did not. More than anything, the seemingly extraneous circular gap hinted at an advanced aesthetic sensibility.

While studying the building she could not avoid imposing her own cultural and historical references on everything from its location to its architecture. It might, she thought whimsically as she moved toward what appeared to be a growth-barred entrance, be nothing more than an elaborate high-rise chicken coop. On closer inspection the dark oval stain at the base of the structure did indeed appear to be an entrance. The shadowy corridor that extended beyond the overgrowth reached far back into the building. Alone and far from camp and assistance, she had no intention of trying to penetrate its unfathomable depths on her own.

As it turned out she did not have to. Though heavily overgrown, the entrance itself offered up revelations of its own.

The bas-reliefs that covered both opposing walls and receded into the darkness were of exceptional quality. It was immediately apparent that they had been created with tools far more sophisticated than hammers and chisels. Several depicted scenes of what she took to be the daily life of the small city. Others—others were unmistakable representations of incidents of warfare between the conurbation's builders and an invading horde. Perhaps it was the latter who were ultimately responsible for the fall of the city and its burgeoning civilization.

The defenders of the city were squat bipeds with oversized heads, eyes, and other facial features. Despite their short arms and stumpy legs, in the reliefs they were shown capable of considerable agility and impressive feats of strength. Whether these were accurate depictions of physical ability or exaggerations due to artistic flattery, she had no way of knowing. The weapons they employed to defend themselves and their community were far more sophisticated than the simple spears and clubs she and her colleagues had observed in use by the sentients living farther to the south. Even a cursory study of the opposing walls revealed the use of explosives, something resembling a compact crossbow, various kinds of flaming liquids, even a crude short-range device that made use of solar heat. That the city-builders had achieved a level of technology far beyond that of the more primitive southerly tribes was already apparent from the size and sophistication of their community. It was only further confirmed by the depiction of advanced weaponry.

Opposing the city's defenders were tightly packed masses of the oddest beings she had yet seen represented on Quofum. They made the physiognomy of the stick-jellies look almost normal. Each of the invading creatures was composed of what appeared to be half a dozen pulpy, pale white balloons. Three tiny black pupil-less eyes were visible in the central balloon. In the absence of arms, fingers, tentacles, or other recognizable appendages, the outermost balloons held on to weapons and other devices by partially englobing them with elastic portions of their bodies. In the absence of legs and feet, the globular creatures advanced not by walking but by bouncing along the ground.

Larger scenes of battle were interspersed with ennobling portrayals of individual squat city folk (local heroes, she presumed) single-handedly fending off attacks by multiple balloon-beings. When pierced or otherwise wounded the urbanites bled blood while the invaders secreted a thick mucus. Instinctively and most unscientifically Haviti found herself siding with the city-dwellers. That was the human in her, inclined in the absence of knowledge to favor battling bipeds against assailants who were as nonhuman as could be imagined. The rationalist in her quickly assumed a neutral stance with regard to the ancient conflict.

She knew nothing of either defender or invader. For all she was aware the mucus-oozing balloon-folk were the righteous saviors of all that was good and noble while the bipedal urbanites were bloodsucking slave-takers. Ever since contact with the thranx, the human-Pitar war, and the subsequent Amalgamation that resulted in the forming of the Commonwealth, humans had learned never to judge an intelligent species on the basis of appearance.

While aesthetically beguiling and of unarguable historical interest, the extensive depictions of fighting were not what had drawn her to the panels depicting combat. It was the detailed portrayals of the combatants themselves. Here were two species that were not only far more advanced socially and technologically than those to the south, but utterly different from them. The squat urbanites were as unlike the stick-jellies as the stick-jellies were to the hardshells. The raiding balloon-beings bore no more relation to the fuzzies than she did to the lazy yet sentient river-dwellers.

Rather than adding any kind of clarification, her discovery only served to further magnify the mystery that was Quofum. Seven sentient species. Seven, existing on a relatively tiny corner of one continent. What would they find if they had the wherewithal to explore the entire planet? Ten intelligent species? Dozens? Hundreds? On Quofum the laws of evolution and biology were as muddled as the surface of a comet-struck moon. What was responsible? Or, she mused as she thought back to discussions she'd had with her colleagues, who?

Magnifying the madness, it was the more advanced of the two new species who had apparently died out and left no local descendants. Though she lacked evidentiary proof, it was hard to imagine that the superior urbanites and balloon-folk had somehow given rise to fuzzies and spikers and stick-jellies. It was equally difficult to imagine the reverse. On Quofum it appeared that the normal process of evolution was as a bystander instead of a mover. What would she find as she traveled farther north? Intelligent arthropods? Cities of social bivalves? Cephalopods in spaceships? For a curious xenologist Quofum was a kind of nirvana.

Or hell.

12

The village of the seals offered a respite of sorts—if finding an eighth intelligent species could be called a respite. By this time Haviti had resigned herself, as a person if not as a scientist, to the fact that Quofum could be expected to yield up an entirely new sentient species or two every couple of hundred kilometers. Having stepped through the scientific looking glass, she saw no point in driving herself crazy struggling to make sense of the biological wonderland on the other side of the fantastical pane.

The coastal locale was as pleasant and inviting a venue as she or her colleagues had come across since their arrival. Compact homes and shops built of gathered stone and rough-hewn wood lined neatly cobbled streets at the bottom of a small canyon that swept gently down to the sea between heavily forested hills. The cove at the terminus of the valley was picture-pretty. Small single-masted fishing vessels, their purpose defined by the nets that draped them front and stern like discarded petticoats, rode at anchor.

By now indifferent to any and all Commonwealth regulations, she landed the skimmer right on the beach in front of the town and just to the north of its single pier. Her first sight of the creatures who came loping to greet her immediately reminded her of Terran pinnipeds who had forgone a water-dwelling existence in favor of living on land. They had large eyes, narrow laid-back ears, small black nostrils, and expressions she could only define as winsome. Except for their dark, slick-skinned faces, their heads, limbs, and the parts of their bodies that were visible outside their simple attire were covered by short brown, black, or gray fur. They were the first Quofumian sentients she or any of her colleagues had encountered in person who wore sewn clothing. Their legs were proportionately much longer than their arms. When they ran or walked they did so by leaping sideways with their heads turned in the direction they wanted to go, giving them the look of puppies skipping on stilts.

As she emerged from behind the skimmer's canopy and started down the extended steps her right hand automatically went to her sidearm. She did not have to draw it. Inherently friendly, the seals (as she chose to call them, following the team's procedure of giving each new intelligent species a preliminary colloquial name) slowed as they drew near. While not complex, their language was a good deal more elaborate than that of the cautious fuzzies, for example, or the raging spikers.

While a handful of the aliens could look her in the eye, most stood no taller than her chest. Keeping her hands at her sides, she let them gather around her. Instead of fingers their hands split into opposing halves, like soft claws. While incapable of fine work, these were perfectly adequate for grasping and lifting. Gaping round mouths revealed inner horny layers easily capable of masticating fish and probably a wide variety of other

Quofumian edibles. She quickly realized that she could identify and remember individuals by noting distinctive patterns of coloration in their fur.

Behind her, several of them had cautiously begun to inspect the skimmer. With the canopy closed they could not get inside, but they could see through the transparency. Their babbling speech consisted primarily of long rolling sentences devoid of consonantal harshness.

This would be a good people to study in more depth, she told herself. If they would allow it, of course. How to open negotiations? She was saved the trouble when the seals did it for her.

The crowd that had gathered on the beach parted to allow others to come forward. The advancing trio was better dressed than any of the natives she had seen thus far. They were neither especially imposing physically nor, insofar as she could tell, of advanced age, but it was immediately evident from the way the crowd made room for them that they were held in high regard.

They halted an arm's length from Haviti, closer than any of the other sleek fisherfolk had dared to approach. Sexual dimorphism was not immediately apparent. Up close, she thought they might bear some superficial resemblance to the more primitive fuzzies. DNA and cell analysis would be necessary to reveal any actual connection. For the moment, though, she was content simply to stand and study the first land-based intelligent native species that did not greet strangers with undisguised suspicion and brandished weapons.

The difference in approach was more profound than she imagined. Lifting a necklace of perfectly transparent shells over its head, careful to avoid getting it hung on one of its narrow, extended ears, the nearest of the respected threesome had to extend itself to its maximum height in order to slip it over Haviti's head. She inclined forward slightly to lessen the strain on the seal's short arms. The gesture was then repeated by each of its companions, leaving her wearing three necklaces: one comprised of delicate shell-like transparencies, a second of small flowers, and a third of roughly but undeniably artificially polished pebbles. Following the presentation, two of the trio stepped back. The third began to speak.

Their speech was gently musical, occasionally rising and falling sharply in the middle of a sentence or phrase. Even in the absence of formal morphological analysis it was evident that their language was far more advanced than that of any previously contacted indigenous species. With the possible exception of the vanished city-dwellers, these were clearly the most advanced inhabitants of Quofum yet discovered.

Though she could understand nothing of their speech, certain gestures are universal among limbed intelligences. Chirping and beckoning for her to follow, they led her away from the pebbly beach and toward the town. She complied, tolerating the hesitant touches of the bolder among the crowd. Placid in lockdown, the skimmer would look after itself. Resistant as it was to penetration by many advanced tools, she was confident these people had nothing in their possession that was capable of forcing an entrance or doing damage to the parked craft.

Proper procedure demanded that she contact her companions and inform them of her latest finding. If she was in the mood, she decided, she might do so later. One of the first things that had been dropped following their abandonment on Quofum by the Qwarm Araza was any concern for or interest in proper procedure. Valnadireb went his way according to his interests and desires, N'kosi did pretty much as he pleased, and so did she. Maybe she would tell them about the jungle-reclaimed city and the village of the seals tomorrow. Maybe she would wait until she returned to the camp. Maybe both would remain her little secret. It was not as if she was exposing herself to official recrimination.

Strange, she thought as she found herself treading the first of the town's well-maintained cobblestone streets. One of the first consequences of the loss of hope was complete freedom.

Unlike contact with the stick-jellies and the fuzzies, the hardshells and the spikers, neither restrained nor overt belligerence was manifested in her direction. Young and old, healthy and infirm, the seals welcomed her with open, highly modified flippers. She wondered how her dropping from the sky fit into their racial mythology or religion, assuming they had either one.

An empty house was opened and presented to her. The inference was clear: it was hers to use. How could she refuse such a touching gesture? Besides, studying the seals from within their community would offer opportunities likely to be missed if she isolated herself on board the skimmer.

Transferring gear from the craft allowed her to equip the small dwelling with adequate security. It was acceptable to like the seals—but not to trust them. The art of patient duplicity was not a skill reserved solely for humanxkind. Still, as the days passed, she grew progressively more comfortable in the company of her hosts and in sleeping among them.

While the shallow, wood-framed ovoid filled with dried and fluffed plant matter that was located in the rearmost room provided a tolerably restful bed, she preferred the expandable she brought from the skimmer. Though her own dwelling as well as every one she visited displayed an admirable level of hygiene, there was no telling what kind of parasites might inhabit the depths of such bedding. Insofar as she could tell, her hosts did not take this preference for her own sleeping platform as a slight. Indeed, they showed the same level of curiosity toward her tools and gear as she did to theirs.

Village society was as evolved as its technology. There were several schools for the young. In the absence of books, knowledge was inscribed on bound sheets of a large echinoderm that was collected by divers. Dried and pounded flat and thin, this organic material had the consistency of flexible cardboard. Paper, she had no doubt, would be the next step up in the advancement of seal writing technology. She did not show them the screen on her communit. Too much magic could overwhelm simple minds. Worse, the history of contact with less advanced species showed how such repeated revelations could lead to suspicion and jealousy.

There were bakeries, facilities for processing the wondrous variety of creatures netted in the depths and gathered from the shores of the cove and the deeper sea beyond, something akin to a restaurant, two gathering places that might on another world have qualified as taverns (a tavern on a world whose oceans were nine percent alcohol seemed decidedly superfluous), and shops for making and repairing clothing, utensils, and other goods. As her knowledge of the local language increased, abetted by relevant programs embedded in the skimmer's AI, she was able to confirm that the villagers obtained the majority of their needs from the sea.

Most exciting of all was the information that there were other seal villages scattered up and down the coast and on offshore islands with whom her hosts engaged in regular trade and social intercourse. Truly, in the absence of the unknown species who had built the now deserted inland city, these congenial folk represented the apex of contemporary Quofumian society.

Occasionally her studies would be interrupted by a perfunctory query from base camp. So as not to unsettle or over-awe her hosts, she would reply only when by herself. Valnadireb informed her that he was hard at work in the forest and staying close to camp. Utilizing one of the expedition's four small rechargeable scooters, N'kosi had chosen to range farther afield. Their respective work was going well. Each was making astonishing discoveries. Though their sporadic conversations were underscored by the kind of calm and composure that attends the condemned, they were devoid of despair or self-pity. Gloom had long since given way to resignation. While she could not speak for her colleagues, Haviti felt like someone who had contracted a terminal disease yet felt no physical pain. Their condition was one to be regretted, but not dwelled upon.

On the morning of the day in the middle of the fifth week she had planned to sit in on one of the local school's most advanced study sessions in hopes of learning more about the history of the town. Instead, when she emerged from what she had whimsically dubbed Cove Cottage, she found herself confronting Ba-fel. Tall for his kind, the male was one of several villagers who had spent enough time in the presence of the pale-fleshed alien to become comfortable with her. Though Haviti's command of the local language was still crude, she could now make simple concepts understood. Talking seal was easier than, for example, trying to speak High Thranx. Haviti likened the latter to gargling without liquid.

"Ti-ah-reh well morning today?" Ba-fel inquired politely.

"Ti-ah-reh well yes." Better to keep exchanges simple and comprehensible than to strive for eloquence and fall on one's linguistic face, Haviti had always firmly believed. Besides, there was little room for elaboration in the seals' language. It was simple and straightforward and functional, which suited her mood just fine. High literacy could come later.

The native gestured. Not in the direction of the town and the school where Haviti was expected, but toward the cove. "Ti-ah-reh has ask often about other peoples. Ba-fel talk with friends. Believe Ti-ah-reh good person." The attenuated, backward-facing ears flapped lazily back and forth, serving to pick up sounds while simultaneously cooling the speaker's body. "Ba-fel and friends think time okay now show Ti-ah-reh place other people leave behind."

Haviti's heart skipped a beat. The chronicle of the town could wait. What the ingenuous Ba-fel seemed to be offering was a history lesson of a different sort.

She closed the cottage door behind her. There was no way to lock it, and no need to. "This place," she asked her friend and guide, "is located in cove?"

"Not in cove." Ba-fel's long legs seemed to slip and slide over the cobblestones as they made their way toward the pier. "Beyond." A short arm rose to gesture northwestward. "Other side Sharp Point. Must take boat."

This would be a first, Haviti realized. Until now, all her time had been spent in the village and its immediate terrestrial surrounds—except for on those occasions when she had gone swimming. Her sporadic bathing excursions invariably drew a crowd, as curious about her method of aqueous locomotion as they were about her unclad form. But no one had offered to take her out on one of the double-prowed fishing craft. Having access to the skimmer, she had not thought to ask.

She had no compunction about making a short journey in one of the native boats. Though unbeautiful and strictly utilitarian in design and purpose, they were broad-beamed and solid. She had seen them riding storm waves, bobbing over big swells like corks as they ventured out in search of a catch or returned heavily laden with water-dwellers who were the equal in biological variety of anything she had encountered on land. Sturdy masts held single or double sails made from dried and treated animal hides. As none of the simple craft had sunk during the course of her visit she felt reasonably safe in anticipating that one would not sink while she was aboard.

She did detour to the shuttle to add a few additional items to her utility belt. Exiting and locking the canopy behind her, she indicated her readiness to the patient Ba-fel and followed him the rest of the way to the pier. The fishing boat that was waiting for them had its nets neatly rolled and stored, ready for deployment. Their presence caused her to smile to herself. While the seals clearly desired to show her something they felt was of significance, they were not about to waste the opportunity to do a little fishing.

Her hosts had timed the departure to coincide with the morning winds that blew outward off the land. Funneling by the narrow cove increased the strength of these warm gentle breezes so that departing boats made good time outbound from the village. In the absence of any moons, tidal action was minimal. There was virtually no surf to surmount.

She had no idea what to expect. Ba-fel had not elaborated and she saw no reason to press him for details. Anything worth discussing would present itself soon enough. The panorama as they rounded Sharp Point and set sail northward was something of a letdown. As near as she could see, the coastline north of the village was identical to the coast south of it. Certainly nothing distinctive presented itself. In the absence of revelation she stretched out on the central deck and allowed the alien sun to warm her.

Several hours passed before Ba-fel approached her and leaned over to declare, "You might want stand up now, Ti-ah-reh. We here."

As she sat up, her visor immediately adjusted to the difference in brightness. Looking around she saw more coastline, more sky, flat sea. The view was no different from the one to be had at Sharp Point. Seeing her confusion, Ba-fel beckoned her to the rail. Those seals not attending to shipboard duties were watching her with interest.

As the morning heat intensified, she found herself growing irritable. Had she wasted a day because some of the natives wanted her company on a fishing outing? "I don't see anything different, Ba-fel. What you here bring me for?"

"Come see, Ti-ah-reh. Here." Leaning over the side of the boat, the native pointed. Not toward the shore, but downward. Stepping up alongside him Haviti peered into the sea—and caught her breath.

The water was clear as crystal. Just below the surface was the top of a building. Beyond, she could see a good twenty meters into the depths. The rest of the building was clearly visible—as were the structures that surrounded it. She turned to her host.

"Who build this, Ba-fel? Not your people."

"No, not mine. We not know. This place always here, since beginning of memory. We come often." He made the seal equivalent of a smile. "Always much here to catch. Is suits your interest, yes?"

"Yes. I am very pleased, Ba-fel." Turning away from him she sought the box where she had placed her boots and service belt. "I am going swim."

"Here?" He looked surprised. "Water is deep. You go deep, Ti-ah-reh?"

"As deep as I can," she told him.

The mask she donned was self-equalizing. Its miniaturized built-in rebreathing system would vent CO_2 and draw oxygen from the surrounding water, allowing her to stay down as long as she wished. Powerfins would allow her to descend and move around with ease. A liquidrive would have extended her under-water range. The expedition had two of the powerful underwater propulsion units, but both were back in camp. She would have to make do.

Ba-fel was removing his simple clothing. So was one of the other sailors. "Safer Ti-ah-reh go with company. Are sometimes dangerous animals here."

"I be all right," she assured him. Her beamer would work just as well underwater as above. But she did not object to the offer of an escort. In any case, it would have been impolite to turn it down.

As usual, the water was warm and faintly aromatic. After hovering near the surface to make sure both the mask's re-breather and the powerfins were working, she arched her back and headed downward. Unable to draw oxygen from the water, Ba-fel and his friend remained near the surface, tracking her progress through their simple glass eyeshades.

Despite the clarity of the water she could not see all the way to the bottom. The structures that rose from darkness and from depths unknown were profoundly unsettling. Touching the side of one, examining it while hovering in the slight current, she could not identify the building material. It was as far in advance of the cut stone of the inland city as the lens of her mask was from the simple sand-glass goggles worn by her hosts. She was

almost certain the wall before her was made of metal. Seamless
and devoid of rivets or other imperfections, it plunged downward in a single sheet, unmarred by windows or other openings.
There was not a speck of rust.

Leaving it and dodging curious ocean-dwellers, she swam
across the open space between the first building and the next.
Structurally, the second edifice was utterly different from its
neighbor. Where the first boasted sides that were severe and
straight, the second was a riot of entwined arcs and curls, free-
ranging, free-flying arches of metal and what appeared to be
some kind of translucent white super-porcelain. Aesthetics
aside, Haviti was unable to divine the purpose behind the radical architectural motif.

It soon became apparent as she let the powerfins push her
through the sunken city that such extreme embellishment was
the norm. The building at whose summit she had been dropped
turned out to be the exception, the only one with simple,
straight sides. No two submerged structures were alike and each
was more fantastic in design than the next. As she swam her survey, Ba-fel and one or two other seals were always with her, par-
alleling her progress and watching from above. The longer she
spent exploring the sunken metropolis, the more comforting
she found their presence. There were ghosts here, in a meta-
phorical if not tangible sense.

It had been apparent from the first that whoever had built
this city had achieved a level of technological sophistication
that dwarfed anything else she or her companions had previously encountered on Quofum. Parts of it appeared to have
been spun instead of built, as if some mad cake decorator had
been given giant tubes of metal and glass and ceramic to work
with instead of buttercream frosting. Touching the smooth skin

of several structures she found herself wishing for more advanced analytical equipment than she had on the skimmer. In its absence she could only guess at the composition of some of the construction materials.

The powerfins drove her through and around edifices that gleamed golden in the bright light filtering down through the clear water. A visitor from an earlier time might have been forgiven for thinking the towering spires were constructed of polished brass. An enormous stadium whose purpose she was unable to construe occupied the entire top of a small seamount. Though increasing pressure at depth only allowed her to swim through its uppermost reaches, the shafts of light that illuminated immense hallways and vast gathering areas reminded her of images she had seen of ancient cathedrals.

While the sunken city was rife with life, with one exception its present population either avoided her entirely or paused at a distance to consider the curious creature that darted through their midst. The exception took the form of a seven-meter-long length of undulating ribbon, silver glazed with crimson, that tried to fasten needlelike teeth on her left arm. A burst from her beamer left it writhing and twisting as it drifted away, its narrow toothy skull seared and smoking. A host of attentive scavengers magically materialized from every direction. They proceeded to quickly and efficiently reduce the writhing, coiling corpse to shards of drifting flesh that filled the water like so much chrome confetti.

Though she learned a great deal in the course of her awestruck, hurried underwater survey, she found nothing that allowed her to identify the creators of the oceanic Oz. Unlike the overgrown corridor she had discovered in the inland city, there were no bas-reliefs, no engravings, no depictions whatsoever of the community's builders. Nor were there any images that might have given a clue as to how the metropolis came to subside beneath the waves. Like its builders, the cause of its fate remained a mystery.

Ba-fel and his friends were looking anxious by the time she surfaced and returned to the boat. She felt guilty. She had not expected to be down so long. As she unsealed and pulled off her mask, shaking water from her hair, she eyed him apologetically.

"I sorry, Ba-fel." She held out her mask for him to see. "With this, my kind can stay underwater long time."

"Was concerned for Ti-ah-reh." The seal's ears quivered anxiously. "Was worth see this place?" he added hopefully.

"Was much worth," she assured him as she picked up a drying pad and began to pat herself down. "Must come back again." With more advanced equipment and the ability to go deeper while avoiding the need for decompression, she added silently to herself.

As sail was raised and the boat turned back toward the village, she soaked up the warm sun and wondered at the sunken metropolis and its origins. Who had built it? What had happened to sink it beneath the waves? Some kind of natural geologic subsidence, perhaps. If the latter, it must have been violent and rapid. Many of the buildings she had investigated looked as if they had been completed only yesterday. Yet if an earthquake or some similar phenomenon was responsible, why had she not found any evidence of the kind of physical damage one would expect to see resulting from such a cataclysm?

More important, what had happened to the city's inhabitants? While her examination had been necessarily brief, she had seen evidence of technology, or at least metallurgy, that approached Commonwealth norms. Certainly the city had not been built by the seals, or for that matter by the fuzzies, or the hardshells, or any of the other sentient species she and her colleagues had encountered thus far. Why had such an advanced culture vanished without a trace? Or had it? She and her friends had spent only a couple of months studying a minuscule portion of a tiny part of a large world. Who knew what remained to be discovered in its other hemisphere? Or even a few kilometers distant in any randomly chosen direction?

It seemed that the longer she and her colleagues remained on Quofum and the more they learned, the greater grew the mystery that shrouded the whole planet in confusion and illogicality.

She could have spent the rest of the day pondering that greatest of all the questions posed by the world on which she and her friends had been stranded. She should have been able to. Instead, the unexpected intervened. Quofum intervened.

The rising agitation among the sailors manifested itself before anyone thought to explain it to her. Before one of them could, she saw the explanation for herself.

Smoke was rising from the village. The first dark puffs, clouds of ash and smoke pushed out to sea by the offshore breeze, were visible even before the sturdy craft rounded the Point. By the time it did so her hosts were breaking out spears and crude projectile weapons. At full sail and working feverishly to tack landward, they made their way back into the cove.

Haviti's spirits fell as she saw the havoc that was being wreaked on shore. Several of the village buildings farthest inland and up the canyon were on fire, sending up streamers of furious smoke. The sounds of battle, of the primitive but still deadly *pop-pop* of gunpowder-fueled weapons, of seals screaming and shouting, of the faint metallic ring of metal on metal, drifted out to sea along with the smoke.

She had no idea who was attacking the village. As soon as the boat reached the single pier, everyone on board leaped off. Long legs eating up the ground in great, loping strides she could not match, they raced up the beach and toward town. In the absence of pikes and swords and guns some of her companions, including Ba-fel, brandished razor-sharp fishing gear. Others vanished into streets and buildings in search of better weapons. No one took the time to inform the visiting alien who was their guest as to the nature of the attackers. She could hardly blame them.

Seeking clarification on her own, she ran toward the village. She was halfway through the town and panting hard as she raced up a familiar sloping street when an apparition came hurtling toward her out of a side alley. Had it not paused in its charge it surely would have crushed her skull with the blocky wooden war hammer it wielded. The sight of her, however, made it hesitate. Clearly, she was no villager.

The being was as tall as N'kosi and twice as broad. From the thick, cylindrical torso protruded a trio of muscular arms that terminated in triple gripping digits. Thick strips of tanned and treated animal hide crisscrossed the body to form clumsy but effective armor. Sustaining the trisymmetrical body plan, the bulbous head sported three slightly oval eyes, a tripartite nostril, and a mouth that was oddly triangular in shape. The creature had no legs. It advanced by jerking its body across the ground on a single thick, muscular pseudopod. In place of fur or hair, the perfectly smooth skull secreted a kind of protective rose-hued jelly. In contrast to the seals it was aggressive in attitude and loathsome in appearance.

She fried it.

Holding her beamer out in front of her she advanced uphill

and farther into the village. The battle had moved from the out-
skirts of town deeper into the community. There were several
public fountains. Approaching the uppermost, she saw that the
villagers had lured their hideous attackers into an ambush. Individually, a singlefoot, as she immediately dubbed the invaders,
was markedly stronger and more powerful than any two seals.
The villagers, however, made up for their physical disadvantages
with better smarts. Caught out in the open square that centered
on the fountain, the attackers were being picked off by the ar-
rows and primitive guns wielded by seals concealed in the surrounding buildings.

Another intelligent native species, a dazed and exhausted
Haviti realized as she stood back and observed the carnage. One
that she felt pretty certain was not responsible for the magnifi-
cent city in the sea. How many sentient species did that make
now? She gave up trying to remember.

Pinned down and caught without cover, the singlefoots tried
to retreat, to no avail. The clever and alert villagers had blocked
off all avenues of escape. One by one the brawny but slower-
witted invaders were cut down. Looking on, Haviti saw a pair
drop their weapons and spread their multiple arms. A dozen
armed seals immediately surrounded the two who had capitu-
lated.

They proceeded to hack them to pieces, displaying a zeal
and enthusiasm that turned her stomach.

Backing up, she holstered her beamer. She had followed the
sounds of combat intending not only to observe and record the
conflict, but if necessary to assist her friends the seals. Patently,
they did not need her help. Observing the slaughter, she found
herself retreating in disgust. Intelligence, as ever, was a relative
term—and on Quofum there were apparently no decent exam-

ples to relate to. The singlefoots might be unsightly, even re-
pulsive in appearance. They were hostile and warlike. But
they were intelligent beings still, and warranted being treated as
such. They did not deserve to be butchered like the daily catch
the villagers hauled up onto the beach every evening.

To her surprise she found that she was crying silently. She
had come to like the seals, to favor them above every other sentient species she and her colleagues had thus far encountered.
The bloodthirsty enthusiasm with which they were dispatching
every last one of the singlefoots filled her with a dismay that
bordered on outright disgust. This was the world on which she
had been abandoned. These were the beings among whom she
was going to have to live. Was it all endless fighting and conflict?
Was there no peace to be found anywhere? No common sense,
no respite from brutal competition?

Competition. The word, the meaning, the potential behind
it triggered something in her mind. Multiple biologically unrelated primitive races fighting for dominance over one another.
Advanced civilizations that had risen and fallen; not one, but
two, and both within a geographically small area. Was it all
nothing more than feverish evolution at work? Or was there
something else? Something they were overlooking. Hadn't
N'kosi once proposed as much? It was a crazy idea. An insane
notion.

With the entire village occupied in massacring the rest of
the attackers, no one noticed her as she made her way back to
the beach. Secure and inviolate, the skimmer sat undisturbed
where she had parked it upon arrival that first day weeks ago.
Upon boarding and resealing the canopy, internal instrumentation responded as promptly and efficiently as if she had disem-
barked only yesterday.

Her idyllic sojourn among the seals was over. Rudely interrupted, she made certain that the last of her recordings had
been properly stored before directing the compact craft to lift,
pivot, and accelerate southward.

Behind her she left the village and its affable populace engaged in exterminating the last of the individually robust but
collectively ill-prepared invaders. As was universally the case,
strategy and intelligence had once again won out over sheer
brawn. Did that mean anything on Quofum? She needed more
information to be certain of anything. Somehow, in the absence
of shuttle, ship, or satellite, she felt that she and her colleagues
were going to have to greatly extend the reach of their knowledge if they were to find any answers.

As the shuttle hummed its way southward along the coast
she could not escape the feeling that things happened unnatu-
rally fast on this world. Species evolved, developed, advanced,
and then went extinct at a rate unknown anywhere else. The
city in the jungle. The more sophisticated city in the sea. The
seals fighting off the singlefoots. Stick-jellies and fuzzies battling
spikers and hardshells. It was becoming clear that biological se-
lection on Quofum did not proceed at a normal, measured
pace: it sprinted and stumbled and spilled madly forward, as if
driven by natural forces as yet unidentified.

Or, she mused thoughtfully as sand and water and forest
whipped past beneath the sleek little craft, by unnatural ones.

13

Valnadireb found it hard being alone. More so even than humans, thranx were social creatures.

Like the rest of his kind, he was not particular as to the species whose company he kept, so long as it was mature enough to engage in intelligent discourse. But where thranx were concerned, variety in conversation was as important as content. Being restricted to repartee with just two companions, and non-thranx at that, was intellectually debilitating. With Haviti away on her north coast excursion, it left only N'kosi to chat with. While the human did his best to be sociable, he had his own research to concentrate on.

It was never expected that the original six-member expedition would have to endure one another's company for more than a month or two. Psychological profiling had taken that into consideration when the team was being assembled. With that number now cut in half and accorded permanent instead of temporary status, it became more and more difficult to find matters of commonality to discuss beyond those immediately germane to issues of survival.

All of which was a roundabout way of realizing that N'kosi preferred to go his own way and Haviti to go hers. This found an increasingly introverted Valnadireb with little choice but to do likewise.

With Haviti having elected to travel northward, N'kosi decided to begin fieldwork off to the south. Utilizing one of the camp's rechargeable single-person scooters he would take off in that direction nearly every day, taking care to return well before sundown lest he find himself outside the perimeter after nightfall. The fact that the camp had not been attacked since it and its occupants had been abandoned by the Qwarm Araza was no reason for the three survivors to let down their guard.

Finding themselves confronted by technology that must have seemed like magic to them, it was possible that the spikers had decided to give the camp and its deadly perimeter a wide berth. Alternately, the extended assault on the village of the fuzzies might have weakened them to a point where additional local depredations would have to await reinforcements, or perhaps another season. Whatever the reason, Valnadireb and N'kosi had been able to go about their work without interference. Not only had the camp not been attacked anew, in the course of pursuing their respective fieldwork neither thranx nor human had seen so much as a single spiker or hardshell. Similarly, on his scoots southward N'kosi saw nothing but simple flora and fauna.

While studying the forest in the immediate vicinity of the camp, Valnadireb occasionally surprised a party of stick-jellies or wandering fuzzies. Despite his attempts to make contact, they invariably fled at the sight of him. He did not think it had much, if anything, to do with his appearance, which to the natives was no more outré than that of his human colleagues. More likely was the possibility that both groups had seen evidence of the camp's deadly defenses and had decided he and his friends were best avoided.

For the present, that suited Valnadireb just fine. Since he and his colleagues now had all the time in the world to pursue their individual interests, they could afford to lavish patience on the matter of indigenous contact. Let the local natives come to them if they wanted to try and communicate, he and N'kosi had decided in Haviti's absence, certain that upon her return to camp she would agree with the course of action they had chosen. There was no hurry. Not anymore. They could sit down and break bread with the fuzzies and the stick-jellies in the natives' own good time.

Meanwhile, Valnadireb immersed himself in the study of the forest. As an area of research it was as frustrating as it was rewarding. He did not try to persuade N'kosi to join him in the fieldwork. By the same token the human refrained from asking Valnadireb to accompany him on his daily trips south. It was a perfectly sensible division of labor. To a thranx, hot and humid defined ideal working conditions. While he did not find the climate at the coast uncommonly unpleasant, unpredictable sea breezes could and often did carry a chill. The same temperate climatological conditions that N'kosi found bracing left Valnadireb feeling irritable and wont to gnaw on the tips of his antennae.

They had settled into a routine. Every morning N'kosi would depart to study the oceanic shallows, narrow intertidal zone, and coastal biota to the south. Valnadireb would walk out of camp to explore the deep forest farther inland. In the afternoon the thranx xenologist would return to the camp's lab module to analyze, record, catalog, and give names to each day's new discoveries. N'kosi would invariably meander in later, his recorder stuffed full of precise notes and fantastic imagery, his collection containers brimming with new biological wonders.

What was the hurry? Valnadireb began to ask himself. Why the need, much less the rush, to record and register and index? In all likelihood no one would read his scrupulous notes until after he was dead—if then. Why was he making the effort to maintain the fiction that his meticulous daily efforts were in any way worthwhile?

As a consequence of such unavoidable thoughts something remarkable began to happen. The work of Valnadireb, knowledgeable and skilled thranx scientist and field researcher, began to slide. He continued to bring in specimens and recordings and discuss the findings of the day with his human counterpart. But while his outward enthusiasm was little diminished, the care with which he had always documented his discoveries started to show signs of indifference. N'kosi gave no indication that he saw anything amiss. Perhaps it was because he had become too wrapped up in his own work. Or possibly it was because he was experiencing some of the same symptoms of self-absorbed unconcern himself.

Valnadireb's fascination with the world on which they had been stranded grew with each new discovery even as he spent less and less time documenting them for posterity. What particularly held him in thrall was the seemingly endless parade of biological contradictions. So rich and diverse was the forest's flora and fauna that after a while he gave up mapping them using the standard field recording grid and took to just wandering through the woods that surrounded the camp.

"Not a good idea," N'kosi told him one night as the two were finishing up an evening meal together. "You should be using a scooter, like me. Even for going short distances. A scooter can carry heavier weaponry than you can on your person, more specimen containers, more analytical equipment, and if you have to make a run from something you've got a lot better chance of getting away clean on a scooter than you do on foot."

Sliding off his bench the thranx began to clean his mandibles, utilizing a special device for the purpose. Sometimes he no longer bothered to search for the traditional tool and improvised the necessary hygiene using a human fork.

"Though the scooter is comparatively quiet, it does make some noise," he contended. "And its presence is disturbing to many creatures. I thank you for your concern, Mosi, but I prefer to walk. I have not been attacked, there has been no sign of hostile behavior on the part of the local natives, and I find that I am more comfortable without the vehicle. It is one less thing to worry about. One less thing to worry about," he concluded, inclining his antennae in the human's direction, "means that much more time I can devote to my work, *irr!lk*. Now tell me true: do you yourself always stay so close to your transport?"

N'kosi shrugged and returned to his dessert. The main food preparation unit had become adept at devising dishes using locally gathered ingredients. The thick, cold paste the researcher was currently spooning into his mouth looked like blackberry pudding garnished with ground glass. The glistening crystalline seeds contributed crunch, and while they added nothing in the way of nutrition to the dessert, they dissolved harmlessly in the human digestive tract.

"Unless you're investigating or collecting macrolife, you really should move around more in order to get a proper sample."

"Exactly my point," Valnadireb declared. "The scooter's presence is restraining. I find it easier to focus on my surroundings in its absence."

N'kosi shook his head. "You're distorting my point to justify your own rashness. I make sure that I'm never so far from the scooter that I can't get back to it in a one-breath sprint."

Valnadireb gestured as he replied. "While thranx are not the sprinters that humans are, I assure you that I remain within an equivalently safe running distance from camp. So tell me then: which of us is safer out in the field? You, who make a daily journey down the coast of up to several kilometers? Or I, who stay within running distance of the camp itself?"

Finishing the last of his dessert, N'kosi put down the spoon and gazed across the table at his insectoid counterpart. "I'm just concerned about your well-being, that's all, Val. Because lately you don't seem overly worried about it yourself. Records show you returning to camp after dark on more than one occasion. You know how dangerous that is."

Light glittered golden off the thranx's compound eyes. "I know how important it is that we obtain samples and recordings of local nocturnal as well as diurnal life-forms."

N'kosi let out a bitter laugh. "Important? Important to who?"

"To those who come after us," the thranx replied quietly. "For those who will recover the records we will leave behind."

"*If* anyone comes after us!" N'kosi was on the verge of shouting. "*If* anyone can find this lunatic world ever again."

"Of course it will be found again. What makes you think it will not?"

"Oh, I don't know." Rising from his seat, N'kosi was rambling wildly now, throwing his arms around as energetically as any thranx but with considerably less exactitude of meaning.

"Maybe the fact that it's often recorded as being located at different coordinates? That it possibly blinks in and out of normal space?" He halted, staring at his friend and colleague. "You stay out collecting and recording after dark. Have you taken a good look at the night sky lately? It's not even just that some of the stars occupy different positions. They're not even the same stars!"

The thranx xenologist remained unruffled, his speech as calm as ever. It was one of the racial characteristics that had first induced humans to overlook his kind's appearance. No matter the seriousness of the circumstances, thranx rarely lost control of their emotions. It was not that they had none. They simply managed them better than did their frequently overwrought human allies. The inflexibility of their faces and concurrent inability to express feelings through facial expression contributed to the impression that they had complete mastery of sentiment. The only clue to a truly emotionally upset thranx was a frenetic waving of manipulative limbs.

"Commonwealth Science Central was aware that Quofum is subject to peculiar astronomical distortions. It may be that these are magnified by atmospheric or localized stellar peculiarities. I have confidence that no matter what the manifold vagaries of local conditions, our work here will not pass unacknowledged. Otherwise, why continue with it?"

Nodding vigorously, N'kosi lowered his arms and turned away from his colleague. His tone was grim. "That thought had occurred to me."

"If it has, and you hold to it with some degree of sincerity, then why *do* you continue with your work?" Antennae quivering like feathery tuning forks, Valnadireb folded both sets of forelimbs as he awaited his companion's reply.

Having given full vent to his frustration, N'kosi now responded with a weary shrug. "Simple. Because if it wasn't for the work, I think I'd go insane."

It was Valnadireb's turn to nod, a human gesture the thranx had long since adopted as one of their own. "An idle mind is like an unattended pupa. If ignored, it reverts to a vegetative state. In one way humans are fortunate. Though mental illness is not unknown among my kind, we tend not to go mad. When the illogicality of a situation becomes too overwhelming, we usually just kill ourselves."

Concerned and engaged once again, an alarmed N'kosi looked back at his fellow researcher. "Val, you're not . . . ?"

"No, *crriik*. Do not mistake detachment for psychosis. Here lately it seems that I am simply preoccupied much of the time. With the very research we have been discussing, if not always with documenting it."

"Okay. Okay, then." N'kosi began to sweep the dirty dishes and utensils into the gap in the center of the table where they would be received, cleaned, sterilized, and stacked on a bottom shelf for use again in the morning. "I just—I worry about you, that's all. Just like I worry about Tiare. I wish we'd hear from her."

"And I worry about the two of you." Valnadireb clicked his concern. "I'm sure Tiare is fine. She is in the skimmer, after all. Even if she does not do so, the vehicle automatically reports on its status every day. Each time I happen to check the relevant readout all its instruments are normal across the board. I am certain that when she finally returns the account of her travels will be full of entrancing discoveries." Pivoting on four trulegs, he started toward the right-hand corridor. "Right now, I have work of my own to attend to."

N'kosi called after his friend as gleaming aquamarine-hued

wing cases and abdomen receded out the doorway. "You're going out into the forest after dark again, aren't you?"

His friend's reply echoed slightly. "I am more comfortable and at home in such surroundings than any human, more aware of my environs, and I take ample care for my safety. When you sprout antennae of your own, then you can pass judgment on the wisdom of my actions, colleague."

Alone in the dining area, N'kosi's lips tightened. Was Valnadireb safer alone in the forest but close to camp than he was far down the south coast with the scooter close at hand? The real truth was one the xenologist preferred not to examine too closely, because it suggested that by going off and conducting research by themselves, on their own, neither of them was exactly behaving in a sensible and prudent manner. He did not dwell on the contradictions.

He had work of his own to do tomorrow.

The more time Valnadireb spent in the outlandish and unfathomable Quofumian forest, the more comfortable he felt in its alien surrounds. This was understandable. Time spent on any fieldwork naturally increases familiarity with a place. But it went deeper than that. He knew the feelings he was experiencing were not a consequence of having to work alone. Like many experienced field researchers he had grown used to spending long amounts of time by himself, even if he wasn't fully comfortable with it. The emotions that welled through him in the forest were an odd mixture of anticipation, expectation, exultation—and incipient revelation.

The latter sentiment was the most difficult to explain. Certainly every day, sometimes every hour he spent collecting and recording, revealed new species of flora and fauna. Yet no matter how many discoveries he made he could not escape the feeling that he was missing something much greater, something far more important. That there was one momentous breakthrough teetering right on the tips of his antennae, and every time he flicked one in its direction it fluttered back just out of reach. It would have helped if he'd had some idea what it was that he was seeking. But if he had known that much, then he would have known it entire.

All he could do was keep to the daily schedule he had set for himself. It was the same with his colleague N'kosi and, the thranx presumed, with Haviti. Perhaps one of them would make the syncretic breakthrough he sensed lay waiting to be unveiled. Humans had a way of making jumps in logic and reason that often eluded the more disciplined but less intuitive thranx. That did not keep him from continuing the search for a unifying rationale for what he was feeling.

On certain days it was hard even to contemplate something like an overarching theme, so rich was the forest in individual new discoveries. He had long since given up exclaiming over findings any one of which would have supplied sufficient material for an entire paper by one of his colleagues back home. It wasn't enough, for example, that the fungal spears he found growing out of a woody tree trunk were unlike anything in the applicable scientific literature. Despite their undeniably pseudofungal form, they had to go and sport tiny purple flowers. And the tree on which they were parasitic reproduced with cones that contained sporicites instead of seeds.

Quofum was not an ecology, he told himself as he wandered through a new quadrant of forest a kilometer or so from camp. It was a circus. Not a biota, but a riota. Every day he encountered and recorded contradictions bizarre enough to convince a senior researcher he was hallucinating. It was good that his studies were vetted and confirmed by his human colleague as well as the camp's AI unit or he would have begun to question his own sanity.

There was the ground-dwelling forest quadruped that clearly scavenged meat but had neither teeth nor beak. How then did it eat? An automated recording unit provided an explanation for the elusive creature's seemingly paradoxical behavior. Coming upon a choice bit of carrion, it extruded its stomach through a frontal aperture until it completely covered the rotting carcass. Secreting powerful gastric fluids, it dissolved the flesh and digested it on the spot. The thranx suggested "Insideouteater" for the common name, which an equally amazed N'kosi promptly placed in the records.

The ioe, to which the name was shortened, was by no means an extreme example of Quofumian fauna. Consumption was often carried out by anatomical designs that seemed more fanciful than practical. What was a sensible xenologist to make of a large herbivore that had two legs on one side and five on the other? How did perpetual lurching to the left enhance the animal's chances for survival? Nor was the forest-grazer the only example of what on any other world would have been classified as mutant structural asymmetry. There was the flying creature that boasted one wing shorter and stubbier than the other, the river-dweller whose limbs constantly backfinned in what appeared to be an attempt to keep it from moving its wriggling form forward, the arthropods who fought one another as often as they cooperated for the sake of the hive, and far too many more to mention.

N'kosi proposed a simple explanation. Evolutionary principles on Quofum were not merely skewed; they had gone insane. In the absence of damaging radiation from the planet's sun, its

interior, or highly radioactive rocks, there was no immediate explanation for the phenomenon. The pink-tinged atmosphere
was more than substantial enough to block or filter out gene-
altering cosmic radiation from deep space. Valnadireb felt that if
they could discover the answer to that question, they would
also gain the explanation for the greater one he could not quite
elucidate.

Thoughts of unifying biological theories and judicious explanations for explosive mutation and uncontrolled evolution
went out the window on the evening he returned from a typical
day of collecting specimens only to have N'kosi point out something strange on the side of his friend's abdomen.

A plant had taken root there. Or at least, it was making an effort to settle in. As a field researcher Valnadireb was used to
working in the proximity of potentially active parasites. With his
chitinous exoskeleton he was safer from such incursions than his
soft-skinned human companions, but he was by no means immune. And humans had the advantage of an epidermis flush with
sensitive nerve endings that was more alert to such incursions.

He felt no pain as a solicitous N'kosi helped to treat the affected area. A dose of general growth killer followed by an anti-
septic bath made short work of the would-be hitchhiker.
Together they examined it inside the analyzer.

"Fascinating." As he stared at the three-dimensional breakdown of the parasitic plant's interior, N'kosi adjusted a sensor to
give a more detailed reading.

"What on this world is not?" Valnadireb's exoskeleton was
not entirely devoid of feeling. The place where they had removed the parasite continued to itch. "It's just one more amazing example of how little on this world makes biological sense,
yet continues to thrive."

Though the parasite looked wholly plantlike and boasted long, attractive green leaves, its inner structure was unmistakably ossiferous. The connective tissue that enabled this seemingly contradictory construction was a wondrous blend of plant and animal, to the point where the two scientists studying it were unable to agree on its taxonomy. It was placed, as had been hundreds of previous inscrutable discoveries, in the continuously expanding file reserved for the unclassifiable.

What would it have done if it had succeeded in penetrating Valnadireb's exoskeleton and reaching the soft tissue within? Would it have spread throughout his system and eventually killed him? Or would it have been content, like more sensible parasites, to stay small and only draw from his body the minimal amount of nourishment necessary to survive?

From then on he paid more attention to himself as he explored the forest. It was quite all right for him to collect from it; quite another for it to collect him. Attempts by alien forest species to co-opt intruders were well documented from many worlds. To such creatures he was merely another tantalizing, wandering food source. As a scientist thoroughly versed in the relevant biology he took no umbrage at the growth's efforts to infect him. Attempts at parasitization were wholly random and only a threat to the inattentive or inexperienced.

If it was random.

Now you're thinking crazy thoughts, he told himself as he pushed through a thicket of tall, single-leaved growths with coppery metallic skins. Parasitism was always random, though certainly on Quofum nothing could or should be taken for granted. It was not as if the grown-bone life-form had been commanded to attach itself to him by some unknown, unimaginable intelligence. That made less than no sense.

But then, didn't this entire world? Was it necessarily crazy to contemplate the preposterous on a planet dominated by irrational evolution? Of course, there was one way to find out. He could allow himself to be parasitized. If not by the grown-bone, then by something even more persistent and advanced. He would not be the first dedicated scientist to study a parasitic life-form by deliberately allowing himself to be infected.

Despite his desire to know and his exhaustive quest for answers, he was not sure he was quite that dedicated.

His upsetting encounter notwithstanding, he continued to feel at ease in the forest. The next time one of its eager denizens took a stab at making a home for itself on his person he was ready for it and brushed it effortlessly away. On returning to camp he took especial care with his personal hygiene, making sure to sanitize himself thoroughly to prevent any kind of infection. Occasionally he was forced to deal with active predators as opposed to slow-moving parasites. Falling to precision bursts from his sidearm, these only added to the growing stock of specimens preserved in stasis at the camp.

But though the forest was unable to get a grip on his body, its wildly eccentric and diverse inhabitants and all that they potentially represented continued to prey on his mind.

Strangely, what appeared utterly outlandish during the day seemed to make more and more sense at night. The cautious cacophony of animal sounds grew almost familiar, an ever-changing alien concert he began to look forward to not only recording for an unknown posterity, but whose weird harmonic beauty often left him just standing and listening in admiration. The songs and squeals and hopeful hooted longings of the night welcomed him and drew him close in a way that more straightforward sight did not.

Though he worried about his friend and colleague's growing detachment, N'kosi said nothing. Absorbed as he was in his own work and as infrequently as he saw his fellow xenologist nowadays, he had little time to spare to play therapist to a thranx. In the absence of facial expression, it was often impossible to tell what his counterpart was feeling, much less what he might be thinking. But by noting and interpreting little hints and small signs, it was becoming increasingly clear to N'kosi that Valnadireb was spending altogether too much time in the great evolutionary experiment that was the Quofumian forest and not enough dealing with the rudiments of daily life in camp. Still, despite the suspicions that were growing in his mind based on the informal observations he could not avoid making, he said nothing. Did not refer to it at all.

Until one night Valnadireb failed to come back.

Fearing the worst, N'kosi set out to look for his colleague. Had the increasingly blasé thranx xenologist let down his guard to the point where he had been overcome by another parasitic life-form? Had he fallen prey to one of the forest's numerous active and unpredictable carnivores? Or had an emboldened group of aggressive spikers or hardshells caught him out after dark and insufficiently alert? The thought of losing half his remaining company, even if it was thranx, frightened N'kosi more than any predator he had encountered in the course of doing fieldwork down the coast.

Fortunately, whatever had prevented the thranx from returning to camp had not damaged his communit. Tracking its signal, N'kosi was able to home in on the beacon without difficulty. The fact that he reached Valnadireb in less than an hour was almost as unsettling as the thranx's overnight absence from camp. If he was not injured or taken prisoner, then why had he failed to respond to N'kosi's persistent queries? Something was not right.

He found Valnadireb sprawled across a surface root beneath a twisted nightmare of a tree. The branchless, upside-down growth thrust a single sap-coated bole skyward. In the absence of leaves, the upper quarter of its length was solid green. Looking like frozen fireworks, a spray of orange-hued surface roots exploded in all directions from the base of the trunk before plunging deep into the rich soil.

The thranx glanced up somnolently from where he was half asleep. "*Tch!!lk*, Mosi. You should be lying on a beach somewhere to the south, indulging in your kind's inexplicable penchant for relaxing in close proximity to water. What are you doing here?"

Still unsure whether to be relieved or concerned, N'kosi gazed down at the recumbent scientist. "More to the point, my friend, what are *you* doing *here?*" He pointed back the way he had come. "You didn't return to camp last night. You didn't answer my repeated calls. I thought the spikers might finally have picked you off." With a sweeping gesture he took in the forest surrounding them. "Or something else."

"I am fine, Mosi. Comfortable, even." On his left side, both truhand and foothand rose to gesture. "In the incomprehensible diversity of this place I have found solace."

N'kosi's gaze narrowed. "That's no excuse for not responding to a call. If I didn't know better, I'd say you were drunk."

"Intoxicated on information, perhaps." Using his trulegs to brace himself and maintain his position on the smooth-surfaced loungelike root, the thranx slid slightly to his right. "I turned off my communit to ensure that I was not disturbed. I'm sorry if this upset you. All you had to do was ignore me. I have no difficulty ignoring you." The triangular-shaped head swiveled almost a hundred eighty degrees before returning to face the staring human. "It is hard to believe that I was once afraid of this place. There are the known dangers with which we are both familiar and the unknown yet to be revealed, but the forest itself does not deserve to be feared."

An irritated N'kosi chewed on his upper lip. "You're coming back to camp with me, Val. I don't know if you need medication, or food, or to immerse yourself in an hour or two of mindless, stupid vit entertainment, but you can't stay here."

Golden-lensed ovals peered up at him. Were they slightly glazed? N'kosi could not be sure. With compound eyes, it was hard to tell.

"Why not?" the xenologist asked his human colleague.

N'kosi held his temper. "Because it's dangerous. Because the signs are becoming clear to me now. There's an ancient human saying for what I think is happening to you, Val. Goes all the way back to old Earth. You're at risk of going troppo. You need to get a bucketful of cold water in the face. Or that entertainment vit." He scrutinized the dense vegetation that surrounded them. "I'm glad you're comfortable here, but I won't let you take root. Something's going on here that we don't understand. Maybe if we persist we'll find out what it is. We surely won't if we 'free our minds,' as certain capricious philosophers say. We're dealing with rogue biology here, not spiritual enlightenment."

Valnadireb's gaze had not shifted. "How can you be so certain, Mosi?" Antennae flicked forward as truhands gave an eloquent flutter. "Humans are always so certain of themselves."

"I'm not certain of myself at all, Val. You know that. I'm a scientist. We're not allowed to be certain of anything." Advancing, he slipped both arms underneath his colleague's thorax and strained to lift. "Come on. Get up. Get off that root before you become one with it. I'm not leaving you here so I can come back in a week and find you covered in sprouted spores."

"But I'm *comfortable,*" Valnadireb protested.

"That," N'kosi informed him grimly, "is why I'm worried."

The human was bigger and stronger. Had Valnadireb really wished to resist he could have done so, kicking and striking out with all eight limbs. But his resistance was as lackluster as his attitude. N'kosi soon had him on his feet. With one arm around the thranx's thorax the human xenologist half guided, half hauled his colleague back to camp.

Once inside the habitation module Valnadireb seemed to come around. Emerging from a daze, a human would have blinked repeatedly. With a thranx, N'kosi had to resort to listening for subtle changes in pitch in his colleague's voice while watching for more active movement of his antennae.

"I—I'm sorry, Mosi." Valnadireb lay sprawled on his lounge in the dining area. "I was so relaxed, so at ease, that returning to camp seemed pointless. Superfluous, even."

Pacing back and forth next to his friend, N'kosi spoke while deep in thought. "If I didn't know better I'd say you had been hypnotized."

"By what?" Valnadireb looked up at his friend. "Plants? Mutant fungi? Silicate pseudosucculents? Wandering arboreals?"

"I don't know. Maybe hypnotized isn't the right term. Maybe seduced is a better definition."

"It won't happen again." Rising from the bench the thranx walked over to the wall where all the food service apparatus was mounted and drew himself a spouted beaker full of dark, honey-colored liquid. "I will continue my research, of course, but I will not stay out all night."

Coming up alongside him, N'kosi put a hand on his colleague's thorax, careful not to cover any of the gently pulsing breathing spicules. "How about not going out at night at all? Put nocturnal research on hold. At least for a week or two." He smiled. "It's not like you won't have adequate time to resume that particular area of study."

Valnadireb considered. The gleaming, valentine-shaped head turned to regard the human xenologist. "My memory is distressingly hazy. Was I really that far gone?"

N'kosi's reply was somber. "For a minute out there I thought I'd lost you completely. I considered stunning you and dragging you back."

The thranx nodded slowly, gesturing simultaneously with the truhand that was not holding the beaker. "So dangerous. So subtle. Such an insinuating environment. Very well. Your caution is well considered, Mosi. No nocturnal research for a while." Inflexible mouthparts prevented a thranx from smiling, but Valnadireb shaped the equivalent expression with animated movements of his hands.

"You promise? I'll be working down the coast as usual and I won't always be able to keep an eye on you."

Antennae stiffened. "I am not a larva, Moselstrom N'kosi. I can guarantee control of myself here as effectively as in a proper hive."

N'kosi nodded his understanding, indicating that his colleague's terse pledge was sufficient assurance.

It would have to be.

14

Despite the promise Valnadireb had given him, N'kosi could not keep from worrying about the state of his colleague's mind as he headed southward to continue his own work. So apprehensive was he that if not for one small matter on which he was most anxious to follow up, he would have stayed at camp just to watch over the thranx. That small matter, however, did more than draw him southward one more time down the coast.

It all but compelled him.

Several hours of travel on the scooter brought him to the temporary campsite he had established. He was relieved to see it was exactly as he had left it. The campsite lay at the extreme southern edge of the scooter's round-trip range. Neither native sentient nor animal had disturbed it in his absence. Not that there was much to disturb. Cobbled together out of driftwood, drift silicates, and other natural materials he had scavenged from the beach and the edge of the forest, the ramshackle lean-to resembled a shelter from pre-technology old Earth.

With its clipped-together plant-leaf roof flapping in the wind and its unmortared rock-and-shell lower walls, its function would have been immediately familiar to one of his own primitive ancestors.

Though not critical to his work, the shelter certainly added to his comfort while he conducted his local surveys and processed the specimens he acquired for the main camp's burgeoning collection. The impermanent walls of loose stone and harvested vegetable matter protected him from the occasionally gusty ocean breezes and the hot, humid winds that blew outward from the depths of the forest. The sandy-floored interior boasted a couple of crude workbenches and rough seats he had thrown together. While inadequate to pass muster at an artisan's gathering, they allowed him to work without having to sit on the damp sand or an exposed log. Used to relying on advanced technology to facilitate his toil, he was inordinately proud of having knocked something together with his own hands and a few simple tools. Still, he knew that his research would have progressed faster had he had the use of the skimmer.

On the other hand, if he had been the one utilizing that speedy, long-range transport, he might not have found the entrance.

The entrance to what, he did not yet know. He fully intended to share his discovery with his colleagues. But first he wanted to find out more about it. As yet there was little to describe scientifically beyond a dark hole in the ground. Well, not in the ground actually, he reminded himself as he left scooter and shelter behind and made his way into the edge of the forest that bordered the beach. More in a hillside than in the ground.

It was a short walk through the usual frantic Quofumian vegetation from the temporary shelter to the discovery site.

Small flying things darted at his face and buzzed his ears as he pushed his way through the brush. He waved at them and they dodged nimbly, whistling their outrage at his persistent refusal to let them land on and suck fluids from his exposed face. With half their ten-centimeter body lengths consisting of long, sharp-pointed snouts, he had no desire to study their feeding method firsthand.

Ten minutes after leaving the shelter and the beach behind he found himself once more standing before the opening. He had discovered it on his previous trip. Searching for some of the exotic Quofumian life-forms that absorbed, concentrated, and then secreted metallic compounds to form protective shells or body armor, he had been startled when the handheld scanner he had been using had unexpectedly gone borderline berserk. Hastily recalibrating the device and following its signal, he had pushed through the forest until he found himself confronted by the hole in the hillside.

It was not all that impressive. Approximately twice his height and width, the gap gave way rapidly to total darkness. Shining a light within revealed only a dark tunnel running straight into the hillside.

Of more immediate interest and the find that had drawn him back was the wide ring of black metal that framed the opening. It ought to have been overrun with vegetation. In-stead, it was completely bare and exposed, as if it had been installed yesterday—or regularly maintained. As neither expla-nation made any sense, he had come back in search of one. A gleaming, highly reflective charcoal-gray, visually the metal frame most nearly resembled a primitive ancient alloy called wrought iron. That it was something else entirely was confirmed as soon as he passed his field analyzer over it. The result was a readout best described as confused. As a xenologist whose focus was biology it was not surprising that he was unfamiliar with the initial readings. An experienced astronomer would have been quicker to recognize their significance, though they would have left him even more bemused.

The alloy of iron, chromium, and titanium was a signature indicative of a rare type of binary system known as an iron star. But the applicable reading for such stellar phenomena were always detected and recorded as emissions, not as a solid. It was as if the metal ring that framed the opening in the hillside had been forged from a particular type of stellar wind. Pure fantasy, N'kosi thought as he read through the analyzer's layman's description of what he had stumbled across. Except—he was looking at it.

And then there were the deeply embossed hieroglyphs.

At least, he assumed they were glyphs. They appeared too elaborate and too diverse to be the letters of an alphabet. There were hundreds of them, minute and perfectly stamped into the metal. If they were letters or characters, they far exceeded in variety the components of ancient Terran languages such as Chinese or ancient Egyptian. On his previous visit he had utilized his beam cutter in an attempt to excise a sample to take back to camp and show Valnadireb, reasoning that it was as important for his colleague to see the material itself as well as just a recording of the inscriptions. His advanced, high-tech tool would not score much less cut the metal. It would not even warm it. That also made no sense. The heat from the cutter had to go somewhere. Either the gray alloy was a heat sink of unique molecular composition or else there was another explanation that exceeded his limited knowledge of metallurgy.

Unable to interpret the hieroglyphs or take a sample of the

metal into which they were imprinted, he had returned to the site with fully charged long-lasting lights. At least he could explore the tunnel. He had also made certain to bring not one but two sidearms with him, both a beamer and a pulsepopper. The tunnel was too welcoming a potential habitat for it to have been ignored by Quofum's fauna, and he fully expected to encounter at least one imposing species as he explored its depths. He had no intention of doing so unprepared in case any current residents took exception to his trespass.

Yet as he advanced deeper and deeper into the passageway he encountered nothing larger than a few harmless, nonambulatory growths eking out a precarious existence on the walls and floor. Though fashioned of the same singular metal as the ring that framed the entryway, the latter were as smooth to the touch as glass. Soil or decomposing organic compounds that might have been expected to have been blown, drifted, or been dropped inside were utterly lacking. Clearly the impenetrable metal was not a hospitable environment for hardy fungi, or even bacteria.

The sensors on his scanner stayed flat, indicating a complete absence of radiation, heat, or other life-inhibiting factors. It was as if the tunnel walls themselves comprised a self-sterilizing environment on which nothing could grow. Nor did he encounter the hypothesized forest fauna that might have been expected to lay claim to such a splendid uncolonized habitat. In addition to life-forms, the tunnel was empty even of hieroglyphs.

Whether tired or not, he stopped every hour to rest, drink something, and eat a small snack to keep his energy level up. The circle of light that marked the tunnel entrance had long since shrunk into oblivion. At least he did not have to worry about taking a wrong turn. There were no side passages, no dark tributaries down which to stumble and lose his way. The perfect straightness of the corridor was almost as startling as its composition.

That it was artificial in origin was a conclusion he had reached long ago. As to who or what had created it and for what purpose he had not the slightest idea. The dark alloy itself corresponded to nothing in the extensive reference archives contained in his analyzer and communit. He remained as ignorant of its nature as he did of the meaning of the extensive glyphs that decorated the tunnel's entrance. Thus far the unmarked, unmarred corridor was nothing more than a horizontal shaft leading deep into the rippling range of low hills that constituted this portion of the unbroken surface forest's most notable geologic feature.

He had been hiking for a little over four and a half hours when his eyes sensed light that was not being given off by the glowbeam attached to his headgear. The faint radiance strengthened as he lengthened his stride. His analyzer confirmed that the light was of artificial origin, so it was not coming from outside. So he had not walked all the way through a hill or ridgeline. Soon it had brightened enough for his glowbeam to shut down automatically in response. He slowed. Though he was unaware of it, his lips parted and left him standing with his mouth slightly open.

Spread out before him was a subterranean panorama of tubes, conduits, relays, light-wave connectors, transmitters, siphons, spigots, emitters, electronic transposers, and a host of variegated apparatus and instrumentation he did not recognize. It appeared to go on forever. Trying to make sense of it all and to compare it to something identifiable, he found himself imagining all the pasta that had ever been produced and consumed by humankind transmuted suddenly into chrome and gold, tossed with a googol-plex of jewels, and then dumped in a vat of soup the size of Cachalot's world-girdling ocean. The technical spectacle sprawled out before him was simply incomprehensible.

He could see through the maze as far as his excellent distance vision allowed. Pulling a scope from his duty belt, he found that even at maximum magnification he could not discern the end of the complex. One unblocked lane allowed him an uninterrupted view through the serpentine maze all the way to the horizon. As near as he could tell, the tortuous byzantine meandering of cables and conduits and flashing lights extended not only to that horizon but beyond. How far beyond he had no way of telling.

He resolved to leave and return with the scooter. It would allow him to explore far more of this temple of connectivity than he could ever hope to see on foot. Unfortunately, the tunnel was too narrow to admit the skimmer. That restriction led him to ponder the lengthy but constricted corridor's purpose. A ventilation duct of some kind, perhaps. Knowing nothing of the size or shape of those who had bored the shaft, he supposed it might be wide enough to admit lesser craft intended for beings smaller than himself.

Despite the unending display of activity that continued to flash and flare before his eyes, there was no sign of whoever had built the visceralike network. Every time he saw motion, whether through the scope or just with his eyes, the source of the activity proved to be automata. Their method of propulsion was as enigmatic as their shapes, and he recognized neither. Blobs of liquid metal or plastic glided through the underground world as effortlessly and silently as if elevated by helium. Animated conduits and serpentine tools slithered like snakes or

waved back and forth like windblown plant stems until they
completed their own necessary connections and disconnects.
Solid transparencies drifted to and fro like so many preprogrammed jellyfish, dipping low or ascending ceilingward to execute designated tasks with bursts of intensely colored light.

More than size or sight, it was the abounding silence that
struck him most forcefully. So much activity, so many things going on at once, and all of it taking place in the absence of any
noise louder than a puff of displaced air or a fleeting electronic
whisper. The utter lack of clash and clamor bespoke a dearth of
friction, which in turn implied a technology sophisticated beyond that achieved by any humanx science. There was much
going on here, he told himself, and not all of it was visible. The
implications of what he was not seeing were more overawing
than the shapes and actions his optic nerves were able to define.

Who had built this place, and why? What was the function
of what appeared to be an endless subterranean ganglion of
tubes and electronics and devices he was unable to identify?
Why did thousands of lines and conduits and photonic tracks
disappear into the perfectly smooth, eggshell-white, highly pearl-
ized ceiling or into the equally featureless floor? All manner of
possible explanations raced through his mind, running into one
another, only to crash and burn on the bumpy, potholed field
of logic.

Whatever its purpose, whoever had built it had arranged for
it to be automatically maintained, cleaned, serviced, and possibly upgraded. A sudden thought made him glance down at his
wrist chronometer. He had been standing and staring in one
place for nearly half an hour. A full hour remained to him before he needed to start back up the tunnel in order to emerge
from its entrance in time to return to his makeshift beach camp

before dark. Not that he couldn't find his way back after dark—all he had to do when he stepped out of the metal-framed exit was turn right and keep walking until he reached the ocean. But he was mindful of the same advice and warnings he had forced on his colleague Valnadireb about roaming around in the forest at night.

What he was looking at now left him even less inclined than usual to engage in any nocturnal rambling.

He could not simply stand where he was on the edge of the tunnel and stare. No scientist in his position could do so and claim to be worthy of the name. In the absence of the scooter he would have to explore what he could as best he could on foot. Tentatively extending his right leg and putting a boot down on the seamless cream-colored floor, he took a step forward.

A pale violet luminescence immediately flared beneath the sole, spreading like ripples in a pond. Hastily he drew his foot back into the tunnel. Spreading outward in all directions, the ripples of embedded light faded away. His feathery imprint had generated no sound.

Bending his knee and bringing his foot up, he felt gingerly of the boot sole. It was perfectly cool to the touch. Taking a deep breath, he stepped forward once again. This time when the radiating light appeared beneath his foot he did not retreat. Bringing his other leg forward, he let all his weight rest on the vitreous, shining surface beyond the tunnel. It was as solid and unyielding beneath him as the metal floor of the corridor or the land outside.

Though the surface was solid enough, the ripples of light that flared outward in concentric circles of energy every time he put a foot down made him feel as if he were walking on water. Or more accurately, he corrected himself, on cream. And just

because he heard nothing, he reminded himself, did not mean
he was not making any noise. His footsteps and the dynamic
technology that now surrounded him could very well have been
generating frequencies beyond his plebeian human range of
hearing. Returning to this place with more sophisticated instruments for analyzing its surroundings would doubtless allow him
to answer many of the questions that were presently crowding
his mindspace for attention.

He set out on a relatively straight line through the hallucinogenic techno-tangle, relying on his communit's tracker to guide
him safely back to the tunnel in the event he lost sight of it. Looking over his shoulder, the black circle that marked the corridor's
location seemed as out of place in the all-glistening weird-wired
whiteness as a hippo on an iceberg. Though he had heard virtually nothing since leaving the tunnel mouth, his ears strained for
sound.

Deep caves were like this, he told himself. Deep and dry and
dead, they were places where the silence was so profound you
could hear your own heart beating. But though the pulse of energy and activity was all around him, he heard nothing beyond
the occasional tantalizing whisper of speeding electrons.

He estimated that he had hiked about a kilometer from the
end of the tunnel when the spheres confronted him.

There were two. Globular in shape with edges that were in
constant motion like the rim of a sun in the process of setting,
each was some two meters in diameter. They came rushing toward him from behind a trio of enormous discontinuous cables
that spiraled upward to tie floor and ceiling together with flicker-
ing blue filaments. Strain as he might, N'kosi could not see anything connecting the intermittent flashes of azure. Some kind of
energy field, he decided, was all that was holding them together.

He started to turn and run, hesitated, then decided to hold his ground. For one thing it was unlikely he could outrun spheres composed of nothing but light. If the approaching shapes wanted to run him to ground he felt certain they could do so easily enough.

Instead of making contact they halted a body length away, hovering in the air, featureless and refulgent. One was a deep pulsing purple, the other an intense throbbing orange. He could not escape the feeling that he was being scrutinized. Like everything else in the immense underground chamber they made no sound.

The confrontation or standoff or examination or however one chose to think of it (N'kosi considered all three and more) continued for several minutes, until the subject of the radiant inspection swallowed and said, as clearly and composedly as the situation and his emotions would allow, "Hello."

There was no reaction from the shimmering spheres. He repeated the salutation a little louder, also to no effect. Taking into consideration that an action should have an opposite if not necessary equal or even comprehensible reaction, he moved to his left with the intention of going around the purple sphere.

It immediately slid sideways to block his path.

This told the wary but fascinated scientist two things. First, the arrival of the spheres was not a coincidence but was directly related to and probably responsive to his presence, and second, hostility was not an initial reaction to his intrusion. His assumption was reconfirmed when he stepped back and attempted to advance in the other direction by going around the orange orb. Replicating the reaction of its darker companion, it too moved to block his path.

He pondered the possibilities. Was there something nearby

that was explicitly off-limits to intruders? Something a nonmachine was not supposed to see? Or by advancing this deep into the complex had he finally triggered some kind of automated response mechanism?

Studying the spheres, he doubted that they possessed the equivalent of high intelligence. They were pure automatons, part and parcel of his immediate engineered surroundings. No effort was made on their part to communicate. They had materialized, confronted him, and blocked his advance, but without any attempt at explanation. He was not being questioned and they exhibited nothing in the way of curiosity or active sentience.

Intelligent beings composed of pure energy had been mooted, of course, ever since the KK-drive had been developed and humankind had taken its first baby steps beyond the bounds of Earth. But no evidence for the actual existence of such creatures had ever been found.

That did not mean, he reminded himself, that their existence was an impossibility. It was just that nothing he had seen thus far inclined him to place the twin spheres in that category. They were closer kin to the other astonishing mechanisms surrounding him than they were to cousin Joe.

It was at the conclusion of this rumination that the orange sphere drifted forward and bumped him.

Contact was soft and cushiony, as if he had been nudged with a thick pillow. There was not enough weight or force in it to push him backward. This being the case and curious to see what would happen next, N'kosi held his ground. When he did not move, the orange orb advanced a second time. Impact was as gentle as before, only this time it was accompanied by a blast of heat. Startled, N'kosi stumbled backward a couple of steps and hurriedly looked down at himself. It felt as if a flaming torch had been jabbed against his solar plexus. There was no sign any such burning had occurred. The top of his jumpsuit was not even scorched. When he cautiously patted the fabric with his fingers it was cool to the touch.

Both spheres came toward him again. Indicating that he now understood their purpose and intent, he retreated several steps. When the orbs maintained their steady forward motion, he turned and started walking away from them. They followed, maintaining a constant distance behind him.

He was within a couple of hundred meters of the tunnel entrance when he whirled sharply and tried an end run around the purple sphere. This time it did not move to block his path. Instead, a crackle of violet lightning burst from its interior to intersect his chosen route. The faint smell of ozone tickled N'kosi's nostrils as he skidded to a halt and began to back up. Rapidly, this time.

The resident instrumentation, it appeared, was losing patience with the intruder. He decided it would not be a good idea to try and repeat the previous maneuver. Earlier intimations of mechanical pacifism notwithstanding, next time the potent electric discharge might be directed through him instead of merely in front of him.

By now he felt he had a pretty good handle on the events of the past hour. He had emerged from the tunnel to marvel at the seemingly interminable underground complex of connectors, links, energy beams, terminals, and Einstein knew what else. As long as he had remained within the tunnel his arrival had been ignored. Once he had stepped out into the room, which for all he knew and could tell or measure ran around the entire inside of the world, his presence had been noted. Appropriate automated apparatus had been dispatched to deal with him. That it had done so gently, if with increasing insistency, bespoke volumes for the conscientious nature of its builders. It would have been a simple matter to blast him to powder the instant he had set foot in the radiant white chamber.

The purple and orange spheres were the highly advanced equivalent of a couple of brooms charged with sweeping out debris that might find its way in from the outside. That they could probably have killed him, if only by enveloping him and depriving him of air, was a realization he committed to memory as decisively as anything he had seen in the endless subterranean chamber. That they *would* kill him if he persisted in his attempts to bypass them was a hypothesis he had no intention of testing further.

At least not by himself, equipped as he was with nothing more powerful than a pair of field sidearms.

Quofum's sun was just beginning to set when he emerged from the far end of the tunnel. He did not kiss the ground when he at last stepped from metal surface onto soil, but his respiration did slow. On the way out he had found himself looking back over his shoulder, half expecting to see a mass of purple or orange light coming up fast and angry behind him. The only danger the pair of patrolling orbs posed now, however, was to his imagination. The last he had seen of them showed their glowing forms receding in his wake as he had hurried away up the tunnel.

Out of sight, out of mind, he told himself. Or in the case of the spheres, once he had left the underground expanse behind, he had passed beyond their programmed awareness.

He reached his improvised beach camp before darkness could close in around him. There beneath the makeshift canopy of harvested native vegetation he replayed and studied the visuals and associated information his instruments had recorded. He had not dreamed it. It was all there: the perfectly smooth metal tunnel, the long walk in darkness, the resplendent and inexplicable underground chamber replete with incomprehensibly advanced technology engaged in unknown and possibly unknowable tasks, and the impassable spherical guardians. He replayed it as often in his mind as he did via the compact projector. Except for the spheres whose actions were not in question, he could not make sense of nor find reason or explanation for what he was viewing.

What were all those thousands upon thousands of energy beams, connectors, tubes, and transits doing in the ground beneath them? What, if anything, were they doing to the surface of Quofum? If he could not get past the patrolling orbs, how could such questions be answered? One thing he knew for certain, and without having to ponder it at length. There was far, far too much here to be interpreted or understood by one individual. It needed, it demanded, the attention of a full complement of Commonwealth researchers. Of an entire department, if such could be transferred. With a softly voiced command he shut off the recorder's projector.

In lieu of such inaccessible resources he would have to rely in addition to himself on the intelligence, expertise, experience, and, yes, the imagination of one female human and one thranx xenologist.

15

N'kosi had hoped upon his return to find a reenergized Valnadireb hard at work within the camp's laboratory complex. His mixed disappointment and concern at not encountering the thranx there was more than mitigated by the cheery salutation he did receive.

"*Iorana*, Mosi." Though she welcomed him with the ancient traditional greeting of her ancestral tribe, the smile that accompanied it struck him as more world-weary than content. He was not surprised. Quofum was a world that could be more than wearying, even for those who did not happen to be marooned on its chaotic, unnerving surface.

"How was your field trip?" he asked her as he drew himself a glass of cold distilled water from the nearby dispenser.

"Informative. Educational. Exciting at the beginning, exhilarating in the greater part, dispiriting at the end." She shut off the scanner she had been studying. "I found two more sentient species and spent time among one of them. They're as different from, say, the spikers and the fuzzies as we are from the stick-jellies. I also came across and recorded evidence of not one but two far more advanced civilizations, also different from anything we've so far encountered."

"Really?" He sipped from the glass. The cold liquid was rejuvenating. "How advanced?"

She looked at him uncertainly. His tone hinted at something unspoken. "One inland. Overgrown by forest. Probably pre-steam but making progress in that direction. The other on a spit of subsided land but remarkably well preserved despite being completely submerged. Far more advanced than the other, possibly to the level of extraplanetary travel but likely pre-Amalgamation."

He nodded, took another swallow, said nothing. Her expression narrowed.

"Pardon me, Mosi, I know we're all getting a little bit jaded by new discoveries here, but don't you find any of this the least little bit electrifying?"

" 'Electrifying.' " Interesting corollary, he mused, remembering the purple bolt the amethyst-hued sphere had spat to block his path. "Yes, I suppose I do. Congratulations."

"Gee, thanks." She made no attempt to mute the sarcasm in her tone. "And you've been doing what here while I was gone? I suppose you found a couple of lost civilizations, too?"

"No." He spoke quietly as he set the glass down on a nearby workbench. "Just one."

The matter-of-factness of his response took her aback, but only for a moment. "Well?" she prompted him impatiently when he did not continue. "What was yours like? Could it be a southern offshoot of one of the two I discovered?"

"Somehow I don't think so." He ran one finger lazily around the interior rim of the empty glass, staring at the contents. "What I found lies underground. How far it reaches and how big it is I can't say. The development extended beyond what the instruments I had with me could measure."

"Really?" In the scientific spirit of the moment her initial displeasure at having her own findings all but casually dismissed was set aside. "Estimated level of technological achievement?"

Raising his gaze from the glass, he looked across at her. "Beyond assessment."

"Beyond . . . ?" She gaped back at him. When she saw that he was neither drunk, joking, or under the influence of recreational pharmaceuticals, she pulled up a nearby chair and sat down. "What are you saying, Mosi? What exactly does that mean, 'beyond assessment'? I don't recall that being listed on the chart approved for determining the various levels of alien technosocial achievement."

He responded with a casual shrug and cryptic smile. "What I stumbled across, Tiare, is at least according to first impressions so far off the chart to which you are referring that a new one will be required to even begin to make sense of it."

She sat for a long moment, silent and thoughtful. Not unlike, he mused, much of the alien apparatus he had encountered at the terminus of the tunnel.

"I'm not sure I believe what you're telling me, Mosi," she declared finally.

Having anticipated this possible reaction, he nodded tiredly. "Come with me," he told her, "and I'll show you."

Later, after they had both watched the floating tridee presentation he had edited and put together in the course of half a day's work, she looked over at him as the final projection winked out and stated simply, "I'm sorry. I shouldn't have doubted you, Mosi."

He chuckled softly as he deactivated the projection unit. "Why not? I would have."

Leaning back in the lab chair, she put her hands behind her head and gazed contemplatively at the smooth pale curve of the ceiling. "Even more than who constructed it and how extensive it is, I find myself wondering what it's all for."

N'kosi nodded agreement. "That's why I didn't take the scooter and try to penetrate farther. Not just because those sweeper spheres would probably have tried to stop me, but because I felt right away that I would be in over my head if I tried to make sense of it all without someone else present to criticize assumptions, make alternative suggestions, or evaluate my hypotheses." Rising from his seat, he walked over to halt in front of her. "It was no place and no subject to try to define with hasty conjectures. I needed intellectual backup. I needed you and Val."

She nodded, then frowned. Sitting up straight, she looked around the room. "Speaking of Val . . . ?"

N'kosi sighed and gestured westward. "These days he spends more time outside the perimeter and in the forest than he does here in camp. One time while you were away I had to practically drag him back and delouse him. The thing of it is, he knows he's spending too much time out there." The xenologist licked his lips fretfully. "I really feel that if I didn't keep after him and force him to check in regularly he would simply sit down on a log or one of those peculiar silicate growths and let the forest take him."

Haviti blinked at her counterpart. " 'Take him'?"

"He'd become one with the woods, let himself be absorbed into it both physically and mentally. Of course, once he was absorbed physically that would be the end of him mentally. He keeps losing focus."

She rose from the chair. "Let's have something to eat. Can't think properly on an empty stomach. Maybe he's just tired."

Falling in step beside her, N'kosi nodded agreement. "If anything will jolt him intellectually and wake him up, it will be this new discovery of mine. For one thing, it's all underground." Gleaming white teeth, half of them artificially regenerated, flashed a broad smile at her. "Being thranx, he should be delighted to go wandering around the place I found. Certainly he'll be more comfortable down there than you or I. Who knows? Maybe he can even persuade the guardian orbs to let us probe deeper." Leaving the laboratory module, they crossed through the entrance dome and entered the residence area.

"Tell me, Mosi: what do you think it's all for?" she asked him. "Surely you've given it some thought. The vast underground network, all those tubes and light-links and connectors? Even if you've been waiting for my opinion and Val's you must have done some speculating by now." Reaching out, she put a friendly hand on his shoulder. "I know you well enough to know that you couldn't avoid doing so."

"Sure, I've given it some thought. Initially I assumed it was a habitat for yet another sentient Quofumian species, only one that was far in advance of anything we've yet encountered. But even though my progress was eventually halted by the spheres, I saw enough to soon realize that what I was looking at had nothing to do with tenancy. It was as if someone had built an enormous wired house and then removed the dwelling, leaving only the wiring behind." He gazed off into the distance, remembering.

"There were hundreds of kilometers of 'wiring,' probably

thousands, but nothing for it to be wired *to* except more of itself. A rat's nest without any rats."

She was a step ahead of him as they entered the dining area. "The vit you made showed hundreds of connections running from floor to ceiling, from subterranean sites toward the surface." He nodded, and she concluded, "Maybe that's what all that massive infrastructure is intended to link together."

N'kosi frowned. "The ground and the surface? Or something in the ground to something on the surface? To what end, Tiare?"

She shrugged. "Who knows? If we're going to find out we're going to have to examine at least some of the instrumentation in detail. That's if your colorful lightning-farting orbs will let us." She glanced around the deserted dining area. "All of us."

He nodded understandingly. "You too hungry to go for a walk? If I just call, Val may not answer. It wouldn't be the first time."

"Try," she suggested. "If there's no response we'll take the hike you're proposing and shepherd him back inside. He needs to see that vit you compiled." She turned suddenly wistful. "Science Central needs to see that vit, and every xenologist in the Commonwealth, but that's not likely to happen for a long time. If ever."

"All we can do is live for and focus on the here and now," he reminded her. "The future is going to have to take care of itself."

A reluctant Valnadireb did not want to return to camp. Though he protested that he was only following through on a normal day's fieldwork, N'kosi could see that the thranx was backsliding again. Just as he had told Haviti, it was plain that they could not leave him alone for several days at a time or their increasingly indolent colleague was likely to simply vanish into the forest, never to return. The next time he did so he might turn off or throw away his communit, making it impossible to find him.

Thankfully and as his friends had hoped, the vit of the subterranean world N'kosi had found seemed to snap the thranx out of his lingering lethargy.

"Unbelievable." As the last glimmer of the hovering presentation faded into the air of the lab, Valnadireb slid off the lounge on which he had been lying. Multiple lenses fixed on N'kosi. "But what can be the purpose, the meaning of so much sophisticated infrastructure? And who built it?"

"That's what I am hoping the three of us, working together, can find out," N'kosi told him. "We may have a more difficult time establishing the identity of the builders than the function of their instrumentation. While I was only allowed a little time for observation before I was eased out, I saw no signs of organic life. It may be that the builders are long gone and that the whole undertaking, whatever its intent, is entirely automated. Function, maintenance, upgrading, expansion—everything."

"Or," proposed Haviti, "the builders themselves may simply be elsewhere. On another world of this system, a different stellar location, or no more than a hundred kilometers distant from the place where you gained entrance."

He nodded energetically. "All questions to which we need to find answers."

"*Tch!lk.*" A newly excited Valnadireb semaphored with all four arms. "We won't learn them squatting here on our abdomens and pushing air." The thranx was truly reenergized. He turned eagerly to Haviti. "What is the skimmer's condition?"

"It's fine. All it needs is a recharge and a standard preflight check." She smiled, an expression as familiar to the thranx as his own hand gestures. "You'll come with us, then, and set your forest studies aside for a while?"

Truhands whisked through the air. "Mosi has found a whole other world. This one will wait."

Despite their impatience to return to the site of N'kosi's monumental discovery, they took their time stocking the skimmer. There was no telling what they might find or how long they would be away from camp. As for the facility that had become their home, it would maintain itself efficiently in the absence of any human presence. Water would continue to be purified, specimens and food and living quarters would be looked after and maintained, and the perimeter fence would continue to keep out curious or hostile natives.

The journey southward in the skimmer was more stimulating for Valnadireb than it was for his companions, both of whom had spent much of the previous weeks traveling up or down the coast. In deference to the thranx's innate unease N'kosi piloted a route that kept the craft inland and as far away from the sea as possible without wasting too much charge on the detour. Though well out of sight of the coast he had no trouble zeroing in on his provisional campsite, having equipped it with a small locator beacon on the day he had originally completed the crude shelter.

Though both of his companions were anxious to set out for the tunnel, N'kosi insisted they pause long enough to eat a regular meal. Not knowing what awaited them underground, the opportunity to dine might not present itself again for a while. Back at main camp they had taken the time prior to departing to ensure that the skimmer was fully charged. It would be irresponsible not to do the same for themselves.

"All right, Mosi." Haviti had risen from the peculiar twisted log that had served as a bench. "I'm rested, I'm hydrated, and

I'm full." She checked to make sure every instrument was in place on her utility belt and that her cap recorder was on. "Time to see this subterranean wonderland of yours."

"Believe me," he told her as he exited the interim shelter and took the first steps inland, "I'm as anxious to see it again as you are to do so for the first time."

For once, none of them slowed or paused to study the multifarious life-forms of the captivating Quofumian forest. While they did not entirely ignore novel sights or sounds, colorful new flora or outlandish alien fauna, their thoughts were focused elsewhere. On something bigger, Haviti found herself thinking. On something of far greater import.

Based on the vit she had watched of N'kosi's discovery, an unknown intelligence had gone to an enormous amount of trouble and effort to undermine at least a portion of the very forest through which they were presently hiking with an immensely intricate ganglion of electronics and automata. To what purpose, she and her companions hoped to learn. As they strode deeper and deeper into the alien woods she found that her respiration was starting to come in shorter and shorter breaths, until she was almost gasping for air. The cause was excitement, not the gentle upward slope they were following.

Easy, she told herself. Hyperventilation would exhaust her more quickly than slow and regular breathing.

The tunnel entrance was exactly as N'kosi had described it and as his vit had shown it. The dark metal shaft pierced the solid rock of the hillside as neatly and cleanly as an antique hypodermic slid into flesh. Detecting and reacting to the darkness, two sets of cap lights and one thranx head flare winked to life automatically when they entered.

Striding excitedly down the smooth-floored corridor, Haviti

was struck by the perfection of their surroundings. The soft pad-pad of their boots on the alien alloy underfoot contrasted melodiously with the percussive clicking of Valnadireb's unshod chitinous feet.

When he had explored the tunnel by himself, N'kosi had proceeded with understandable caution. Having a known destination in mind this time, the three colleagues made much more rapid progress. The first glimpse of light at the end of the passageway impinged on their retinas barely two hours after they had entered.

They slowed deliberately. Advancing with caution while trying to make as little noise as possible, they approached the egress. N'kosi looked on with satisfaction as an expression of awe and disbelief came over Haviti. Valnadireb's antennae inclined forward as the thranx strained for the utmost perception of their immediate surroundings.

Everything was as N'kosi remembered it: the enormous underground chamber stretching off into the unplumbed distance, the flashing and blinking channels of intense radiant light, the softly pulsing tubes and conduits and cylinders that linked ceiling to floor and to one another like some immense synthetic spiderweb.

Haviti swallowed. " *'E mea maitai roa,*" she whispered in her family's ancient language. "It's fantastic. Recorded images can give the appearance, but no way can they begin to convey the scale."

Standing alongside her on four trulegs, Valnadireb gestured with a foothand. "This is indeed vaster than I imagined, despite Mosi's strenuous attempts to convey the expansiveness. The mere sight of it proclaims it incredibly sophisticated, immeasurably advanced, and extraordinarily well maintained." His left antenna flicked back over his head while the right dipped forward. "But the biggest question remains. What is it all *for*? What does it *do*?"

N'kosi started forward. "Let's have a look and see if we can find out."

As she paced him, Haviti found herself looking around uneasily. "What about those guardian globes?"

"All we can do is try to be as quiet and work as inconspicuously as possible." He singled out a dense conduit consisting of layers of light pulses that sped in opposite directions between two glowing sheets of foil-thin metal. "Why don't we start by analyzing this small energy flow here? Readings of strength, speed, and composition should tell us something."

While Valnadireb and Haviti unpacked equipment, N'kosi kept watch. Having encountered the sweeper spheres in person, he felt he might be more attuned to their approach than his newly arrived companions. At the first sign of the sentinel orbs they would pack up their equipment and race back into the tunnel.

The more time that passed and the longer they were left alone, the more accurate and detailed the readings his companions were able to take. The only trouble was, they were not making any sense.

Rising from where they had been crouched around the conduit, Haviti and Valnadireb compared readouts and personal notes. Her expression and tone reflected her confusion.

"These don't make any sense." She was holding her analyzer up next to Valnadireb's. "For one thing, they're way too high." She nodded in the direction of the energetic conduit whose continued existence and ongoing functionality blatantly belied her comment. "It's not possible to contain that much energy in so confined a space."

"There may be methods of compression of which we are

unaware and are therefore incapable of measuring with our instruments. Indeed, such appears to be the case," Valnadireb opined.

She eyed him dubiously. "You don't compress energy in a coherent beam beyond what that beam is capable of containing." Once again she pointed toward the conduit. "That's a perfectly ordinary, visible flow, not a seep from the heart of a neutron star."

"Still," Valnadireb started to argue, "it is theoretically possible that . . ."

Neither of them being physicists, it was unlikely that the disagreement was going to be easily resolved to their mutual satisfaction. It did not matter, N'kosi knew. At least, it did not matter now. Having materialized in the distance, the orbs he had just detected at the limit of his vision were definitely coming their way.

This time there were five of them.

Two were purple, two orange, and one a bright, almost cheerful turquoise hue. Even as he spun to alert his companions he found himself wondering at the significance of the different colors. Were they indicative of specialization? Individual powers? Rank? He had no intention of lingering to voice the question.

Haviti and Valnadireb hurriedly reassembled their gear. Turning, the three visitors broke into a sprint back the way they had come. Looking over his shoulder, N'kosi saw that the quintet of glowing globes was not gaining on them. That in itself was odd. One would expect that should they desire to do so, spheres composed of pure energy could accelerate at speeds no creature of flesh and blood could match. On the other hand, he told himself, there was no especial reason for the guardian orbs to hurry. It was evident that within the complex nothing was beyond their ken, and therefore there was no place for intruders to hide.

He and his companions could run partway up the tunnel
back into blackness, wait for the guardians to grow bored or
move elsewhere, and then try to enter the complex again. It was
a sensible, conservative plan of action. One he and his colleagues
had worked out prior to making their initial entrance. One that
took into account everything he had observed and recorded on
his previous visit. One that he had presumed would account for
everything.

Unfortunately it did not take into account the possibility
that the way out might be blocked.

The sentinel orb that hovered in front of the tunnel entrance
pulsed a deep, ominous magenta. Its lambent fringe extended
beyond the edges of the tunnel as well as below the base and
above the ceiling. There was no room, no space, to squeeze between it and the wall and into the metal shaft. Haviti looked
back. The five other spheres were drawing close. They displayed
no signs of impatience. There was no reason why they should,
she realized. She and her friends were trapped.

Given the existing options, she did not hesitate. Neither, she
saw out of the corner of an eye, did Valnadireb. Drawing their
sidearms almost simultaneously, they took aim and fired at the
center of the dark reddish sphere that was blocking their only
way out. While the thranx wielded a pulsepopper, she employed a more conventional beamer. From the muzzles of both
weapons, fire, as diverse as it was destructive, lanced out to strike
the sphere.

A pair of small circles appeared on the lustrous curvilinear
surface where their shots struck. These briefly glowed a more
intense color than the surrounding area. Then they faded.

N'kosi had his weapon out and was now firing also. The ag-
gregate effect of their combined attack was to produce three

ephemerally glowing circles on the surface of the sphere instead of two. Recognizing the futility of the assault, Haviti holstered her weapon. Stepping forward, she attempted to squeeze herself between the tunnel wall and hovering sphere. Making contact with the orb, she let out a yelp of pain and drew back sharply, grabbing at her left side. Looking down, she expected to see scorched fabric and burnt skin beneath her clutching fingers. Instead, there was nothing. She and her clothing were both unscathed.

Except for her exclamation of distress and the sound of her companions' weapons repeatedly discharging, the entire confrontation was played out in complete silence.

Slowing to a halt behind them, the quintet of multicolored orbs had formed a line blocking any retreat in that direction. The three scientists were now well and truly trapped between the five spheres they turned to face and the larger one that continued to block the entrance to the only exit. Instinctively, they crowded closer to one another. Valnadireb's natural perfume was stronger than ever. Haviti kept glancing down at her side, still not quite able to accept the fact that her body and clothing showed no evidence of the searing sensation she had experienced on contact with the shimmering magenta globe.

"Why aren't they crowding us out?" She found herself whispering without knowing why. "You said the two that blocked your path before pushed you out."

"I don't know," he muttered apprehensively. "I don't know, but at the moment I'm glad they're not." He indicated the five orbs that continued to hover in a glowing line before them. "If they were pushing, we'd be squeezed between them and the one you touched."

Valnadireb did not whisper. "You're certain, *trr!lk*, they are not intelligent?"

"I'm not certain of anything." N'kosi shook his head. "I didn't see any conclusive signs of it before, and I don't think I'm seeing it now. They act more like devices than sentients." He looked to his right as Haviti let out a sharp, nervous laugh.

"Toilet plungers. That's what they are. And if that's the case, then we are simultaneously redefined."

"Take it easy." Without thinking, he put an arm around her shoulders. As a gesture it was mildly condescending, but she made no move to shake it off. "They're not exhibiting aggression."

"Perhaps trying to decide what to do next." Skittering to his left, Valnadireb attempted to dart around the outermost orange sphere. It did not move to block his path.

N'kosi frowned. "That's strange." His arm still around Haviti's shoulders, he tugged gently. Keeping a careful eye on all the guardian spheres but most especially on the leftmost orange one, the two humans mimicked the action of their thranx colleague. As with Valnadireb but unlike on N'kosi's previous visit, the orbs did not move to intercept.

The three of them found themselves standing, untouched and unharmed, behind the six spheres. The way into the depths of the incredible subterranean complex was open and unblocked. They could not really revel in their achievement for the simple reason that the only way back to the surface was still barred.

"What now?" N'kosi wondered aloud.

Slipping free of his arm, Haviti studied the line of spheres for a long moment. Then she turned to let her gaze rove free among the fantastical technology that filled her line of sight as far as she could see.

"There's an old saying among my family. If the current is too strong to paddle against, go with it. If you are lucky, it will swing around and take you back to where you want to go." She started off into the complex. N'kosi and Valnadireb were barely a step behind her.

Hardly a moment or two had passed when Valnadireb announced, "They're following." A glance backward revealed that the half-dozen multihued spheres were indeed trailing the intruders. As she recalled the pain of contact with the dark red orb, Haviti experienced a surge of anxiety. She worked to mute it. They could do nothing about the spheres. Only do their best, by exerting considerable effort, to ignore them.

"They're not bothering us," she noted apprehensively. "Maybe if we don't bother them, or damage anything, they'll just observe and leave us alone."

N'kosi frowned, trying to make sense of it all. "Then why did they push me out before?"

Valnadireb made a joke his pre-Amalgamation ancestors could never have imagined, so alien had they originally found human beings. "Maybe they're all male guardian spheres, and they're more interested in keeping Tiare around than they were you."

It raised a smile on the faces of both humans, one that in the context of the moment was invigorating as well as welcome. "Well, it won't do them any good," a somewhat less uneasy Haviti declared. "I don't go out with radiant orbs."

"Shame," N'kosi chided her, trying to join in the heartening spirit of the verbal byplay. "Shape prejudice has no place in Commonwealth society."

"All right then," she corrected herself. "I don't go out with *nonsentient* radiant orbs."

Having succeeded in lightening the mood, however slightly,

Valnadireb turned serious once more. "Do you think they have individual AI, or are they controlled by a central source?"

"Impossible to say." Halting, N'kosi began fumbling with the equipment attached to his utility belt. "If we're lucky, maybe we can pick up something like a recognizable carrier wave. One that is passed from sphere to sphere, or from sphere to somewhere else." He indicated a row of what looked like clear glass ovoids standing off to their left. Three meters in diameter, each massive egg shape pulsed with light. Their interiors were furious, seething clouds of glassy multicolored shards speckled with fiery dots of dancing plasma.

"Meanwhile, let's see if we make some sense of that display." He glanced at the hovering sentinel orbs. "It will be useful to see if our guardians allow us to proceed with our work."

Valnadireb looked the nearest ovoid up and down, his valentine-shaped head bobbing on his short neck. "It could be some kind of energy pump. Or highly advanced composter. Or anything in between."

Keeping a wary eye on the six drifting orbs, they began to break out the instruments necessary to take the measure of the pulsating alien ovoids. Clustering behind them, the spheres formed a tight semicircle a modest distance from the visitors. The space separating each from its neighbor, Haviti noted, could not have varied by as much as a millimeter.

Eyeing them charily as she began to set up her own equipment and despite what N'kosi had said about their perceived lack of independent intelligence, she could not escape the feeling that the shimmering orbs were engaged in an intensive examination of their own.

16

As the day wore on, the two humans and one thranx accumulated a body of information and recordings a small portion of
which would have been sufficient to astound the most venerated
gathering of scientists the Commonwealth could muster. No matter where they went, no matter what they did, the silent glowing
orbs did not interfere. They followed, and in their own singular
eyeless way doubtless observed. But they did not interfere.

However, when individual chronometers indicated that it
was well past nightfall on the surface outside and the trio of visitors attempted to leave, they once more found their way
blocked. Not at the tunnel entrance this time, but the very route
leading toward it. Their freedom of movement to go forward
was in no way restricted, but the energetic spheres resolutely refused to allow them to retrace their steps back the way they had
come for more than a few meters. When Valnadireb tried to
make a quick dash around the outermost orange orb, it swiftly
darted into his path to cut him off. Fleeting contact was made.

Like Haviti before him, the thranx was subjected to the same sharp burning sensation. And as had been the case with the human female, he incurred no actual physical damage as a result of the brief convergence.

"They're herding us," Haviti mumbled unhappily as she sat down on the narrow path that ran straight as an arrow between clusters and ranks of gleaming, incomprehensible instrumentation. "Forcing us farther and farther away from the exit."

Plumping his daypack into a pillow, N'kosi stretched out on the floor nearby. "It's too early to be jumping to those kinds of conclusions. We've only been here for part of a day. It's light but it's late. Let's try to get some sleep." He squinted at the omnipresent luminosity that filled every square meter of the never-ending underground space. "Put a collection cloth or something over your eyes and try to turn off your thoughts." He forced a smile. "At least the noise won't keep us awake."

"*Tch!lk,*" Valnadireb concurred. "It has been an eventful day. We have accomplished much, learned much. The mind needs rest as well as the body. When we reawaken we can turn our renewed energy to devising a means of circumventing our persistent escort."

Haviti was certain she would not be able to fall asleep under such conditions and such stress. Her fatigued body was equally certain she would have no trouble doing so. Somewhere between the two extremes of certainty, truth emerged, so that she eventually did fall asleep but tossed and turned while doing so. The hard, unyielding floor was probably as responsible for her uneasy slumber as was any mental distress.

When they awoke, almost simultaneously, the six spheres were still there. Hovering, Haviti saw, and watching, she was sure.

Wordlessly, the three scientists sat and consumed a quick breakfast, thankful for the technology that made self-heating food and self-cooling drink easy and portable. The meal concluded, they rose to resume their research. This time, instead of advancing deeper into the underground complex, they restricted their studies to their immediate surroundings. The last thing they wanted was to be pushed farther into the facility so that they ran the risk of not being able to find their way back. The locator signals from both N'kosi's temporary camp and the skimmer had been lost, though whether this was due to direct interference by the guardian spheres or the insulating properties of the complex itself, they could not say. It was vital they travel no farther from the metal-lined tunnel than they already had.

Thankfully, the attendant orbs showed no inclination to force them deeper into the underground world. They were not being "herded," then, despite Haviti's oversensitive remark of the previous day. They were simply not being allowed to leave—yet. N'kosi remained hopeful.

The seriousness of their situation did not begin to really hit home until days later, when they started to run out of food. Despite the low humidity within the complex, drink remained available via the emergency portable condenser N'kosi had brought with him. But unlike water, they could not conjure sustenance out of thin air.

Already weakened from having spent the preceding day on reduced rations, Haviti chose a moment when she thought the spheres were at their least attentive to try and dash around the attentive semicircle of hovering incandescent globes. She might as well have tried to outrun a beam of light. As soon as she broke in the direction of the tunnel one of the purple globes

darted sideways to block her path. Anger and frustration contributed to poor decision-making. This time she did not brush
the sphere but ran straight into it.

The fiery shock of contact knocked her to the floor.

As she lay there on her back, crying, Valnadireb crouched at
her side while a concerned N'kosi helped her to sit up.

"We're not going to get out of here," she sobbed softly.
"Never. They're not going to let us go. Whatever 'they' are."

Fumbling within his pack, N'kosi pulled out a square of ab-
sorptive synthetic and handed it to her. She used it to give her
eyes and nose a couple of desultory wipes.

As a species, Valnadireb's kind were no more fatalistic than
humans. But he had started to prepare himself.

"It is a possibility we must face." Looking up, he shifted his
gaze from his colleague to the hovering spheres. "If only we
could establish some kind of contact, explain that we can't survive on air alone and that we have to be allowed to leave. We
could even take them with us as insurance against our return."

If by voicing his anxious thoughts out loud the thranx
hoped he might inspire some reaction in the glowing orbs he
was mistaken. More than ever, their utter nonresponse to what
amounted to a desperate plea confirmed their nonsentient
status.

After a while N'kosi and Valnadireb helped Haviti to her
feet. They suggested finishing the last study they had begun.
She waved them off, no longer interested. In her own mind she
and her companions, her friends and colleagues, were already
dead.

Several days later they nearly were—the key descriptive being "nearly."

One by one each of them lay down and stretched out on the

smooth, porcelain-white floor, ostensibly to rest. Haviti and N'kosi on their sides, Valnadireb on his abdomen. Nothing was said, no words were spoken. None were necessary. As xenologists whose general specialty was biology, albeit alien biology, they each knew full well when their own bodies were failing. Eyes were closed. Breathing grew shallow.

For a long while nothing happened. The only sound in that part of the whole unimaginably vast underground complex was the increasingly feeble breathing of the three offworld visitors.

Then the glowing, gently pulsing spheres began to move.

When Haviti woke up the first thing she wanted to do was scream. Only when she realized that the hundreds of hair-thin tubes and lightwire filaments running in and out of various parts of her naked body were causing her no pain was she able to stifle the rising panic that threatened to overwhelm her. And there was a second factor that served to mitigate the initially horrifying sight.

She felt wonderful.

In fact, she felt better than she had in weeks. Gone not only was the gnawing hunger that had overcome her and rendered her unconscious, so too was the despair and the stress of fearing she would never again see the light of day. As she sat up she realized that might still be the case, but somehow it no longer bothered her nearly as much.

A sharp stridulation nearby announced Valnadireb's awakening. The noise stopped as he stilled his wing cases and glanced around. Looking at her colleague, Haviti was able to see how precisely his body had been penetrated and pierced by the multitude of fixed lines and beams of coherent light. There was no bleeding, no seepage of bodily fluids. Peering down at herself, she could see no marks or scars, no signs of alien surgery. Tentatively, she reached down and pulled ever so gently at one of the hair-thin cables that protruded from her stomach. She felt only the mildest of tugging sensations, less than if she had pulled on and popped the knuckle of one finger. Bravely, she pulled harder on the strand. It would not come loose and the mild discomfort did not intensify.

She tried to grab one of the lightwires. As her hand passed through the pale yellow beam, she experienced a slight tingling sensation in her clutching fingers. At the same time, nausea flared in her gut. Hastily, she drew her hand back. Both the tingling and the nausea went away.

Filaments disappeared into her belly and chest, her back and legs, arms and feet. Several sprouted from opposite sides of her neck. Her head was unadorned, a fact for which she was unreasonably grateful. After all, with the rest of her body exhaustively and apparently irreversibly entangled, what mattered another line or two running from her skull? But she was thankful for the omission nonetheless. She thought she might try to stand up.

She was shocked when the exertion proved almost effortless. The hundreds of lightwires and lines and cables helped her up. With the intention of seeing how well her nutrition-starved muscles were working, she took a little jump. A small gasp escaped her lips as she rose all the way to the ceiling before dropping back to the floor. Her bare feet made contact with the slick, lustrous surface as lightly as if she had been no more than a feather.

Possibly it was at that point that she first became fully conscious of her nakedness. Or perhaps it was immediately thereafter, when a voice complimented her on the comely and effortless leap.

"Nicely done."

Looking to her right she saw Moselstrom N'kosi standing in front of the row of ovoids that were the last component of the underground complex she and her companions had been investigating. Though he was equally naked she neither blinked nor turned away. As a general rule scientists did not suffer from nudity phobias. Valnadireb, of course, never wore anything more than utility belt and packs.

"You look better without clothes," N'kosi added. Mastery of scientific detachment notwithstanding, Haviti felt herself blushing slightly. But then, why shouldn't Mosi be direct? They had nearly died of starvation only to find themselves revived and—and what? Bound, experimented upon, entwined with strange devices? What had happened to them? What had been done to them?

Valnadireb ambled toward her. Cables and lines followed him, trailing behind. Studying them, she found herself wondering how much range of movement she and her companions would be allowed. Keeping his truhands folded in front of him, the thranx gestured with both foothands.

"We have been given new life by these machines." With a truhand he gently lifted one of the thin lines running from his thorax. "I think there is no question but that they have provided us with sustenance, adequate hydration, and quite possibly a good deal more."

N'kosi proceeded to duplicate Haviti's ten-meter vertical jump. "I don't think you'll get much argument on that, Val," he murmured when his feet hit the floor. The xenologist looked down at himself. "I'm assuming that our clothing was in the way of the procedures that were performed." One hand tugged on a metallic thread that emerged from the vicinity of his spleen.

"I'm starting to think that the alterations, adjustments, and modifications necessary to save us are more than temporary."

Haviti pursed her lips. "I don't understand. Why bother with us? Why interfere? Why not just let us die? We're intruders in this place." She turned a slow circle. The lines and cables running from her body adjusted themselves to turn with her. "The guardian spheres are gone, but we're still here."

Valnadireb speculated aloud. "Perhaps we are no longer perceived as a potential problem."

"We'll only find the answer if we look for it." Starting forward, N'kosi resumed walking deeper into the complex. No pulsating radiant orbs materialized to guide his path. Looking back at his friends, he smiled.

"Come on. If we're lucky, maybe we'll get to see what's on the other side of the proverbial mountain."

The guardian spheres never showed themselves again.

By that afternoon one of the questions that had been burning at Haviti had been unambiguously answered. No matter how far they walked there always seemed to be enough cable and line length to allow them ample range of movement. Whether these were the original threadlike connections or whether they were being passed from one link to another, she could not tell. Looking back, the slender filaments always appeared seamless and unbroken.

Having been stripped of their chronometers and gear and in the absence of daylight, they were unable to tell with certainty how much time passed, but it was agreed among the three of them that the better part of a day had gone by when they finally chose to call a halt.

"Notice anything?" N'kosi was grinning over his tangle of threads.

Haviti and Valnadireb exchanged a glance. It was the thranx who replied, gesturing surprise as he did so. "I am not hungry or thirsty. I have not felt any such urges since I awakened."

A look of amazement came over Haviti's features. "Neither have I." She looked down at her elaborately wired self. "I don't know how or with what, but we're being fed."

"And kept healthy," N'kosi surmised. "And who knows what else?"

"But to what purpose?" Valnadireb marveled at the alien life-support system with which he had been involuntarily integrated.

N'kosi's smile faded. "I don't know. Maybe we've been prepared to be the human equivalent of lab rats and are to be subjected to study by an as yet unknown sentience—Quofumian, cybernetic, or otherwise. Maybe keeping us alive is nothing more than untainted automated altruism." Lifting his gaze, he nodded at the way forward. "Maybe if we just keep going, we'll find out."

Haviti would have shuddered at several of the prospects her friend's conjectures called to mind, only—she felt too good. Was whatever intelligence that was sustaining (she refused to think "maintaining") them supplying their bodies with more than just nourishment? A steady injection of synthesized endorphins would go a long way toward explaining her persistent sense of extreme well-being. But how would an alien intelligence, artificial or otherwise, know about human endocrinology? For that matter, how did it know what kind of nutrients they needed and in what quantity to supply them? It was clear she and her friends were dealing with a biotechnology knowledge base that was easily the equal of the astounding physical engineering they had already encountered. Where did it come from? Had it originated on Quofum, or elsewhere? And most important of all . . .

What did it want from them?

For days, then weeks, they explored the endless underground complex. Freely and without hindrance, the hundreds of lines and cables and lightwires somehow roamed freely with them. Haviti counted two hundred forty-three entering or emerging from her own body. In the course of their wandering they stood on the edges of immense chambers crowded with incomprehensibly advanced machinery and tried to puzzle out their purpose. Once, they found themselves wading waist-deep through a shallow lake of considerable extent. A simple check revealed that the liquid was not water but a soupy brew of glutinous proteins and other organic matter existing in a continual state of disintegrating and recombining. The tepid fluid had no effect, detrimental or otherwise, on their respective tangles of manifold connectors.

Later (weeks later, months later—Haviti could no longer tell) they found themselves standing on the rim of an enormous open space, an artificial underground valley crisscrossed with horizontal tubes and conduits some of which exceeded in diameter that of the average starship. A multitude of brilliantly refulgent geometric shapes darted and flashed throughout the colossal chamber, efficiently executing tasks whose purpose was as unknown as the mechanisms they serviced. Standing on the barrier-free edge looking out over incomprehensible vastness, Haviti found that she was still capable of being staggered by the scale of the subterranean alien technology.

Out of the corner of her left eye she saw N'kosi take a long stride forward and deliberately step off into emptiness.

"No!" She and Valnadireb rushed toward him, but they were already too late. Then they both stopped, and stared.

Pivoting gracefully in midair, a smiling N'kosi looked back at them. "Since nothing we have experienced or seen so far leads me to believe that our own personal life-sustaining apparatus is anything less than flawless, I thought I would push the limits a little to see what, if any, restrictions there might be." Turning, he resumed his stroll out into emptiness, capably supported and held aloft by the hundreds of wires and cables that pierced his still human body.

"Come back here!" an anxious Haviti yelled. Taking his time, a sauntering N'kosi transcribed a gradual circle before returning to the solid footing of the overlook.

"Don't do that anymore," she growled at him. "No more radical experiments—at least, not without mutual discussion beforehand."

"Why bother?" Grinning at her, he reached down to grab a handful of the lines running into his body and lift them slightly. "If there was a sudden and unexpected alien equipment failure while I was walking on air, I'd be the only one to suffer the consequences." His grin faded and his tone turned abruptly and unexpectedly serious. "Would you miss me, Tiare?"

Valnadireb had come close. "We would both miss you, Mosi. As I would miss Haviti, and as I suspect she would miss me." Pivoting on four trulegs, the thranx xenologist gestured to indicate the immensity of the chamber spread out before them. "I cannot vouch for your emotions or feelings on the matter, but I believe that I am still thranx enough to know that I would not want to wander onward and onward through this place—alone."

Nothing more was said about N'kosi's stroll through emptiness, but he did not do it again.

The weeks rolled into months, the months into years, and the years into time without end. They never grew hungry or thirsty, they never felt ill or fell sick.

Throughout it all they did not, as Valnadireb remarked on a day like the one that had gone just before and would with absolute certainty be just like the one that would arrive tomorrow, age.

With time to travel and explore and in the absence of noticeable fatigue, they covered great distances on foot. In the course of their travels they were never able to determine whether the linkages that kept them nourished and healthy and young constantly renewed themselves or were extensions that by now must have been hundreds of kilometers long. It did not matter. There was so much to see, so much to try and absorb, that they never grew bored. Lonely, yes. Homesick, occasionally. But never bored.

There seemed no end to the extraordinary subterranean technological fantasy. For all they knew it might run all the way around the inner rim of the entire planet. The location of the metal shaft that had provided access to the surface had long since been forgotten. They encountered drifting blobs of purposeful energy the size of cities, found their way around or through ranks of conduits large enough to channel small seas, and crossed artificial gorges that consisted of hundreds of levels whose foundations lay beyond their range of vision. And still they never saw another guardian orb.

Their absence made perfect sense to Haviti. There was no need for the complex to be on guard against wandering organic components that had by now become part of its own structure.

Then there came a day, quite unexpectedly, when certain things were revealed.

They were strolling, purposefully and without fatigue, through a forest of spiraling crystals of varying color and refractivity. Above the crystalline spires fist-sized balls of energy were sparking briskly back and forth. The forest might have been a mechanism for channeling power, an advanced apparatus for analyzing the underlying nature of matter, or a game akin to chess. They had no way of knowing.

What they did know was that without warning or preamble, their surroundings suddenly went dark.

It was the first time—indeed, the only time—that the light had gone out since they had originally entered that long-forgotten, long-since-left-behind tunnel. Confused and bewildered, they used the sound of their voices to draw anxiously close to one another.

"What now?" an uneasy N'kosi murmured.

"Patience." Valnadireb's terranglo was calm and steady as always. "Illumination will return."

"I wish I possessed your sense of certainty," the other xenologist muttered.

"I have no choice but to be certain," the thranx replied evenly. "To believe otherwise would, I think, lead quickly to madness."

Something had attracted Haviti's attention from the moment the light had died. Perhaps her vision had become more sensitive than that of her companions. Or maybe she just happened to be looking in the right direction at the right time.

"I see something."

"Where?" N'kosi asked. She sensed that her friend was very close to her.

A moment more and he did not have to ask for directions, nor did Valnadireb. The burgeoning glow became visible to both of them.

From a bright pinpoint in the distance the light expanded until it filled the space directly in front of them. Images had begun to materialize within the darkness. No sound accompanied

them. Their appearance did not violate the interminable still-
ness and silence of the underground world.

No accompaniment was necessary. As trained scientists they
had no difficulty comprehending or interpreting what they
were seeing. It was an unmistakable panoply of biological pro-
gression. Not an allegory, but a realistic representation of the
evolutionary modus as it was being played out on Quofum.

First came the empty, waiting, open world that all but begged
to be seeded with life. Single-celled creatures appeared, swiftly
multiplied, advanced and fractured and fledged. Since the presentation was not taking place in real time Haviti and her colleagues had no way of judging the pace of the process. They did,
however, appreciate the incredible variety of developing life-
forms and the insane speed with which they emerged, diverged,
and speciated. Haviti let out a little cry of recognition when the
ancestors of her seals first appeared. All three of them identified
the progenitors of the fuzzies and the spikers, the stick-jellies
and the hardshells.

A cavalcade of other intelligent races rose and fell. Some,
like those who had built the sunken city Haviti had explored,
achieved admirable levels of refinement before falling back,
overcome by disease, war, internal dissension, or their own lack
of drive. Most never reached such heights.

The depiction of Quofum's wildly diverse evolution abruptly
vanished, to be replaced by a portrayal of one species. Individually they were small and physically unimpressive; multiarmed,
soft-bodied creatures who moved about on a quartet of sticky
pseudopods. Their four eyes were horizontal in shape with
matching longitudinal pupils. What they lacked in size and physical strength they made up for according to their description with
a ferocious intelligence, curiosity, and intensity.

Representations of individual star systems appeared, then entire galactic arms. The inoffensive but dynamic beings were shown spreading from system to system. Their persistent inquisitiveness led them to explore ever farther outward in every direction. Then one of their earliest, most far-reaching probes encountered something outside the Milky Way. Something immense, something inconceivably vast. Something evil.

Something coming this way.

The multiarms did not panic. That was not their nature. They deliberated, analyzed, evaluated, and considered. Reaching a decision, they then embarked on not one but on a pair of sophisticated and highly structured schemes for dealing with the unprecedented oncoming menace. These were now depicted in more of the softly shimmering imagery. Haviti and her companions caught their breath at the scope of not one but of both the contemplated solutions.

The first consisted of running away.

The multiarms accomplished this by a means as direct as it was breathtaking in scope. Utilizing everything from chaos theory to a mastery of the hard science of multiple dimensions to a knowledge of the true physical makeup of the universe, they constructed machines that could generate folds between dimensional planes. They then proceeded to move their entire civilization of billions upon billions of souls from the present universe into another. If the universe that contained the impending evil was eventually consumed by it, they would be immune from the resulting catastrophe.

But concurrently with the escape mechanism they employed, they also constructed another device. Accelerated through a dimensionally altered variant of space-minus, it was sent at a velocity faster than one that was even mathematically compre-

hensible toward a portion of the universe occupied by an astronomical phenomenon known as the Great Attractor. This diffuse
concentration of matter some four hundred million light-years
across was located two hundred fifty million light-years away
from the Commonwealth in the direction of the southern con-
stellation Centaurus, about seven degrees off the plane of the
Milky Way—allowing for red-shifting.

The device built by the multiarms arrived there safely, situated itself at the center of the Attractor in the region known to
humanxkind as the Norma supercluster—and waited. Waited to
be directed at the oncoming threat, and activated. Even though
the multiarms had successfully escaped to another universe,
they still retained an interest in trying to stop the vast malevo-
lence that threatened to annihilate all the other less fortunate
sentient species of the galaxy they had forsaken. In accordance
with this desire they had left behind warning devices and ac-
cessways to enable them to be alerted in the event of a change
in the course or behavior of the Great Evil. They had very recently been so alerted and so warned. In response, they prepared to activate the device now waiting at the center of the
Great Attractor.

And failed.

In constructing it and carefully positioning it in the universe
they had left behind, they had neglected to append the final
means necessary for its activation. In the immensity of time that
had subsequently passed, information had been lost, mechanisms
no longer required had been forgotten, and the need for backups
had been overlooked. Hurriedly (by their standards), they set
about trying to reconstruct the vital, indispensable, final component that was necessary for the activation of the galactic defense
mechanism they had built. They were still trying.

On Quofum.

Quofum, an unimportant planet that slipped in and out of Commonwealth notice. Quofum, an entire world that was nothing but one long extended attempt to replicate a core element of the solitary device that had been drifting in the center of the Norma supercluster for the preceding four hundred million years. Quofum, where even the incredibly advanced science of the multiarms had so far failed to reproduce the problematical final factor that would allow the half-forgotten instrumentation to become activated and respond to the incoming threat.

Quofum, where their lofty but imperfect science had failed to evolve it.

That, the presentation explained, was the driving force behind Quofum's outrageous riotous biota, behind its uncontrolled runaway speciation. The multiarms were trying to evolve something that was essential to the activation of their now incredibly ancient apparatus. In the absence of critical long-forgotten knowledge they had thus far failed. In the meantime, the evil that was racing toward the Milky Way had entered a state of steady, continuous acceleration. Given present projections it was likely to arrive before the determined but regretful multiarms could succeed in their work. The multiarms would be safe in their other universe. As for the universe they had departed . . .

In the universe they had departed, the Commonwealth and everything in it would be destroyed. The Great Evil would sweep through and continue on to the next galaxy, and the next, ever onward, all-consuming, until the entire sum of the universe itself was a black and dark and empty place. The multiarms would sorrow for what they had left behind and could not save, and go on with their lives. All this, Haviti and N'kosi and Valnadireb saw, would come to pass.

Unless . . .

Unless the device the multiarms had left behind in the heart of the distant Norma supercluster could be activated. It preserved its programming, it retained its functionality, it was ready. All it needed was to be triggered.

But not by the three marooned visitors. They had been maintained, and helped, and even improved by the machines of Quofum in the hope that they might provide, if not a solution to the great ongoing conundrum of the previous four hundred million years, at least a hint in the right direction. From their distant and difficult and other-dimensional vantage point the multiarms had been studying both thranx and humans, along with every other intelligent species that had arisen independently in or near the Commonwealth. A few of the most hopeful among the otherwise pessimistic watchers thought they detected the tiniest flicker, the briefest glimmer of promise among both allied species. To date, that was all they had glimpsed. That hope, if little else, remained alive.

The images faded. The all-pervasive illumination returned. Around the three artificially enhanced friends the machine world that underlay the natural world of Quofum hummed silently; kindling development, nudging progress, enhancing evolution among thousands of competing species. Not realizing that some among their kind were already aware of the oncoming Great Evil and were desperately trying to do something about it, Haviti and N'kosi and Valnadireb regretted that the destiny that had overtaken them prevented them from conveying a warning.

"Why show us *that*," Haviti wondered in reference to the

recently concluded presentation, "and continue to keep us alive?" Her expression was drawn and her tone had turned deeply cynical.

Valnadireb was less scornful, more philosophical. "As you saw. They hope that one day we may be able to offer a useful suggestion." Gesturing truhands conveyed mild humor. "Even if we cannot ourselves evolve into one."

Both of them looked over at N'kosi, who was being quiet. Such unusual reticence was enough to prompt an acerbic comment from Haviti. "What's this, Mosi? Nothing to say, not even on matters of cosmic import?" Bitter humor did not allow her to fully accept everything she had just seen—but it was a useful temporary defense. And a very human one.

"I was just thinking," her friend and colleague and companion for what was looking more and more like an everlasting future replied, "that those cute little wiggly-limbed supermen are probably experimenting on us even as they're keeping us alive and well." His eyes met hers. They still looked plausibly human, as did the essence behind them. "My only regret is that we can't share what we've just seen with Science Central."

"Perhaps they are better off not knowing," Valnadireb observed, unaware that the peril in question had already been documented. "There is nothing anyone could do about it. The Commonwealth is prepared and able to defend itself against external threats such as the AAnn. Coping effectively with a maliciousness that is galactic in size and scope, I fear, will remain beyond the capability of both our kind."

Turning, Haviti resumed walking. As ever, it required barely perceptible effort and no strain. She found herself wishing that there was a way she could hurt herself, could feel real pain once again. It was not to be. The mechanisms the multiarms had left

behind would not allow it. She and her friends were too valuable intact. Much of her adult life had been spent in collecting
specimens for research and study.

She had never expected to become one herself.

Maybe they'll get tired of working with us, she mused as she
strode along assertively between Moselstrom N'kosi and Valnadireb. *Maybe they'll release us from this planetary laboratory of
theirs and let us find the tunnel again.* But what good would that
do? They would still be trapped, marooned here on Quofum—
a world that much of the time could not even be found at
the suggested coordinates in the Commonwealth galographics.
Which was the better fate? To live on, nourished and maintained by the multiarms' machines? Or to die a slow and natural death up on the frenzied, chaotic surface?

There was a third possibility, she reminded herself. What if
one of the multiarms' multifarious ongoing evolutionary experiments succeeded? What if the means necessary to trigger the device implanted deep within the Great Attractor was found? *If*
that eventuated, and *if* successful activation resulted, and if the
device worked and the vast onrushing menace was subsequently
countered, there would be no more need for them on Quofum.
If despite being preoccupied with weightier matters the multiarms deigned to remember their three insignificant humanx experiments, might they not in their scientific brilliance and moral
munificence find a way to send them home? Or at least to alert
others of their kind to their continued survival and existence on
Quofum, thus prompting a possible rescue expedition?

That was the possibility, however remote, however unlikely,
that convinced her it was worth staying alive. That was what
persuaded her companions to do likewise. She was not particularly proud of her decision. It was entirely selfish. She wanted

someone to save the galaxy because in doing so the action might also save her and her friends. Whether that was likely to happen she did not know and had no way of predicting.

She knew only that she and Valnadireb and Moselstrom N'kosi had best continue to get along with one another in their enhanced and transformed states because the wait to learn the final answer was likely to be a long one.

ALAN DEAN FOSTER has written in a variety of genres, including hard science fiction, fantasy, horror, detective, Western, historical, and contemporary fiction. He is the author of the *New York Times* bestseller *Star Wars: The Approaching Storm* and the popular Pip & Flinx novels, as well as novelizations of several films, including *Transformers, Star Wars*, the first three *Alien* films, and *Alien Nation*. His novel *Cyber Way* won the Southwest Book Award for Fiction in 1990, the first science fiction work ever to do so. Foster and his wife, JoAnn Oxley, live in Prescott, Arizona, in a house built of brick that was salvaged from an early-twentieth-century miners' brothel. He is currently at work on several new novels and media projects.

ABOUT THE TYPE

This book was set in Berling. Designed in 1951 by Karl Erik Forsberg for the Typefoundry Berlingska Stilgjuteri AB in Lund, Sweden, it was released the same year in foundry type by H. Berthold AG. A classic old-face design, its generous proportions and inclined serifs make it highly legible.